DEADLY CONDITIONS

DAVID WOLF BOOK 4

JEFF CARSON

CROSS ATLANTIC PUBLISHING

DAVID WOLF NOVELS IN ORDER ...

Gut Decision (A David Wolf Short Story)– Sign up for the new
release newsletter at
http://www.jeffcarson.co/p/newsletter.html and receive a
complimentary copy.

Foreign Deceit (David Wolf Book 1)
The Silversmith (David Wolf Book 2)
Alive and Killing (David Wolf Book 3)
Deadly Conditions (David Wolf Book 4)
Cold Lake (David Wolf Book 5)
Smoked Out (David Wolf Book 6)
To the Bone (David Wolf Book 7)
Dire (David Wolf Book 8)
Signature (David Wolf Book 9)
Dark Mountain (David Wolf Book 10)
Rain (David Wolf Book 11)

CHAPTER 1

THE MAN LEANED over the wheel, squinting through the windshield as another powdery gust of wind hit the side of his truck.

All he saw was a swarm of snowflakes illuminated by his headlights, and he felt his eyeballs twitch back and forth as he tried desperately to get his bearings. When he instinctively let off the gas, the truck lurched and stuttered, rocking him in the seat. He kicked the clutch and downshifted to first, and then he felt the truck meander to the side, though to which side was impossible to tell.

It was useless trying to orient himself. Like looking through the eyepiece of a twisting kaleidoscope. Just as he was about to stomp the brakes, the whiteout let up and the two pinpoints of red light flitted back into view on the otherwise deserted county road ahead.

Dammit. He turned the wheel left and got back into the twin ruts in the snow he'd been following, hoping to God they were somewhere near the center and safe from drainage ditches, roadside boulders, and anything else hidden under the blanket of ever-thickening white that could derail his plans.

County 15 was a desolate, winding dirt thoroughfare with steep drops off the left shoulder in a few spots. Houses were few and far between. If a driver got in trouble here, it was a long walk to get help, and an even longer one in weather like this—overall a stupid place to be driving tonight.

He was waiting for his quarry to call it quits, turn around, and coast back down the hill before the deepening drifts stranded them. Maybe they would take the girl back to one of their places or go to a hotel or something.

He looked at his watch—11:26 p.m., Saturday night, on the eve of surely the biggest powder day on the mountain in years. Fat chance of getting a hotel room. Out-of-town skiers on the mountain today would have sensed the opportunity and snatched up any vacancies after the big gala.

What a night to have a big event on the mountain, he thought with a shake of his head. It was going to be mayhem for people getting back down the gondola and to their homes and hotel rooms.

He scratched his nose and grasped the wheel with a two-hand white-knuckle grip. The defroster howled, blowing hot air on the highest setting against the windshield. Regardless of the wipers' speed, an immovable arc of water remained on the glass. The red taillights ahead illuminated it, and it reminded him of oozing fresh blood.

For the past day he'd seen red, and the way this girl was acting was only driving him madder as the seconds ticked by. Picking up two men in the span of half an hour? She'd simultaneously proven herself a bigger whore than he'd already thought and killed his entire plan in one slutty move.

He shook his head and gripped the wheel even tighter, and

then spat onto the floor of the passenger seat and growled aloud. He'd never felt more disgust with any human beings than with those conniving behind the scenes of Rocky Points.

Well, he'd felt a similar disgust once before. And that? That had ended badly. Was he going to remember anything after this? Or was he going to wake up in blood again? The thought made him nervous and his hands were slick on the wheel.

Because the memory of his first time was buried deep in the cave of his mind and he didn't have a map to find it, he knew this was going to be like his first time all over again. It had to be done. He would not fail. He turned the heater knob down and the cab quieted. The digital clock changed to 11:30. This was looking to be futile. They were going to her house, if they could make the last mile, and then what? It was sure to be full of roommates, and the neighbors who lived in that line of six houses in the middle of nowhere, and no opportunity. The driver bared his teeth and shook his head.

Ahead, the taillights rounded the corner and disappeared from sight. All he could see was the thick curtain of swollen flakes flying into the lights, the windshield and the twin tire grooves.

Damn, it was deep, he thought, looking to the left and barely seeing the trees in the forest. The snow had started at sundown, and really ramped up after nine. By the looks of the ruts, at least twenty inches had accumulated already, and the storm was still coming in full force.

Enough was enough. He should quit and get back home while he could. He started scanning for the widest part of the road to turn around.

Ahead, the lights flared red and he jammed his foot down on his own brake. The truck had stopped.

He shut off his headlights and the chaotic scene outside

went black. He squinted and blinked as his eyes adjusted to the darkness. Finally, he could see the twin grooves running up the road, disappearing into a television-static night, and then the faint lights of the motionless truck.

It was almost impossible to see—the snow and wind were relentless—but he swore that the cab light flicked on and then off. The tail lights shone as the truck backed and K-turned, and then the truck's headlights were coming straight at him.

His pulse jumped as he considered his next play. He flicked on his headlights and shifted into first. His knobby tires spun briefly and then caught. He shifted into second, following the tracks ahead. Less than a minute later the truck's headlamps glared into his cab as it passed. He squinted and held up his hand to cover his face, figuring the truck's occupants might be pressed against their windows and wondering who in their right mind was out in this weather along with them.

He sighed and looked in his rearview mirror. The taillights disappeared around the corner without braking.

It was over, he decided. He followed the ruts to the point where the truck had turned around. There was no sense breaking new ground and risking falling over the edge of the road, sitting in a snowdrift overnight, and possibly dying for his carelessness.

As he drove, he tested the high beams. Visibility was worse, so he shut them off.

He leaned forward again and squinted. When he'd flicked off his lights, he could have sworn he'd glimpsed a dark figure along the right shoulder several yards ahead.

He blinked rapidly, then squinted again. And when the shape moved, his pulse jumped. *It was a person.*

"Holy shit," he whispered to himself, and sat up straighter in his seat.

It was her. There was no mistake. She was waving, and then she held up a gloved thumb.

The man swallowed, letting his brain process the opportunity standing in front of him. His mission, melting away moments ago, had now dropped in his lap, and he found himself wondering what to do.

He slowed down and stopped next to her. Before he knew it, her face had filled the passenger window. As she pressed against the glass and peered inside, the driver opened up the center console, grabbed the gun's rough plastic handle, and pulled it out.

If he shot her when she opened the door, would he black out and wake up a few hours later? Just sitting in a car, engine running, door open, and a bloody corpse lying nearby, waiting for early-morning plows to discover them? Was he even conscious now? Was he dreaming?

His breathing was frantic, and his skin tingled as sweat glands opened up all over his body.

She pounded on the window and yelled something too muffled to hear.

He clicked the lock and she opened the door. The dome light went on and a blast of snow and cold swirled into the cab as she bent inside. He tucked the revolver in between his legs way too late, but she didn't seem to notice.

"Hey, it's you! What the hell are you doing up here? Don't answer, I don't care. Can I get a ride?"

"Yeah, get in," he said. His voice sounded a mile away in his own ears. He reached into the center console again, pulled out his leather gloves, and put them on.

She jumped up onto the seat butt-first and knocked her feet together out the door to drop off the snow, and then twisted into the chair and shut the door.

The cab was suddenly filled with her sniffling and breathing and a flowery scent. She pulled off her wool hat, flipping snow all over the dashboard.

"Oh, I'm sorry. Shit. Thank God you're up here. Oh, man ... do you think you can get up the rest of this hill to my house? Do you know where I live?"

The driver stared at her and smiled. Or was he sneering? He couldn't tell.

She looked at him and frowned. "Are you okay?" she asked.

The driver picked up the revolver and pointed it at her face.

"Oh, God!" She twisted and grabbed for the handle, and then put her hands up and shut her eyes. "Please. Please. Don't hurt me. What are you doing?"

"You know you killed her, right?"

"What?" she said, still cowering against the door. "What?"

Every muscle in his body tensed as rage overtook him.

"Unzip your coat," he said, flipping on the cab light.

Her eyes were wild and wide, pupils tiny, mascara running down her cheeks. She nodded profusely. "Yeah, okay," she said, fumbling to take off her gloves. At first, she moved quickly to unzip her jacket. Then she looked up at him as if a sudden brainstorm had given her an idea, and she slowed down, arching her back a little and taking a calming breath. "Yeah, let's get comfortable."

He set his jaw and inhaled deeply to contain his rage. It figured this whore would think if she puts out, he would punch her ticket out of this. He kept his aim steady and pulled up on the emergency brake, shifted into neutral, and let up his feet from the clutch and brake.

"Now pull open your jacket with both hands, and pull it down your back, and push out your boobs again."

She smiled and gave him a wink, and then slowly did as she was told.

He unbuckled his seatbelt and scooted his chair all the way back, watching her closely. She was now sitting with her hands effectively wrapped against her sides, but he would need to make sure she couldn't fight back, so he put the gun to her head and climbed on top of her, and then put his knees on her arms.

She gave him a smile and closed her eyes, trying to look like she was enjoying it, unconvincingly so.

He dropped the gun on the driver's side seat and grasped her neck. First, he just gripped her and started squeezing. And then she started to squirm.

There was no preparing for this moment, and her fierce counter-attack startled him. She thrashed and twisted underneath him, and he tightened his grip until his muscles shook, and then he gripped harder still.

She sagged down in the seat, like she was trying to escape by sliding underneath his legs, but he just leaned on her harder and a gurgling sound bubbled from her lips. Even through the leather gloves, he could feel the pounding of the blood in her neck. Then, after what seemed like an eternity, she went still, and the pounding stopped.

He gripped her for a while longer, knowing she was already dead, but just wanting to make sure. He finally eased his grip, the leather of his gloves peeling off her skin as he pulled away.

He had almost forgotten. With a quick movement, he opened the center console again and pulled out the tube of Ruby Fire lipstick. He removed the cap, carefully twisted the tube's base to expose the right height of color, and then applied the mark to her forehead. He leaned back and assessed his work. *Maybe not exactly like the original,* he thought, *but close enough.*

He wiped a tear from his cheek before it dropped onto the warm lifeless body. It was strange. As the seconds ticked by and he replayed images of the past few minutes, a persisting adrenaline spike spawned an airy sense of wonder. *I did it. I strangled her. I killed this pathetic excuse for a human being. Maybe my mind is playing tricks on me,* he thought. *Maybe I am out cold, lying on a dead woman in a running vehicle on a deserted road in the middle of the night.*

He slowed his breathing and looked around, watching the flying flakes and listening to the windshield wipers squeal behind him. Then he felt the warmth on his knee and jumped over onto the driver's side. She had pissed herself, and it was all over the seat.

He reached over, pulled on the door handle, and then shoved her out. She ended up hanging out the door with her legs still jammed inside on the floor, so he crawled onto the passenger seat, feeling the warm liquid soak through his jeans, and then rolled her out into the deep snow.

For a few seconds he stared, watching the snow cover her body like a lace veil, and he again wondered if this surreal scene was a dream. The bitter-cold wind and his sticky wet jeans reeking of urine convinced him otherwise. It seemed real because it was real.

He climbed back in the driver's seat and decided that even if it were a dream, the prudent thing would be to dream about getting the hell out of there. So, he turned the truck around and did just that.

CHAPTER 2

THE ANTICIPATION on the pass was electric. If Wolf had not been cocooned in his winter duty gear—hat, gloves, fully zipped coat, pants, boots—he was sure his body hair would have been standing on end.

"Waiting on you, Sheriff," the distant-sounding voice crackled through everyone's radios.

Wolf looked at the other bundled faces and wide eyes of the people around him, and then shifted his gaze up the snow-blanketed highway that bent out of sight behind the pillowed pines. It was the day after a huge dump of snow, and a beautiful morning on a bluebird day, as skiers called it—a cloudless, radiant sky. Despite the crowd surrounding him, Wolf regarded the scene as desolate and peaceful. For the moment.

He turned to look past the congregation of official personnel that surrounded him. A few hundred yards down the highway, a line of still vehicles puffed exhaust behind a closed gate arm. For five minutes now, people had been abandoning their vehicles and huddling on the roadside next to the fresh wall of plowed snow, jockeying for position to see, cell-phone cameras swinging between the bright mountaintop and the congregation of Sluice County sheriff's deputies, Rocky Points Rescue volunteers, and Colorado Department of Transportation workers milling in the cold shaded road above them.

An RKPT-News 8 crew had set up next to the road gate, with an expensive camera mounted on a tripod, lens aimed high up the mountain.

"Stand by!" Wolf shouted, a puff of cloud jetting from his mouth. He thumbed the radio button and brought it to his lips. "All clear."

The uniformed men and women surrounding Wolf swiveled in unison to look up, and he gave a final glance to the line of vehicles down the road. They reacted to the synchronized commotion and stared up. He watched as motorists nearest the front shouted down the line and people began sprinting toward the gate for a better view.

Wolf felt like he had just opened a cage containing a wild beast.

"Fire in the hole," Bob Duke, longtime director of the resort's ski patrol, said through the radio.

Even through the tiny speaker, Wolf could hear Bob's high-pitched excitement, and it coaxed Wolf's body to tense and tingle. He resigned himself to the moment, and assured himself that they'd taken every precaution so that no one would be in harm's path. Wolf had taken CDOT's recommended perimeter around the slide zone and doubled it. He had discussed the terrain above the motorists in detail with the avalanche specialists. There was nothing more to do but ...

Two sharp-edged blasts thumped the air, and Wolf looked up.

The deputies nearby started to whoop as a white cloud began billowing from the bowl high above.

On a normal blast day, when the conditions on the resort's

southernmost bowl were just right to slide, a triggered avalanche would make its way down a third of the mountain, and stop in the relatively flat zone at the bottom of Brecker Bowl along the southern boundary of the resort.

But if snow conditions were just right (or just wrong) and an especially deep layer of powder lay over a weak layer of sugar snow, the slide could ride through the flat zone and spill into the treeless chute that had been gouged out over the millennia by other slides. An especially big avalanche could get as far as the highway. That specific zone was a safe distance up the road, clearly discernable by smaller, younger trees and an open glade.

According to Duke's earlier assessment, backed by over thirty years of experience with the Rocky Points Resort ski patrol, there was a small chance they were going to see a slide reach the road, or something even bigger. The official accumulation from last night's storm was twenty-seven inches at the peak, and conditions had conspired to prevent CDOT and ski patrol from preemptively blasting the bowl. Topping that, the wind had shifted and come strong out of the north all night, loading at least nine feet of wind-deposited snow underneath a freshly sculpted cornice, all on top of a layer of depth-hoar crystals, or sugar snow, a result of the resort's dry and sunny conditions over the past month.

For ski conditions on the rest of the mountain, and the skiers who would be enjoying them all day, the new snow was a godsend. But as Wolf watched the white cloud explode from the bowl above, he wondered if this wasn't something sent from hell.

The deputies and personnel surrounding Wolf began to shift at the sight of the pyroclastic flow-like explosion traveling down the mountain, and everyone, including Wolf, let out a gasp of amazement.

The billowing mass rumbled, and the hundred-year-old trees cracking into millions of pieces inside the torrent were muffled pops.

At the front of the cloud, a white streak shot forward at startling speed, then another, and another, reminding Wolf of streamers coming out of a napalm explosion. They were snow and ice-covered rocks, ejected at hundreds of miles per hour, and they were a definite surprise to Wolf.

Wolf watched as one of the streamers struck a tree a third of the way up the mountain, wrenching it out of sight in a twist of green branches and a puff of powder.

"Heads up!" Wolf yelled, certain, though, that every spectator had seen the new danger and was acting accordingly.

Wolf looked up, wondering whether any invisible rocks were headed right for them. He couldn't see any, so he looked back to the front of the rolling monster.

The barrage seemed to be gaining speed, which was hard to believe since it was moving so fast and now so low on the mountain. It was going to hit the road with full force, Wolf thought. As quickly as the thought came, the thundering mass shot across the road. Trees cart-wheeled out of the cloud and crashed into others on the far side of the road, and the mayhem continued onward.

"Holy mother of ..." Wolf heard Rachette say somewhere nearby.

The trees to the immediate left blocked everyone's view as the slide reached the flat valley below, but the roar and snapping and cracking were still there. Then the white steam came back into sight, climbing up the other side of the valley, as if it were a huge bucket of water splashing from one side of a bathtub to the other.

The spectacle was short-lived, however, because a cloud of powder was descending on them, traveling down the highway at more than a few over the speed limit.

"Holy shit," someone said.

Wolf turned his back and jumped as the cloud hit, half expecting to be knocked into oblivion by a wall of snow, rocks, and trees. But the feared deadly impact never came, and Wolf fell onto his butt, jarring his spine, as the millions of hissing ice crystals collided with his back and then invaded every crack in his winter armor. Shutting his eyes and holding his breath, he shoved his face inside his coat and waited for the tempest to pass.

When the air stilled, he popped his face out and watched the others around him do the same. The air was sweet with the stench of pinesap. Rachette had huddled into the airplane-crash position and was now uncoiling himself from the ground. Wolf stood up and scanned the group through the still swirling air.

"Everyone all right?" Wolf yelled.

"Okay."

"Yeah."

Expletives flew from everyone's mouths, and there was a faint cheer from the crowd below gathered on the road.

Wolf started accounting for every person that had been there before. Eleven … twelve … thirteen bodies, all moving and talking excitedly to one another.

"Oh. My. God," Rachette said. "Did you see that?"

Wolf blinked in response, and then took a glove off and began wiping the fine powder from his upper and lower lashes. His skin was beading with moisture, and he palmed his entire face and pulled down, raking the melting snow off his beard with his shaking hands. Yes, he'd seen that, and for a second, he'd thought that he'd killed thirteen people.

...

It took a full five minutes for the cloud of ice crystals to fully dissipate, drifting on a small breath of wind that came in striking contrast to the howling blizzard from the previous night.

Thirty minutes later, after three more charges had failed to slide any more snow high above on the bowl, officials deemed the slide zone safe for CDOT workers to clear the road.

Wolf looked up as a growling front-end loader crunched its way through the snow toward the wall that now blocked the pass. Another tractor rattled to life and beeped, and the deputies made way for the awakening machines.

"... I gave him a roadside last night." Deputy Baine was giving Rachette an earful about something.

"Did he pass?" Rachette asked.

Baine looked up at Wolf and nodded, as if including him on the conversation. "Yep. Passed with flying colors."

Taylor Hunt, a burly man who had seen real napalm streamers in Vietnam, drove by in a lurching yellow Volvo tractor. He wore a wide smile with a cigarette between his teeth, and he waved at the crowd of men and women from behind the glass. Just like everyone else who had witnessed the avalanche, he looked excited to be alive, and excited about the stories he'd be able to tell over a beer that night.

"That's not a normal-sized slide, right? That was, like, a hundred-year slide, right?" Rachette was grilling Patterson.

Patterson avoided eye contact and responded with a shrug. For the first time, Wolf noticed that she seemed shaken up.

Rachette detected it, too. "You okay?"

"Yeah," she said. "I just don't like avalanches."

Rachette gave Wolf a quick glance. "What, you have history with avalanches or something?"

Patterson looked at Rachette and then to the ground. "Yeah." Her tone said, *Let's drop it*.

"All right, everyone," Wolf said. "Let's huddle up. We have a lot of work to do, and now that we have three of our snow movers stuck on the pass for"—Wolf turned around and looked at the tractors who were picking away at the wall of snow. At one point, it was taller than two of the big machines stacked one on another—"most of the day at least. That means driving conditions are going to be more hazardous. Get started on the patrols we talked about this morning. You know your assignments. And keep an eye on all our plowing friends."

Wolf looked at Deputy Yates, who nodded back. Wolf had given Yates the task of keeping an eye on the Hosfeld twins, brothers who loved to rage through town with their plow-wielding four-by-fours each and every snowstorm, providing more community terror than service.

"And, again,"—Wolf took a deep breath—"the funeral service starts at two-thirty. Get there early, or just do not get there. Stay out in the parking lot if you can't make it on time. Am I clear?"

Wolf moved his gaze from one deputy to the next, and each nodded in turn.

Wolf smacked his gloved hands together. "All right, let's get out and help our community today, people."

The uniformed crowd scattered and walked back down the road to their waiting vehicles.

"Rachette, Patterson," Wolf said.

"Yeah?" Rachette turned and stopped. Patterson did the same.

"First thing: go to Edna Yerton's place and check on her. Her wood pile is going to be buried, I doubt she'll have a fire lit, and she probably won't have enough groceries to make dinner tonight." He took off his glove, pulled out his wallet, and gave Rachette a twenty. "Get some food and take it up to her, get a fire going and plenty of wood inside to dry, and make sure she's got what she needs for the next few days. Be careful on the way up—the plows probably haven't done her road—and don't try pulling into her drive. Park on 15 and shoe the hundred yards or so to her house."

Rachette pulled the edges of his mouth down and nodded. "All right." He glanced at Patterson and then back at Wolf. "So, not that I'm against this, but doesn't she have a neighbor who could help her out?"

"No," Wolf said. "He's dead."

"Oh," Rachette said. "Wait, dead? Who was that? When was that?"

"I'm glad you keep up on town current events." Wolf started walking down the road.

There was a bright piercing light near the gate, and they all slowed when they saw a television camera and a reporter speaking into a microphone and gesturing toward them.

"Rachette, you up for doing an interview with Renee Moore?" Wolf asked.

Rachette stopped in his tracks. He went pale, almost green, and by his shifting body language looked like he might vomit, lose control of his bladder, or both.

"What?" he said, staring into the distance.

"Mitch Casper," Wolf said.

"What? Mitch Camper?" Rachette looked at Wolf. "What?"

"Mitch Casper died. He was the neighbor. Who died?"

"Oh. Yeah ..."

Patterson looked at Wolf and smiled for the first time of the day. "I never heard about that either. Never knew the guy."

Wolf nodded. "His family found him this fall. Ninety years old. Natural causes. Was dead for a week. I don't think he left his house much for the past ten years. Not a social guy at all." They started walking. "Sarah has the listing. She can't sell the house apparently. Is having trouble getting the banks to lower the price or something like that. Hey, Rachette, you ready?"

"What?" Rachette looked at Wolf in horror.

Wolf slapped him on the shoulder. "Rachette, under no circumstances, ever, would I allow you to be the spokesman for the Sluice County Sheriff's Department on television."

Rachette almost collapsed from relief. "Oh, good. Thank God."

CHAPTER 3

"THE ROAD IS COVERED by at least ten feet of snow, trees and rocks, and it's going to take some time to clear the pass to the south," Wolf said, feeling the heat coming off the light panel mounted on the expensive-looking camera.

Renee Moore was confident and pretty, and smelled like expensive perfume. Her face was perfect, made up with the lavish precision only seen on television stars, or so Wolf assumed, since he'd never seen a television star this close. Her thick red lips sucked in the light, her face was tanned with rosy cheeks, her eyes giant blue orbs surrounded by thick eyelashes so long she could have used a curling iron on them. Her shoulder-length blonde hair peeked out beneath her hat and framed her face just so. She was downright attractive, holding a look of attentive interest for Wolf's words. With the reflecting camera lens two feet from his face, he had to concentrate to control what was coming out of his mouth. Since this was his first television interview, he had no clue how it was going—no other moment to compare with.

"… on the pass?" she asked.

Wolf realized he'd been zoning out and felt his face flush.

His five-day beard itched like hell, but at least the dark hair obscured the lower half of his reddening face. "I'm sorry, pardon me?"

She flashed a facetious smile and pulled the microphone back to her mouth. "I was asking, have you ever seen an avalanche like that before on this pass? It was amazing-looking from where we were standing."

Wolf shook his head. "No, I haven't seen one that big. We had some conditions come together that were pretty rare, resulting in quite a lot of snow coming down the mountain."

"And how long will it take to clear that snow off the pass?" she asked.

"I would say Williams Pass will be closed for at least the day, even with crews working from both sides of the slide zone."

"And surely a great thing for the ski resort, which is reporting twenty-seven inches of powder at the top. Do you get to make a few turns up there yourself, Sheriff?" She gave a little wink, which made Wolf's lips curl. She was good.

"Ah, no. All of our deputies have a lot of work to do now, helping dig the town out from the snow, and making sure everyone is healthy and safe from the cold temperatures that have settled in for the day."

"Thank you, Sheriff Wolf." She turned to the camera. "And there you have it. We were just talking with Sheriff David Wolf of the Sluice County Sheriff's Department, after an absolutely huge avalanche, triggered by CDOT and the ski patrol of Rocky Points Resort, all caught on camera by our excellent camera crew here. I'm Renee Moore, reporting …"

Wolf decided to walk toward his car rather than stand next to her like a dumbass. For the first time of the day, he walked out of the dull light of the shadowed valley and into the sun's morning rays reflecting painfully off the white snow. He pulled his sunglasses down off his head. They were glazed over with a thin layer of frost, so he put them back up, and then broke into two quick sneezes. The air was a balmy zero degrees, biting into the inside of his nostrils when he sniffed.

"Excuse me, Sheriff?"

Wolf wiped his nose and turned around, hoping he was presentable.

"You just gonna leave without saying goodbye?" Renee Moore jogged toward him, swishing her powder-blue pant legs together with every step. She held out a knitted-mitten hand and Wolf took it.

"Oh, sorry," he said. "Goodbye. Be careful on the trip back to Denver. You do a great job on television. My son is going to flip when he knows I talked with you."

She laughed. "Oh, really?"

"Yeah, I think he's a big fan."

She mock frowned and gave a little laugh. "You *think* he's a big fan? So you aren't sure."

"Well, it hasn't come up. But he's thirteen, and he tends to quickly develop crushes on attractive women, so I'm quite confident that he's either a fan or will be when he sees the interview."

She stared at Wolf for a second and then narrowed one eye and smiled. "And your wife, what will she think?"

"Ex-wife," Wolf said, "and she'll probably hate you."

She laughed, this time more naturally—and attractively— and then she looked down. "Well, thanks."

"You're welcome." Wolf turned to his SUV and hopped in, and then gave her a quick wave as he drove away.

He smiled at the interaction and looked in the rearview mirror, seeing the Colorado-famous Renee Moore looking after his receding vehicle. He wondered why he didn't ask her out, or at least get her number, and then pondered why he would have. She lived in Denver, over two hours away—and that was if there was no traffic—a distance that had already been proved impossible for a relationship to endure.

Had she been hitting on him? Not really, he concluded. It was just easy politeness between two individuals that had morphed into a nice interaction—one with no future in it.

That seemed to be the recurring theme of his love life nowadays. As he drove past the dwindling line of cars on the pass, he thought about seeing Sarah the night before. She had looked extremely good, to put it mildly, with her snug blue dress that hugged her athletic curves and her braided blonde hair pulled back with shiny silver clips. And her eyes, as always, had been mesmerizing—brighter blue than the sky was today.

They had gotten along well last night, too. They'd attended a gala held atop the mountain at the Antler Creek Lodge, an ultra-exclusive restaurant open for dinner, only accessible by snow cat from the top of the gondola. In the little interaction they'd had, Wolf had laughed at her gossip about various people in the dining room, and they'd exchanged funny glances from across the room a couple of times. It was how their relationship had been lately. With their past as complicated as it could get—a marriage, a kid, her drugs, her alcohol, her sobriety, and her now defunct relationship with Mark Wilson—their present was going well. Just like his interaction with Renee Moore, though, he wasn't ready to expect anything for the future. What was holding him back from pursuing the only love he'd ever known in his life again, he couldn't say. But he was definitely hesitating because of some feeling he couldn't put a finger on.

"Sheriff, do you copy?" It was Tammy Granger on the radio.

Wolf plucked the radio from the console. "Go ahead."

"I have a visitor here at the station who wants to speak to you." Tammy was using a quieter-than-normal voice.

"Not exactly a good time. Who is it?"

"It's a Mr. Irwin, from the Irwin Construction Corporation. He's one of the—"

"Yeah, I know who he is. What does he want?" Wolf knew Tammy was using a tone of voice that suggested the man could hear what Wolf was saying, but Wolf didn't really care. It was a bad day to drop in and request a little chat with the sheriff.

Tammy paused. "He wants to speak to you today and is wondering when you'll be back in. He seems adamant. What would you like me to tell him?"

Wolf was coasting down the final straightaway of the pass into town. "Listen, I'm on my way past the station now. I'll just drop in. Tell him to sit tight."

"Thanks, honey," Tammy said in a sing-song voice.

Wolf was unsure how to respond to that, so he didn't.

Highway 734 from the Williams Pass gate to the southern edge of town was relatively easy driving, despite the snow from the night before. The men plowing the town for the past eight hours had made sure of that.

There were only a couple of cars parked in front of the small shops lining Main, and ahead a green John Deere front-end loader was toiling away, grabbing an oversized bucket of snow, turning and dumping it on top of a ten-foot mountain in the center of the street that ran the length of a football field. *The great wall of Rocky Points*, Wolf thought.

As Wolf passed by the tractor, he waved at Greg

Nanteekut, who sat in the cab. Greg pointed at Wolf and nodded, not moving his mouth, which bulged with tobacco. Wolf watched in his rearview mirror as the bucket of the loader swung past the rear of his SUV with barely a few feet to spare and dumped another load onto the center mound of snow.

Wolf pulled off Main into the station lot and parked next to the only other SUV in the fleet still there. Despite the conditions, they still needed at least one deputy at the station, and Wilson had been the lucky one to get it because he had drawn duty at the gate earlier. After sucking in exhaust, fielding hundreds of questions from the line of drivers trying to get out of town to the south over Williams Pass, and then dealing with the complaints following the news of the indefinite closure, Wolf had felt that Wilson deserved a little coffee-and-warmth time.

There was another vehicle parked in the lot, a black Range Rover with tinted windows, billowing exhaust into the arctic air.

Wolf turned off his vehicle, donned his winter cap and gloves, and stepped out into the biting cold. His boots squeaked on five inches of powder in the parking lot. Greg Nanteekut had cleared out the lot at some time in the dark hours of the morning, before the snow had stopped completely. Good enough.

Wolf walked straight past the purring Range Rover without slowing. The tint of the windows afforded Wolf no view inside, and he wasn't one to approach tinted windows and knock, just like he wasn't into speaking to people who wore sunglasses indoors.

Wolf entered the station and stomped his feet inside the door, sloughing off geometric chunks of snow onto the mat.

Inside was quiet, save the humming of the fluorescent bulbs overhead, and warm. Way too warm, Wolf thought. But this was Tammy's territory, and if she wanted to operate the reception area with a short-sleeved shirt on when it was zero degrees outside, then that was her business, and anyone in the department knew second-guessing anything Tammy knowingly did was a bad idea.

The man Wolf remembered from the night before as Ted Irwin sat at the far end of the window-enclosed anteroom of the station. Last night his bone-gray hair had been shinier and neatly plastered to his head, but now it stuck up in the back, as hair tended to do after taking off a winter hat, which sat on top of a wadded winter jacket on the chair next to him.

He looked at Wolf with bark-colored eyes and smiled, creasing his wrinkled, yet taut, skin. He stood up and held out a hand to Wolf.

Irwin's small, soft hands were adorned with silver-colored jewelry that was almost certainly made of an exotic metal. He was thin and just under Wolf's six-foot-three height, in his early sixties, and had a complexion and physique that suggested he ate a lot of plants and exercised regularly.

He seemed to mirror Wolf's sentiments about the room's temperature, as he was stripped down to a long-sleeved polo shirt—rolled to his elbows—and his face was so red that it looked like he wanted to press it against the glass.

"Mr. Irwin," Wolf said.

"Sheriff Wolf," Irwin said with a smile. "Thank you for seeing me."

Wolf turned to the door to the squad room and the locking mechanism clacked just before he reached for the handle and twisted it open.

"Thank you," Wolf said to Tammy, acknowledging her

unerring ability to push the access button mounted on the edge of the counter in front of her with perfect timing. Every time.

"Mmmm," she said, keeping her eyes on her *Guns and Ammo* magazine.

A cool whoosh of air flowed out of the squad room into the reception area as Wolf held the door open for Irwin to enter.

Irwin's eyes lit up for an instant. "Oh, it's ..."

Wolf walked behind him and let the door shut. "Cooler in here?"

Irwin smiled wide, revealing big, solid, white teeth. Veneers, Wolf guessed. No one's natural teeth were that perfect.

"Yes. Much cooler in here."

The relief in Irwin's voice made him smile. "Well, you might have to put that jacket back on when we get to my office."

"Gladly," Irwin said.

Wilson was standing in the middle of the desks of the squad room with a steaming cup of coffee. "Sir," he said with a nod.

"Wilson, how's it going in here?" Wolf asked.

Wilson gave a smile and looked around. "Quiet, sir."

"That's good. Follow me, Mr. Irwin." Wolf padded across the low-pile carpet through the line of desks, and then took a left down the hall at the back of the room.

Irwin walked silently behind him and cleared his throat as they passed the coffee machine standing on the oak-television-stand-turned-coffee-station against the wall.

"Would you like a cup?" Wolf asked.

"Uh, if you don't mind, I would love one."

Wolf shook a styrofoam cup off the stack and held it out to Irwin.

Irwin grabbed a cup and pulled the coffee beaker from the machine, then filled Wolf's cup before pouring his own.

"Thanks," Wolf said. "Sugar there, cream's in this little fridge here." Wolf took a sip and watched Irwin expectantly, but Irwin just raised an eyebrow and took a sip.

"Ah,"—Irwin smacked his lips—"I like it black, too."

Wolf stepped through the open door of his office and flicked the light on, unnecessarily, as it was bathed in bright sunlight slicing through the blinds. The fluorescent lights overhead stuttered on and buzzed. A green-and-gold plastic CSU Rams clock ticked on the wall.

"Please, take a seat." Wolf unzipped his jacket and threw his hat and gloves on one of the empty built-in shelves; then he hung up his jacket and sat in his chair facing Irwin.

Irwin sat down and placed his hat and jacket on the chair next to him.

"Did you have fun at the gala last night?" Wolf asked.

"Yes,"—Irwin smiled and gazed into nothing—"it was a lot of fun. Great food."

Wolf narrowed his eyes and took another sip, remembering how Irwin had been sitting next to Sarah at one of the many real-estate tables. Wolf had been a few tables over with Hal Burton, the ex-sheriff of Sluice County who liked to think of himself as Wolf's mentor, the Sluice County Commissioner, the County Attorney General, and a few other political higher-ups from neighboring Byron County.

He and Irwin had met only briefly. It was probably a flicker of memory for Irwin, but Wolf had kept a close eye on him all night. Irwin's infatuation with Sarah had been clear early on.

"What can I do for you?" Wolf asked.

Irwin hovered the cup over the edge of Wolf's desk and glanced up for approval. Wolf nodded, and Irwin set it down.

"Well, I have a little bit of a problem, and I was hoping you could help me out."

Wolf took another sip.

"As you may know, I have a helicopter at the resort."

Wolf did know. The service of cat skiing off the backside of Rocky Points Resort had grown in popularity over the past two decades and, last year, the corporate bigwigs in Denver had decided to exploit even more of the terrain. They'd followed in the steps of Silver Mountain—a tiny resort in the San Juan mountains in southwest Colorado—and begun offering heli-runs for a *reasonable* hundred bucks and change. That is, a reasonable price when compared to a normal day of heli-skiing, which could run to over a thousand dollars per person.

The helicopter and pilot that ferried skiers from mountaintop to mountaintop were leased from a company in Aspen called Irwin Construction Corporation, which was owned by the man who now sat across from Wolf.

Wolf nodded. "Yes, I haven't been up in it, yet, but I've seen it flying all winter."

"Well, I came into town two days ago for last night's gala, and a few other engagements, and to entertain some clients"—he waved his hand—"etcetera, etcetera." Irwin took another slurp of coffee and set it down. "Last night, my helicopter pilot, a man named Matt Cooper, picked up a client of mine from the gondola, to take him back to where he was staying."

Wolf remembered Deputy Baine's side remark on the pass and began to suspect he knew where this was going.

"When Matt got into town," Irwin continued, "a Deputy Baine pulled him over and all but yanked him out of the car, and then proceeded to give my pilot a roadside test for drunkenness."

Wolf looked into his coffee cup and tilted it, letting the grounds settle to the corner; then he sucked down the last drops. "What can I do for you, Mr. Irwin?"

Irwin sat up straight and smoothed his shirt. "My pilot wasn't found drunk by your deputy last night, but he was given a ticket for rolling through a stop sign, something my pilot says he certainly did not do. He slid to a stop. May have been a foot over the line, but the line was also buried under a foot of snow, so I'm not sure how your deputy even gave the ticket."

Wolf lifted his hands. "I don't know—"

"And two nights before that, he was found to be driving sober after a roadside test. By the same deputy. And four days before that, he was given a ticket for rolling through a stop sign by, you guessed it, Deputy Baine. A couple of days before that he was given a speeding ticket by Deputy Baine."

Wolf leaned back in his chair and looked at the stripes of sunlight gleaming off the oak shelving.

"Your man has a personal vendetta against my pilot," Irwin said. "Deputy Baine's actions, and last night's episode in particular, are regrettable and concerning."

The truth was, Wolf didn't put it past Baine to do such a thing. Six or seven years ago, Wolf had witnessed Baine rough up a customer coming out of the Beer Goggles Bar, and it had forever shaped how Wolf viewed Baine professionally.

Wolf and Baine had been on their way in for a bite to eat, and a young man, a college kid, had come barreling out of the bar straight into Baine's chest. The kid had looked up, held up his hands, and apologized profusely, slurring the whole way through. In the process, a fleck of spittle had come out of the kid's mouth—a fleck of spittle Wolf never saw. Before Wolf knew it, Baine had thrown the kid on the ground, his knee pressing on one side of his face, attempting to bury his head into rocks and dirt. Baine had gone nuts, and Wolf had had to pull him off.

It turned out that Baine had messed with the wrong kid that day. The kid's father was ex-DA and ran a prestigious law firm in Denver. In the end, Baine had to endure a month's suspension without pay, apologize, and complete a one-year probation. That was all fine and good, but never once had Wolf seen an ounce of regret in Baine about the matter—not then, and not any time since.

"Sheriff Wolf?" Irwin said.

Wolf took a big breath and swiveled back to face Irwin. "I'll look into this," Wolf said, and stood up.

"What assurance do I have that—"

"I'm sorry, but I can't give you any assurances," Wolf said. "But you have my word that I'll look into this."

Irwin frowned for a second and stared at the carpet, then stood up and nodded in resignation. "Thank you, Sheriff. I appreciate it. Of course you'll have to check the facts yourself before you go making me any promises."

Wolf nodded and stepped around the desk.

Irwin gripped his hat with two hands and looked down. "I was sorry to hear about the mayor's wife. I take it you'll be at the service today?"

"Yes, I will."

"Then I'll see you there," Irwin said, turning around and letting himself out of the office door.

Wolf followed Irwin through the squad room, taking in a whiff of his strong cologne as they walked. Wolf twisted the knob to the reception area and let him go first.

"Sluice County Sheriff's Department," Tammy was saying into the phone as they entered the blasting furnace of a room. "Just a minute, honey."

Wolf looked over. She pointed the phone receiver at Wolf, pushed a button, set it down, and flipped a page in her magazine.

Irwin finished putting on his coat and nodded to Wolf. "Thank you for your time." He turned and ran straight into the glass door, backed up and stared it down, then gave a final wave and left.

Wolf couldn't keep himself from smiling at Irwin's exit. Irwin seemed to be a good man, and he could see why Margaret Hitchens spoke so highly of the well-to-do bachelor, even if Irwin did ogle Wolf's ex-wife.

Irwin jogged across the parking lot and got into the passenger seat. The Range Rover backed up and drove away, leaving behind a cloud of exhaust.

"Who's that on the phone?" Wolf asked, walking back to the door.

"Your girlfriend," Tammy said. "How are you two doing by the way? She come up here lately?"

Wolf ignored her and gripped the handle. When nothing happened, he looked up and gave her a warning glare.

The door clicked and Tammy turned the page on her magazine.

CHAPTER 4

FOR A NUMBER OF REASONS, Deputy Heather Patterson loved days like these—blue sky with heaps of snow on the ground and sagging off the trees. First, they reminded her of her youth and fun on the slopes of Aspen Mountain, Buttermilk, and Snowmass. And that reminded her of skiing with her brothers and parents, oh yeah, and her Aunt Margaret too, because her family used to visit her in Rocky Points.

In short, sunny winter days reminded her of her family, and she was feeling a little homesick. It always happened that way on sunny winter days. It was a mental trigger that had always been there, like how the smell of a man's cologne could remind her of romances past.

Romances. Past. Those two words went hand in hand, she thought.

Her heart thumped in her ears and her breath came fast as she slogged through the thick snow. They were almost all the way down the pine-tree-lined driveway and just a stone's throw from Edna Yerton's porch.

Edna Yerton's home was a no-frills A-frame brown box with two drape-covered windows on either side of a brown front door. A covered porch ran the full length of the house in front, and in the yard was a mound of snow the general shape and size of a Lincoln, or older-model Cadillac. Regardless of the make, the car was worthless for navigating these dirt roads most of the year.

Patterson stopped and turned around to check on Rachette's progress. Correction: *She* was just a stone's throw away. Rachette was still closer to the SUV parked up on the county road than to her.

"Are you okay?" she called.

Rachette had his gloved hands wrapped around the top of his right thigh. To an untrained eye, it would have looked like he was trying to pull his leg out of the snow. But in Patterson's recent experience, she knew he was massaging his gunshot wound from seven months ago.

It was one of three shots he had taken in order to save Patterson's life, and by God, it wasn't something she was ever going to forget. But for a while now, she'd been wondering whether Rachette wasn't playing the whole injured card a little too much. Every time the thought came up, she felt like she was betraying her partner, but she swore she'd been catching him in an act recently.

For instance, when they'd gone skiing the other day, Rachette had done the same thing. What's more, it had been when she was talking to the lift operator—that cute Australian kid who was way too young but had an interesting cocky charm nonetheless. That day, she had skied up to the front of the line and stopped, waiting for Rachette. While waiting, she had struck up a conversation about how cold it was for an Aussie in the mountains of Colorado, or something stupid like that. When Rachette hadn't shown up, she'd turned around, and he had been in this same pose, massaging his leg and looking at her.

"Do you want to go back to the truck and rest, and let me do this?" she called up to Rachette.

Rachette looked up at her and mumbled something. Then his snowshoe lifted, as if finally breaking free from sucking quicksand, and he marched toward her with high steps, kicking up powder that glittered in the sun.

Patterson turned and continued to walk, a smile creasing her lips. She'd used a similar variation the other day. *Do you want to sit this run out? I can meet you in the lodge.*

"Hello there!"

Patterson turned and saw an old woman in the doorway.

"Mrs. Yerton?" Patterson called.

"Yes?"

"I'm Deputy Patterson, from the Sheriff's Department." She turned around and pointed at Rachette, who was now getting close. "This is Deputy Rachette. We were ... can we come talk to you?"

Edna Yerton nodded. "Sure, yes. Come in. Come in from the cold!" She laughed gaily, reminding Patterson of her grandmother. "So much snow out there. It's so deep."

When Patterson's snowshoe scraped against a wooden step hidden beneath the snow, she knew she'd reached the edge of the porch. She stepped up, digging the teeth on the soles into the old pine. She bent down, unbuckled the straps, and then stepped out of them and stomped the snow off her boots.

Edna watched quietly, and Patterson turned to help Rachette up the steps. She held out a hand, but Rachette ignored it and tripped on the submerged step.

"Shh—" he hissed, thankfully cutting his expletive short.

Patterson turned to Edna. "Do you have a wood pile?"

Edna raised her eyebrows and tilted her head, her face contorted with confusion.

"A wood pile?" Patterson repeated. "For a fire?"

"Ohohoho," she laughed. "I thought you said *worthwhile*."

Patterson swallowed. "Oh, no. I—"

"It's around the side of the house," she said, and a hand materialized out of the heap of layered clothing and pointed to the right.

Patterson took a hard look at Edna. The woman's gaze was distant and her lips were curled in a small smile, as if she were thinking of a favorite movie she'd seen forty years ago. Her hair was matted to her head and she was bundled in thick layers of clothing underneath a wrapped blanket. A lot of clothing. Patterson could see a plaid bathrobe, a green knit sweater, two flannel shirts, a hooded something, a turtleneck, plaid pants, candy-striped wool socks and fuzzy slippers.

"I'll get the wood," Rachette said, taking off his backpack and clunking it at Patterson's feet. "You go inside. Dump this stuff in the fridge."

Dump this stuff in the fridge. "All right. You okay?"

He walked away through the thick snow to the side of the house.

"May I come in?" Patterson asked. Edna stepped aside for Patterson and she entered.

"It's cold in here," Patterson said. Her breath was still visible inside the entryway.

Edna shut the door, locked it with two latches, and then walked down the hallway toward a darkened kitchen.

"Uh, can we keep that unlocked? Deputy Rachette needs to ..."

Edna disappeared around the corner. Patterson could hear

canned laughter coming from a television somewhere in the depths of the house.

Patterson unlocked the door, opened it again, and stuck her head out. Rachette was headed back with an armful of logs. "Just come in when you're done," she whispered.

"What?"

"Just walk in when you're done," Patterson said louder, and then she shut the door and walked into the kitchen.

It was filthy, and in mind-boggling ways. A dead mouse lay next to the scratched-out floorboard near the refrigerator. There was a broken ceramic bowl underneath the kitchen table from which four beat-up wooden chairs were pulled out at all angles. Junk mail covered every square inch of the tabletop. Dead mice, chunks of mud, straw, wires hanging out of the ceiling, grass clippings ... *Where was the food mess? The empty cans of soup, spent packages of pasta?*

Patterson stood still, letting her eyes pass over the litter, attaching a sad explanation to every element. She felt her eyes tear up and her breath constrict, and then she cleared her throat.

The front door opened all the way and bashed into the interior wall, and Rachette stumbled inside with an armload of lumber.

He kicked the door closed and then walked down the hall toward Patterson. He gave her a double take and then stopped, looking around.

"Where is she?" he asked quietly.

Patterson nodded to the flickering room where Edna had gone.

"This is a nice place," Rachette said as he made his way past her.

Patterson felt her face redden with anger at Rachette's

insensitivity, but then figured she wouldn't have expected him to tear up like she had. She'd long suspected that Deputy Rachette's tear ducts secreted dust.

Patterson took off the backpack and set it on the table. The leaflets, flyers, and envelopes shifted, and a few dropped on the ground. She picked them up, pushed everything into a pile she would deal with later and walked into the room after Rachette and Edna.

Rachette was already digging in the black stove in the corner, making no attempt to talk to the woman.

Edna sat on a recliner chair, nibbling from a bag of potato chips that sat next to her and watching an episode of *Seinfeld*. At least she was eating.

"Have you had any food today, Edna?" she asked. "I mean, besides the potato chips?"

She looked at Patterson with that same look of confusion.

Patterson backed away and went into the kitchen, unable to take whatever was about to come out of the sad old lady's mouth. She shook her head, unzipped the backpack and began unpacking. Everything went on the counters, which were relatively clean compared to other surfaces. Canned veggies, beans, bread, peanut butter, pasta, soup, a six-pack of soda, and a bag of fried chicken—all in plain view, so Edna would know it was there after they'd left.

She took a deep breath and held it, then opened the refrigerator. Six, no, seven bundles of blackened bananas were stacked on the shelves amid a clutter of condiments stacked two high on each shelf. Bread bags with science experiments growing in them. At least four dozen eggs.

She shut the door and exhaled, then caught the stench she'd unleashed on her next inhalation.

She opened a cupboard and pulled a plate off the stack,

thankful she'd opened the right cupboard on the first try, and relieved that didn't look more depressing inside. No dead squirrels.

She put a chicken drumstick on the plate, pulled off a soda from the six-pack, and walked back into the room.

Rachette was kneeling down in front of the open furnace door. His eyes were narrowed and his face glowed orange as the fire crackled and popped inside.

Patterson walked to Edna, who was oblivious to the life-giving heat now filling the room, and held out the plate. "Okay, Edna. Here's some chicken. Eat up."

Edna looked up and smiled, and then took the plate. She set it down on her thin stomach, tipping the bag of potato chips over, and started devouring the chicken.

There was a framed picture on the wall of a tanned couple with three children, all lounging on the deck of a yacht with different colored drinks in hand. She narrowed her eyes and walked closer to it. It was definitely a yacht, not a cruise ship. The man wore a gold watch and a dangling gold chain hung around his neck. His eyebrows were arched and he smiled with one side of his mouth, like *Hey, you seein' all this?*

"That's my daughter's family," Edna said with a dreamy smile. "They live in Miami."

"They ever come visit?" Patterson curled her lip in a snarl and Rachette looked over at her. She hadn't meant to make the question so loud.

Edna put the chicken to her mouth.

Patterson sighed and closed her eyes, and then returned to the kitchen. She went to the sink and turned on the water faucet, letting out a breath of relief when the water came out in a steady stream.

Opening the cupboards and checking underneath the sink,

she saw that someone had wrapped the pipes in blankets and duct tape, and it looked to be keeping them above freezing. Maybe Sheriff Wolf had done this on an earlier visit. Now, if they could do the same for Edna—wrap her up and keep her from freezing ... Rachette seemed to be handling that part well, so Patterson decided to do what she saw fit to improve Edna's situation.

For the next thirty minutes, Patterson went on a cleaning and tidying rampage. There was no way she was going to leave this woman in this place looking like it did.

She found a few trash bags and doubled them up, and then dumped all the bad food from the refrigerator; then she got started on the rest of the kitchen. After she'd finished—the strange debris cleared and vital things set out on the counters for Edna to find later—she moved on to the other rooms. She vacuumed with an old Dirt Devil she'd found in the closet, and she scrubbed, swept, wiped, threw away, and organized. Patterson went into machine-mode, doing all that was necessary for this woman without an ounce of emotion, like she was cranking out a particularly tough cross-fit workout and kicking its ass.

Rachette took the same time to re-educate Edna on the workings of the stove. Edna didn't look like she'd been paying attention, and another tinge of concern hit Patterson in the gut like she was on a bumpy boat ride on the ocean. *On a yacht.*

By the time they left, however, the air inside Edna's was sauna-like compared to before, and Patterson felt good that they'd set her up for at least a few days.

"I'll check up on you in a couple days," Patterson said to Edna as they shut the door, and she meant it.

...

Rachette two-fisted the wheel of the SUV, sticking to the ruts they'd made on the way up as they crept down County Road 15, which led into town. The dashboard heater was working overtime, sounding like a jet engine, and the sun flickered through the trees into Patterson's window, making it a comfortable ride after enduring the elements outside for so long.

"You got pretty emotional in there," Rachette said.

The comfort was short-lived.

She turned and glared at Rachette. "That didn't disturb you? That a resident of our town lives like that? Barely clinging to life, completely helpless? And did you see that picture of her daughter's family? They're loaded, hanging out on a luxury yacht."

Rachette smiled and shrugged. "There's a shit-load of people like that in the world. You can't save everybody, Patterson. It's gotta be, like, eighty percent of people living like that. And look at the mayor's wife. Just because you have a boatload of money doesn't mean you're happy and don't off yourself."

Patterson twisted her face and looked at him, then turned away and shook her head.

"Easy," Rachette said. "I'm just saying, some people choose to live differently than others, and it's not up to you to save them."

"You think Edna lives like that by choice? She doesn't know what the hell is going around her. She can't even light a fire. Can't even see that there's a dead fucking mouse on the ground that needs to be scooped outside. And her shit-bag family ignores her from life in paradise. And as far as the mayor's wife goes ... just shut up about that."

Rachette held up a hand. "O-kay."

Patterson rolled her eyes. Sometimes she wondered why she talked to her partner.

Up ahead was a little mound that ran across the road, and beyond was freshly plowed the rest of the way down. Rachette slowed, broke through the snow, and then let off the brake and coasted a little faster on the packed powder.

"Listen," Rachette persisted, "we'll go check on Edna again in a few days." He curled his lips down and nodded. "Yeah, get her fire goin' again. You can cook her some ... ramen noodles."

Patterson laughed in spite of herself because Rachette was ribbing her, and doing a good job of it. What he knew was that Patterson was a self-proclaimed terrible cook, and had proven so on two occasions to the entire department. The first time was when she'd made a seven-layer Mexican dip for the Sheriff's Department Halloween party, accidentally adding relish instead of green chili, and catching some serious flak from everyone. The second time was when she'd brought a pasta salad to the Christmas party, and the pasta was rubber-like-chewy-to-rock-hard, thus solidifying her reputation as the worst cook in Rocky Points.

Patterson looked at Rachette. His cropped blond hair stuck up at the back, there was a glint on his face where five days of blonde stubble had grown in patches, and he wore his confident "dreamy" look that worked on no woman, ever. She rolled her eyes and looked out the window, suppressing a smile for fear of encouraging him. She had to admit, he'd gotten better at steering conversations away from the yelling matches they'd had early in their partnership. Just a little.

"Shit," Rachette said.

The SUV began shuddering, anti-lock brakes struggling to keep the truck from skidding on the packed snow.

Patterson sat up and gripped the ceiling bar as she watched the pines twirl past the windows. As the truck stopped spinning at three quarters of a revolution, exactly why they were spinning became clear to Patterson.

She looked out the window and gasped. They were headed straight for the black underside of a truck that had upturned on its side on the right snow bank.

The tires of the SUV squealed as they continued gliding on the slick road.

Patterson leaned toward Rachette as the truck got closer to impacting her door. They were slowing, but it looked like they were going to connect. She pulled on the seatbelt to get away from the door as much as possible, but it had locked itself in place.

Just before they hit, Rachette revved the engine and the SUV lurched forward, narrowly avoiding the collision. Rachette overcompensated, jerking the wheel to the right. They spun in the opposite direction and rammed into a waist-high snow bank beyond the upturned truck, abruptly stopping the SUV.

"You okay?" Rachette asked with wide eyes.

"Yeah, you?"

"These guys with their piece-of-shit trucks and their piece-of-shit plows." Rachette pushed on his door, unable to open it against the snow. He looked over at Patterson. "I gotta climb out your side."

Patterson opened her door and got out.

Rachette climbed over the seat, kicking the dash computer

in the process. "Shit. Ah!" As he stepped onto the ground, he cried out and clenched his leg.

That was real pain.

Rachette slammed the door and marched toward the truck.

"Make sure everyone's all right," she said, half warning him to keep his cool.

The truck was an older-model Chevy, painted sky blue and rusted-out brown near the window wells. On the front was a large yellow plow that now stood straight up in the air, and it looked like the crash had wrenched and bent it to an awkward angle. The old Chevy lay on its passenger side, leaning toward the roof with all four tires off the ground. The deep snow looked to have saved the truck from flipping onto its top.

The wheels still rotated lazily.

Rachette jumped over the snow bank and waded past the plow to the cracked windshield. "Jeff, you all right?" he asked.

There was some movement inside and Patterson couldn't make out what she was looking at for a second; then a scraggly looking man she didn't recognize peered out of the glass. He was standing on the inside of the passenger door, with his head stooped against the driver's side.

"You okay in there?" Rachette asked.

"Yeah," Jeff's voice was muffled. "No!" he yelled.

Rachette and Patterson exchanged looks.

"Roll down the window above your head and climb out," Rachette said.

Jeff reached up and hand-cranked the window open.

"Just a second," Rachette said, and then he high-stepped over to the roof and put both hands on it. "Patterson, get over here."

Patterson took a step and plunged down, the snow reaching her hip, and not for the first time in her life she wished she was a taller human being. A few seconds later, she waded into position and placed her hands on the roof.

"If this starts tipping, move fast," Rachette said.

Damn right, she thought, but just nodded.

Jeff was scrambling around inside the cab and Patterson could feel the truck moving,

"What are you doing in there?" Rachette asked. "Climb out the top!"

"I gotta get my ..." said the voice, fainter this time.

"What?"

Patterson looked at Rachette. "I think he said, 'I gotta get my smokes.'"

Rachette pounded on the roof. "Get out of there, now! This thing could catch fire, damn it!"

Jeff climbed up and out of the window with the help of weak-looking arms, judging by the shaking they were doing underneath his camouflage jacket. He wore a hunter-orange winter cap and his greasy long brown hair protruded over his ears. He grunted, hoisted his butt to the shelf provided by the driver's door, and then kicked his legs over the roof toward them.

The truck wobbled a little, but held steady under Patterson's gloved hands.

"Jump!" Rachette grunted.

Patterson flexed every muscle and pushed against the roof with all her might, wary that the beast could topple onto them —and then she would be shorter than ever.

Jeff jumped down between them and landed with his face buried in the snow, but neither Rachette nor Patterson made a move to help him up. After a few seconds, he pushed his way to his feet, his once brown wispy beard now caked white, and scrambled back up to the road.

Rachette and Patterson let go and followed him, reaching the road as fast as they could.

"What the hell happened?" Rachette demanded.

Jeff was turned away from them and walking up the road.

"Hey, I'm talking to you!" Rachette said, marching after him.

Jeff wasn't having any of it. He was acting as if Rachette and Patterson weren't even there.

Rachette began jogging, Patterson close on his heels. After a few steps, they caught up and got in front of him.

Jeff stopped and stared past them. His lips parted and his chest heaved.

They followed his gaze to a frozen corpse lying partially submerged in the snow bank with impossibly twisted legs. Her torso was striped with maroon, which further inspection revealed to be cracks in her skin showing dark-red flesh and guts below, like she'd been frozen and then ripped open ... which was exactly what had happened, Patterson realized. If that wasn't enough to take in, her neck had rotated independently of her body so that she faced them, tongue protruding and bugged-out white marbles for eyes.

And on her forehead was what looked to be a painted maroon X.

"Oh my God," Patterson said.

CHAPTER 5

"LINE ONE!" Tammy yelled just before the door clicked shut.

Wolf shook his head and walked through the squad room.

"Everything okay?" Wilson asked, looking up from his computer screen.

Wolf nodded. "Yeah, you?"

Wilson shrugged and looked back down at his computer.

Wolf shut the door of his office and sat at his desk, then took a deep breath and picked up the phone. "Wolf," he said.

"Wolf? That's how you answer the phone now?"

Wolf smiled and swiveled the chair to look out the window. "How are you? How are things in Denver?"

"They're going well. I can't complain. A lot more action than Glenwood Springs field office, that's for sure. I hear it's been rough up there lately for you guys in Rocky Points."

"Yeah," Wolf said. There was a beat of silence, and Wolf realized she wasn't talking about the weather.

"Did you go to the call?" she asked quietly.

Wolf took a deep breath, remembering the sight of the mayor's wife sitting in an office chair, dead of a self-inflicted gunshot wound to the head. It was something that had robbed him of sleep the past two nights, and something he would vividly remember for years to come.

"Yeah, I was the first responder."

"Jesus," she breathed into the phone.

"Yeah, we've got the funeral this afternoon, and a huge storm hit last night, so not the easiest of days ahead."

"I saw that about the storm. And, hey, listen, on that note, I'm horny now, and it's all your fault."

Wolf raised his eyebrows. He could always count on FBI Special Agent Kristen Luke to say the unexpected.

"I ... don't know what to say to that. Thank you?"

She laughed. "I just saw your interview on television. Nice work. If you're ever out of a job, you know what field to enter next."

"Really? Thanks. Television, though? I couldn't wear all that makeup."

"I was thinking cameraman," she said.

Wolf smiled and sensed Luke smiling at the other end, probably drawing longing eyes in a room full of male FBI agents. "How are you?"

"You already asked that." Her voice dropped in volume and her tone went soft.

"Give me the real answer," Wolf said.

"Well, I do miss you, if that's what you're fishing for. But, really, it's good. I like the people I'm working with. There are a lot of women in the Denver FO, which is nice for my sanity, and a lot more opportunities for advancement than in Glenwood Springs, that's for sure."

"And how about living down in the big city?"

She blew into the phone. "Chicago was a big city. Denver's manageable. I like it, lots to do. I've gone out a few times for drinks with a few agents. Otherwise, I eat, sleep, and then get up and do it all over again. I've also had to go up a couple of times to see my mom."

Wolf nodded and let the silence settle for a second. He could have said something like *You drove all the way up to Glenwood Springs and didn't drop me a line? I could have met you for dinner.* But Kristen Luke and David Wolf had had a good few months, and the call of duty, and their commitment to their respective jobs, was stronger than their ability to hold a relationship together, and they both knew that trying to force anything was pointless.

As a couple they hadn't exactly been doomed from the get-go; instead their relationship had been destined to become something else besides what other people considered normal. Even when they had been going steady (as steady as it could get), being separated by fifty miles of mountainous terrain had meant they never slept in each other's beds more than a few times a month, and neither of them was going to push for more from the other. Each already had enough pushing from their jobs, and then from what waited for them off the job.

They had enjoyed each other's company for six months, and when federal budget cuts shut down the Glenwood Springs FBI field office, Luke was given a choice between Salt Lake City and Denver. In the end, proximity to Wolf, or any consideration for Wolf and his feelings, was never a part of her decision to transfer to Denver. She was there to be closer to her ailing mother, just a two-and-a-half-hour drive away on I-70; and just as importantly, the Denver assignment gave her the best opportunity for advancement in the Bureau.

"So, you seeing anyone?" she asked.

"Nah, you?"

"Mmm," she said. "Nobody yet. I think you raised my standards to unattainable heights."

"Yeah, well, television star, sheriff, incredible buttocks … good luck topping that."

She laughed. "What about Sarah?"

Wolf paused. "What about her?"

He gazed across the street at Margaret Hitchens's real-estate office, where Sarah Muller had hung her newly acquired real-estate license and was already proving to be a huge asset to the company.

"I heard she broke up with her boyfriend," Luke said in a nonchalant tone, "and he skipped town to Vail."

Wolf shook his head. "How are you getting this information?"

She kept silent.

"Are you talking to my mom down there?" He was dead serious for a second, and then puzzled out the truth. "Oh, yeah. Your new buddy. Patterson."

One night, when Luke had come into town to visit him, they'd gone down to Beer Goggles to join some deputies in the department for a beer. That night, Luke and Patterson had formed a close bond at what he considered unnatural speed. It was like Luke suddenly had the little sister she'd always wanted, and Patterson the big one. Apparently, they still kept in touch and Wolf's love prospects were a topic of discussion.

"So?" Luke asked.

"So, what?" Wolf answered. "Look, I gotta get going. We've got a lot of snow on the ground, and—"

"All right, all right. Relax, I'm just looking out for you. I think you two still have a future together."

Wolf sighed. "Okay, thanks for calling, Mom."

Luke chuckled into his ear, and then a man called her name in the background. "I've gotta go. Later."

"Later."

Wolf set down the phone and stood up. He'd dicked around enough for the type of morning it was outside. There were probably people out there in need of help, and he was playing footsie on the phone with girls. He slipped on his jacket, grabbed his hat and gloves, and walked out into the squad room.

"I'm heading out," Wolf said to Wilson.

Wilson looked up from his computer screen with watery eyes and a clenched jaw that was hiding a yawn. "Okay, boss. I'll be here."

The door flew open and a puff of heat hit Wolf. Tammy's imposing figure stood in the doorway to her reception office. "Rachette and Patterson just called in a 10-79 on County 15."

"Get your stuff on," Wolf said to Wilson. "You're coming with me."

CHAPTER 6

WOLF STOOD in the cold air on County Road 15, watching the ambulance crawl up the road past the line of department SUVs.

He cursed as he dug his fingers into his five-day beard. Again. Every winter he grew it, despite remembering the hell his face had to endure the year before. But it was something men in the mountains did in the winter; men everywhere did. As he pulled off his glove for a better tool to dig into his fur-covered jawbone, he wondered whether the insulation from the bitter temperatures was worth it, and decided no.

Wolf put his glove back on and looked at Rachette. "You ever talk to her?"

Wolf stood with Deputies Rachette, Yates, Patterson, and Wilson near the fluttering crime tape sectioning off a large area around Stephanie Lang's body.

"No, not really. I've just seen her around. She's out at the bars most weekends."

"Yeah, same here," Yates said.

Rachette and Yates were two of the more social deputies in

the department, and that meant spending time off like many young men did—in bars, drinking and chasing women. When they'd produced the driver's license from her wallet and ID'd her as Stephanie Lang, Rachette and Yates had come forward as knowing her. Wolf, on the other hand, had thought she looked familiar but couldn't place her.

"Who'd she hang out with?" Wolf asked.

Yates smirked and nodded. "Guys."

Wolf looked at him. "What does that mean?"

He shrugged. "She's always with a different guy, like every night I've seen her. I've heard she gets around. Sorry, got around."

"Yeah, that she did," Rachette said.

Wolf closed his eyes behind his mirrored sunglasses and willed his skin to pull as much warmth from the blaring sun as possible. It was mid-morning, and the temperature was as high as it was going to get. And according to his dashboard computer when he'd driven up here, that was negative one degree. Somehow talking to Rachette and Yates about this dead woman wasn't helping any.

"And I take it you guys had personal experience with her?" Patterson asked in a serious tone.

Rachette sniffed. "I might have cuddled with her—"

"Let's just remember that this is someone's daughter lying dead in the snow and shut the hell up about it for a few minutes, okay?"

Rachette looked at Wolf and swallowed. "Yeah, sure. Sorry, Sheriff."

The sound of crunching tires coming to a halt and the diesel engine going quiet signaled the official arrival of the medical examiner.

Wolf walked away from the others and down the road.

The passenger door of the ambulance squeaked open. Dr. Lorber, the Sluice County Deputy Medical Examiner, stepped out and stretched his lanky arms overhead.

He left the door open and leaned back inside, and then pulled a Russian-style fur hat with earflaps over his lengthy pony-tailed hair and straightened his glasses. "Oh, man, it's freezing!" he said, zipping up his jacket and slamming the door.

Wolf stalked closer, watching Lorber go to the back hatch doors of the vehicle cleverly called *The Meatwagon*. An assistant Wolf recognized as Dr. Joe Blank stood behind Lorber holding a black canvas bag.

"Dr. Lorber," Wolf said. "Dr. Blank."

Lorber twisted and looked at Wolf. Wolf knew there were gray, intelligent eyes hidden underneath the painful squint. Lorber's eyesight wasn't the best and for some reason he'd decided against prescription sunglasses, something Wolf didn't envy of Lorber at this altitude, especially on a bright day like today.

Lorber ripped off his glove and stepped toward Wolf with a wide brown-toothed smile, the product of too many cigarettes washed down with coffee.

"Fancy seeing you again," he said, tucking a strand of long hair back into his fur hat. "Good God, man, Rocky Points is producing some dead bodies lately."

Wolf took off his glove and shook Lorber's long, thin hand. Lorber was one of the tallest men Wolf had ever met; had Lorber stood straight, he would have been around six-foot-seven. However, because of his posture, Wolf didn't have to look up to meet his eyes. Wolf didn't know whether this was caused by a spinal defect or self-consciousness, or something else, but the effect was that of greeting a large stoop-necked bird, like a condor or a vulture.

Lorber pulled his glove back on and nodded. "Right, show me what you've got."

Wolf turned and walked, and Lorber loped next to him. "Lucky we got here at all. That slide on the pass looks like it was something else. The CDOT guys had a little canyon dug through, and we barely fit. Were you there to see it?"

"I was," Wolf said.

Lorber looked over at the upturned pickup truck with the plow and gave a soft whistle. "The driver okay?"

"Yeah, just shaken up."

The driver of the plow truck was already gone, having already been interviewed in a warm vehicle, and then driven to town.

"Deputy Patterson!" Lorber shouted, like he always did when he saw her.

Patterson looked down with a blushing smile and kicked her feet.

Lorber had been at the department a few months previously to improve the forensics lab, and in doing so had worked closely with Patterson. From their first hour together, Lorber had loved her, and now couldn't shut up about her or stop himself from embarrassing her with praise whenever they saw one another in public.

"Hope you're keeping these bastard men in line," Lorber added.

Patterson chuckled without smiling and turned to lift the crime-scene tape.

Lorber looked around at the somber-faced deputies and then gave Wolf a sideways glance.

Wolf was keenly aware that he'd just vanquished any

morale that may have built up among everyone with his tongue-lashing. But, then again, he wasn't sure that this was a situation for chipper morale, anyway.

Wolf followed Lorber under the tape.

"Ah, there she is," Lorber said as the body came into view.

It had taken almost two hours for Lorber to get here from County Hospital on bad roads. During that time, Wolf had studied the girl's body several times, but frequency wasn't making it any easier for Wolf to see.

Wolf had never gotten too disturbed or squeamish by corpses, but this one was particularly gruesome. The woman's face was pale gray, almost white, and her eyes were open and frozen solid, obscuring the true eye color, though there seemed to be a hint of blue faintly visible through the iced-over corneas. Only a few streaks of black were visible under the otherwise white-encrusted head of hair. Her lips were glacier blue and her mouth was open, tongue frozen solid.

Then there was the red X marked on her forehead, giving Wolf the feeling her death had been part of a satanic ritual or something. Shivers ran through Wolf every time he looked at the body, and not because of the arctic temperatures.

Tracking his eyes down only led to more disturbing sights. She wore torn-up black slacks revealing frozen and shredded meat underneath the fabric. One of her feet was next to her head, which said less about the woman's flexibility and more about how much of a number the plow had done on her. Her white blouse was also torn to frayed strips, revealing a snow-white belly, twisted at the waist, and striped with red openings in her flesh. Her head had been wrenched around one hundred eighty degrees, like an owl's. The final thing that kept attracting Wolf's attention was a green tattoo of a bird and a one-word caption on her exposed lower back. *Happy.*

Lorber bent down close next to the corpse. Craning this way and that, he studied the head and neck; next, he leaned toward the dead woman's crotch, and then ran his eyes up and down her contorted legs. Finally he stood back up.

"Strangled," he announced. "At least it looks like it."

Wolf had seen the bruising on the woman's neck, and how the tongue protruded, but he'd also noticed the body's unnatural twist, and it was so mangled, he had to admit that the cause of death wasn't as obvious to him. "She's pretty chewed up. Are you sure?"

"The plow got her good. She was probably originally back there"—Lorber pointed at the line of department SUVs—"and then she was pushed up the road by the plow and deposited here. Who knows how far she tumbled against that steel." He turned and glanced at the upturned plow truck. "None of these flesh injuries happened before she died. She was frozen stiff when these happened, and long dead."

Wolf nodded.

Lorber looked down at the truck, teetering on its side, then up the road and back to Wolf. "I take it this guy plowed her and didn't notice, then noticed on the way back down the road and crashed?"

Wolf nodded. "You've solved the traffic accident. Now what about her?"

Lorber smiled and looked back down. "I'll get her back to the hospital, thaw her out, and do an autopsy. On this leg, it looks like the fabric has frozen straight onto the skin. I think that's urine. Along with the ligature bruising, that's why I'd put my money on strangulation. I'll check what the hell that is on her forehead. You're right, though—she's torn up, and I could be wrong about the strangling. I've got myself a puzzle here."

Wolf looked at him and narrowed his eyes, swearing he'd heard a hint of excitement in the medical examiner's voice.

"You ID her?" Lorber asked.

"We found her coat with her wallet in her pocket right there." Wolf pointed at the jacket half dug out of the snow bank, a yellow evidence marker next to it. "ID inside. A local girl named Stephanie Lang."

Lorber nodded, apparently not recognizing the name. "You get a cell phone?"

"Yeah, dead and damaged though. We're working on it."

Rachette walked up behind Wolf and cleared his throat. "Sir, we found the current address for our vic."

"Yeah?" Wolf asked.

"What," Lorber said, "the license not current?"

Wolf shook his head.

"She lives right up the road." Rachette pointed. "A half-mile up on the right. Tammy just called me with the address. Says she's been renting with two other roommates."

Wolf turned back to Lorber.

"Go," Lorber said, bending down to study the body again. "Joe and I have this."

Wolf nodded and followed Rachette underneath the tape.

"Patterson, Rachette, with me," Wolf said. "Baine, secure the scene with Yates. Wilson, you can head back to the station. And I'm sorry I snapped earlier. There's a lot of death lately, and it's—"

"No problem, sir," Rachette said. "I was out of line and I apologize."

Wolf nodded and walked away, certain that in his twenty years in the department he'd never once heard his former boss apologize like that. Burton would have disapproved if he were here. But he wasn't here. He was at home, undoubtedly in bed, waiting for the Scotch to metabolize out of his system while he watched fishing shows on TV.

CHAPTER 7

WOLF PULLED up to the address for Stephanie Lang and got out of his SUV. Rachette and Patterson pulled up behind him.

Thirty years ago, a man named Walt Wiggit had built six identical one-story ranches, and to this day he still owned and rented them out.

The house in front of them, sitting at the end of a long, narrow, shoveled walk, was the first in the row. It was painted dark brown and featured a front-facing picture window, through which Wolf and his deputies had an unobstructed view into the living room. Inside there were a few young people shuffling around, looking outside with wide-eyed glares as they urgently talked with one another.

"Anything on that cell phone?" Wolf asked Patterson.

"No, sir. It's damaged. Tammy is getting records from the phone company, but as far as looking at the phone itself, it's toast."

"The plow didn't help." Wolf looked at Rachette. "You know her roommates?"

Rachette shrugged. "I don't know."

Wolf, with Rachette and Patterson in tow, walked to the

porch. The cold froze his nostrils for the hundredth time that day. He pinched the zipper on his jacket with his gloved fingers and pulled it to his chin, careful to not catch any beard hair.

They stepped up onto the porch and Wolf pushed the bell.

There were frantic noises coming from inside—fast footsteps on hardwood floors, a dish slamming against a countertop, the hissing of voices to shush one another, and then silence.

Wolf sniffed and wiped his dripping nose once again, catching a whiff of marijuana smoke from inside.

"Oh, here we go," Rachette said, smelling the same thing.

Wolf reached up to push the bell again, but the door rattled and the doorknob turned.

A red-eyed man in his early twenties peeked out, opening the door only enough to reveal his face "Hello?"

"Good morning. I'm Sheriff Wolf. These are Deputies Rachette and Patterson. Does Stephanie Lang live here?"

The kid's bloodshot eyes narrowed. "Yes. What can I do for you, Officers?"

"We need to ask you a few questions. May we come in?" Wolf asked.

"Uh," the kid said. "I don't know. I ..."

Hot air streamed out of the door, wafting the thick stench of marijuana smoke outside.

"We-we-we—"

Rachette put a hand on Wolf's shoulder. "Hey, if you guys are smoking weed in there, well, guess what? It's legal. So quit freaking out and let's talk, huh, John?"

Wolf stepped aside. Rachette's time off spent at the local bars was finally paying dividends.

"Hey, Tom. Uh, okay." He opened the door wider and looked down. "What's this about?"

"We just said," Rachette said, walking into the house. "Stephanie."

"She's not here," he said, looking at Rachette.

"We know," Rachette said.

John frowned and ruffled his thick head of sandy-blonde hair. He was dressed in baggy blue ski pants, suspenders hanging off his waist, and a zip-up sweater on top.

Wolf stomped his feet against the doorstep and walked in after Rachette, Patterson taking up the rear.

"Of course, driving while high is not legal," Rachette said, looking into the house.

Wolf looked into the living room and saw why Rachette had said as much. There were two more people in the house— a woman and another man, both in their ski pants and under-clothes. Soft music was coming from the television, and there were skiers jumping off cliffs on the screen. It was clear that they were gearing up to get a late-morning start on one of the biggest powder days on the mountain in recent memory, and it appeared that a bong-load each was to be their final step before piling into the car.

"And you two are?" Wolf asked, nodding to the young man on the couch and the young woman on the chair.

The guy on the living-room couch was in his late teens or early twenties. He wore black ski clothing five sizes too big, plastered with duct tape covering rips in the fabric. He had a long ponytail of knotted hair draping over his shoulder and a wispy beard that made Rachette's facial growth look down-right *GQ*. The guy's eyes were narrowed—whether from the weed or defiance was unclear.

"Tyler," he said, shaking his head. "Tyler McClellan."

Defiance, Wolf decided.

The woman sitting on the chair looked up at Wolf with chocolate-brown eyes. Her hair was greasy blonde and hung behind her ears, looking like it hadn't been washed for days. She wore a beaded hemp necklace that draped onto a pink fleece; black ski pants and pink socks completed her outfit. She was probably attractive after a shower, Wolf thought, which looked to be a rare occurrence.

"Jamie," she said. "Jamie Bancroft."

Patterson had her notebook out and was writing furiously.

"John," Wolf said. "What's your last name?"

"Cameron," he said. "What's—"

"Was Stephanie here last night?" Wolf asked.

The guy on the couch blew air out of his lips and looked out the big window.

"Did I say something interesting to you?" Wolf asked.

The kid put his elbows on his knees and scratched the back of his head. "Nah."

Wolf looked at them and held up his hands.

"Uh, she didn't come home," John said. "She texted me and said she was getting a ride home from some guys, so we didn't go pick her up. But she never did show up here."

"Pick her up from where?" Wolf asked.

"Sometimes we'll pick her up from the shuttle stop at the bottom of the road, in town. She works up at Antler Creek Lodge," John said.

Wolf realized where he'd seen Stephanie Lang before. She'd been walking the room last night, waiting on tables.

Jamie looked up from the cloth chair and lifted a finger. "Why are you asking about her? Did something happen?"

Wolf turned to John. "Could I see that text message, please?"

John unzipped a pocket on his ski pants and produced his cell phone. After a few taps on the screen, he held it up.

Wolf read the last incoming message from Stephanie: *I got a ride from two dudes tonight. You don't need to pick me up.*

John had replied: *Okay. You have to bring more beer if they want to drink anything.*

Wolf nodded. "Who was here last night?"

John gestured to the couch. "Just us three."

"And how long were you guys here? From approximately what time to what time?"

John shrugged. "All night. From sundown on. We were just riding out the storm with a few beers, chillin' out, you know?"

Tyler scoffed and shook his head again.

"Is Stephanie seeing anybody? Dating anybody in particular?" Wolf asked.

This was the last straw for Tyler, who leaned his head back and started laughing.

Wolf watched the display, then asked, "Why's that funny, Tyler?"

"Oh, sorry. Yeah. It's just funny because you asked if she was seeing or dating anybody in particular."

"Why's that funny?" he asked again.

The kid put up finger quotes. "Anybody in particular. No. She isn't seeing anyone in particular." He sat back and concentrated on a fingernail.

"Um,"—John looked in between Tyler and Wolf—"no, she wasn't seeing anyone in particular."

"What's going on?" Jamie asked, this time with more conviction.

"Yeah," Tyler stood up from the couch and swiped his ponytail with a hand. "This is straight BS. You have to tell us what's going on. You're, like, entrapping us into making

Stephanie look guilty for something, and we don't even know it."

"We found Stephanie's body a half-mile down the road this morning," Wolf said.

Tyler's face dropped, and he sat back down on the couch. Jamie smothered her face with her hands and started whimpering.

"What? Her ... body?" John said. "Are you serious?"

"I'm sorry," Wolf said, studying their three faces as they withdrew into their own worlds of shock. Although they were all high as cirrus clouds and had been hard to read up until then, they seemed to be reacting genuinely to the news. No *acting* like they were concerned; it was the real deal.

Wolf cleared his throat. "Tyler, why did you laugh and say that about her seeing someone in particular?"

Tyler swayed his head back and forth a few times then looked up at Wolf with glassy eyes. "I ... I, she ... she just sees a lot of different guys." He sniffed and a tear rolled down his cheek.

"Were you dating her, Tyler?" Patterson asked.

Tyler looked up at Patterson, his eyes now streaming, his teeth bared, and Patterson offered a sympathetic gaze in return, which seemed to soften his contorted face.

"Like I said, she doesn't really date anyone ... didn't really date anyone in particular. But, yeah, we were kinda seeing each other. We were getting pretty close. So you can see that I was kind of pissed this morning that she was out with a couple of guys all night last night." He shook his head and shut his eyes. "Oh my God. What happened to her?"

"We're looking into it," Wolf said.

"Was she killed?" Tyler pointed at the phone in John's

hand. "It was those two guys. Whoever those two guys were, it was them."

Wolf pointed down the hall. "We need to search her things. Is her room back there?"

John nodded. "Yeah." He went over and crammed himself next to the girl known as Jamie and put an arm around her.

Wolf looked at Patterson and then flicked his head toward the three kids. Patterson nodded and took out a pen and paper notebook from her pocket.

Rachette pointed at a door in the hallway and looked at John.

"It's the last door on the right," John said.

"Thank you," Rachette said, and started walking.

Wolf followed him down the hall and into the room. It was completely dark inside, the window covered by a thick blanket fastened to the wall with screws.

Rachette flicked on the light and whispered to Wolf, "What do you think?"

Wolf shrugged. "Not sure yet."

He went to the window, pulled aside the blanket, and saw there was a hook on the wall to hang it on, so he did so. The room faced east, and the blazing, snow-reflected sun lit it up like stadium lights on a football field.

Thick brown shag carpet covered the floor, and the boards underneath squeaked with every step. The unmade bed was centered against the wall opposite the window.

Wolf eased open the top drawer of the chest of drawers set under the window, and saw neatly folded socks and under-wear. The second drawer held T-shirts, and the third, miscella-neous stuff: a leather folder, a notebook, various letters, and credit-card statements including some charges by merchants

Wolf didn't recognize. Sex toys. A half-empty box of condoms. Massage oils and candles.

"Hey," Rachette said, pointing in the top drawer of a small desk set in the corner.

Wolf walked over and looked inside at a stack of hundred-dollar bills. He picked up a pencil and pushed them with the eraser, fanning them out. They were crisp and had successive serial numbers, looking like they had never seen the inside of a wallet.

Wolf counted the money by sight. "That's twelve hundred in cash."

"Yeah," Rachette said, "and that's not from waiting tables. No way."

Wolf nodded. "Could have brought a stack of smaller bills and traded them in for fresh hundreds at the bank ... I guess," Wolf said, but not believing his own words.

"Drugs?" Rachette asked.

Wolf shrugged. "Bag it," he said.

A thorough search of the rest of the room revealed nothing significant; nothing like twelve hundred in crisp cash.

Wolf and Rachette walked back into the living room. Patterson looked up, closed her notebook, thanked the three kids quietly, and nodded at Wolf.

"Did Stephanie sell drugs?" Wolf asked no one in particular.

They looked at each other and shook their heads.

"No, she didn't," John said.

"She was clean. Didn't like drugs anymore," said Tyler.

"What do you mean, anymore?" asked Rachette.

"She used to do all sorts of stuff, like weed and other stuff, and then she quit. Cold turkey. It was like a big deal for her.

She went to a counseling group about it and everything," Tyler said.

"Where did she do that?" Wolf asked.

"At the old bank building," Tyler said. "Mondays and Thursdays."

Rachette, Wolf, and Patterson exchanged glances. They all knew that was where Sarah—Wolf's Sarah—counseled a group of troubled young men and women, and they knew those were her nights. It had been a memorable quip by Rachette—*Mondays and Thursdays? Those are football nights. I'd just have to stay an addict*—and Wolf knew his fellow deputies were remembering the same thing right now.

"Thank you, guys," Wolf said. "Deputy Patterson?"

Patterson nodded and waved her notebook. *Yeah, I have everything we need here—names, phone numbers, addresses.*

Wolf pulled a stack of business cards out of his pocket, peeled three off and handed them out. "Please stay available for us. We'll probably be back soon, but we'll call first. And in the meantime, if you need to talk, remember anything of importance, please either call us or come down. Any time, all right?"

They nodded, and Wolf ushered Rachette and Patterson out.

The sun was a little higher in the eastern sky, but it was still nostril-freezing cold out, and they walked in silence to the cars, all zipping and pulling on fabric to stave off the invading air that jabbed at their faces, necks, ears, and wrists.

"You get the next-of-kin info?" Wolf asked, holding out a hand.

Patterson shook her head. "There is none."

Wolf frowned. "No parents?"

"Nope. No one, as far as the kids knew. They said her

parents were killed when she was a child, and they didn't know about brothers or sisters. Nothing about grandparents. Nothing."

Wolf nodded. "Okay. I'm going back by the scene. You two make your way up to Antler Creek and find out who she left with last night."

Rachette nodded and opened his mouth like he wanted to ask something, then thought better of it.

"You going to see Sarah?" Patterson asked, looking up with a curious wince.

Wolf looked at her and narrowed his eyes, thinking about his earlier conversation with Special Agent Luke, and how she had been so in the know about Sarah's breakup with Mark Wilson, and how her source of gossip must have been Patterson. "Yeah," he said. "I'll talk to her about Lang."

"Tell her 'hi' from us," Patterson said cheerily, and turned and walked to the SUV.

Rachette watched her leave and then looked back at Wolf.

"Antler Creek," Wolf said.

"Yeah," Rachette said, and turned around and left.

CHAPTER 8

PATTERSON, Rachette, and Deputy Brent Wilson sat in the six-person gondola car, suspended at least sixty feet over the flat slope below. As it traveled over the wheels on the tower, it pulled up and bounced, and then dropped back down.

As this happened, Rachette closed his eyes again, a prolonged blink that was much more than an involuntary movement to moisten his eyeballs.

It was not lost on Patterson that Rachette was scared to death of the gondola at Rocky Points. Each time they rode it, he would pause every sentence, straighten his posture, and fake every smile as they bounced past a tower or swayed in a particularly strong gust of wind. At least it beat the catatonic state he got into when, God forbid, they went on a chairlift without a safety bar to pull down.

Wilson looked at Patterson and grinned, seeing the same thing Patterson had, and they exchanged knowing smiles.

Patterson liked Wilson, and was glad Wolf had radioed for them to pick him up at the station on the way to the mountain. Wilson was only two years in the department, so he was a relative rookie, just like Rachette and Patterson. But he was at least ten years their elder, and with two kids, so he brought a completely different, more mature perspective to the table. Patterson, for one, welcomed Wilson's adult sensibility. Being stuck with Rachette, day in and day out, took its toll on her.

Wilson was a quiet man, tall and gentle-looking like a big teddy bear. Just like his physique, his face and expressions were always soft—a constantly friendly guy. But she knew his physique belied his strength. Everyone in the department treated Wilson as their resident strongman. His thick limbs lent tremendous lifting, pushing and twisting power.

"How's your skiing coming, Rachette?" Wilson asked, his blond mustache bouncing on his face when he talked.

Rachette sucked in a breath and looked out the window, then put on a cool look and shrugged. "You'll have to ask Patterson."

Wilson turned to her and raised his eyebrows, the side of his mustache curling up.

"He's doing very well for his first year skiing," she said. And she meant it. "With his bum leg, I didn't expect him to improve as quickly as he has."

Rachette smiled and nodded to Wilson. "There you go."

The gondola entered the top terminal, plunging them into shadow. It slowed from full speed to almost a dead stop in less than a few feet, sending Rachette grabbing for the bench he sat on. Since he was sitting facing downhill, he'd really been caught off-guard this time.

Patterson and Wilson laughed and buried their faces in their hands.

Rachette's face reddened as the doors opened, and Patterson got out quickly to help him save face. She stepped a few paces, turned around, and slapped him on the shoulder. "The lifts take a little getting used to," she said.

Rachette gave her a deadly look, and she knew immediately that she should have just ignored the whole thing.

They stepped out of the terminal and into the thin, bright air at the top of the mountain. The view was spectacular, with all the peaks coated in white as far as the eye could see in all directions, save the south where miles beyond Williams Pass the terrain flattened into a vast plain valley lined by tall mountains on either side, like a half-pipe for the gods. Up to the north, they could see past Cave Creek and beyond. To the west stood peak after peak, and she picked out the ski runs of Aspen Mountain and Snowmass, looking like powder-green sundaes drenched in streams of white chocolate.

The sight gave her a tinge of homesickness and, at the same time, comfort that she could see home at that very second. She loved it up here.

"Howdy, Deputies." A tall man with mirrored glasses crunched toward them with an outstretched bare hand.

Patterson took off her glove and shook hands. The man pulled up his sunglasses, revealing beautiful sea-green eyes set under thick, dark eyebrows.

"I'm Scott. Scott Reed," he said.

"I'm Heather. Heather Patterson."

His smile seemed to brighten the day even more, and she was glad she had her sunglasses on because she was certain she was staring like an idiot. They parted grips, perhaps a second too late, and he swiveled to Rachette and Wilson.

"Hey Tom, hi. I'm Scott," he said.

Patterson raised an eyebrow. Apparently Rachette knew this guy. How come she'd never seen him before?

Scott led them toward the snow cat parked near a trail sign a few hundred paces away.

Patterson followed behind in silence, watching Scott converse with Wilson and Rachette. They swerved between throngs of skiers dropping skis, clacking boots in bindings, and clanking poles, but Patterson didn't hear or notice any of it. She found herself entranced with other things, a rare occurrence for her.

Reaching the snow cat, Rachette and Wilson stepped inside the side door and sat down along the benches on either side of the rear hold.

Scott turned to Patterson. "You want to sit up front with me, Heather?"

She shrugged and tried to look nonplussed. "Sure."

Scott smiled at her, looking at her like he knew she was hiding something, or maybe it was like he was looking into her soul. She felt her breath accelerate as she sat down on the cold torn leather of the seat.

"How fast can this puppy go?" Rachette said, thankfully drawing any awkwardness in the situation toward himself.

Scott turned the key and the engine growled to life, rattling the interior. He slapped the steering wheel and turned to Rachette with a serious look. "Twenty-one miles per hour."

Patterson laughed aloud. Scott glanced her way with a smile and then shifted into gear.

"Aw, weak," Rachette said.

Scott turned the wheel and started down the catwalk, which ran straight ahead along the ridgeline toward a big pine-log structure perched in the distance. It was a flat trek on skis, and a long walk on foot, which was the reason for Scott Reed's employment, Patterson mused.

"Yeah. It's not the top of the line,"—he knocked on the

dashboard—"like most of the stuff we're working with at Rocky Points, but she does the job." He flicked a glance at Patterson again.

Patterson smiled easily and looked out the passenger window, admiring the view of the peaks to the west.

"Not a bad office you have up here," she said.

"You got that right," he said. "The view is amazing today."

She nodded and then looked over at him; he was staring at her with a look as serious as a heart attack. She rolled her eyes a little, looked back out the window, and felt her skin go red hot.

Patterson rode the rest of the few-minutes' ride in silence, listening to Rachette's incessant questions and Scott's patient answers. At one point there was a lull, and Patterson half-expected Rachette to whine, "Are we there yet?"

When they stopped, she got out and gave a quick wave to Scott.

"I'll wait here for you guys," he said.

She didn't look back as she walked to the lodge, fearing she might reveal her growing infatuation for him in a one-second glance, and he would think she was desperate or plain psycho.

Instead she exhaled and studied the building in front of them.

Antler Creek Lodge was tall, made of sturdy logs that must have been taken from hundred-year-old trees. Though unseen from the front of the building, she knew there was a roomy lower level that opened to the rear of the building, housing the top-of-the-mountain ski-patrol station. She had heard that one of the major perks of a patroller being assigned to the Antler Creek station was the availability of gourmet coffee and left-over world-class dessert pastries.

It was empty of skiers, in stark contrast to the other lodges around the mountain at noon on a weekend, because it was only open for après ski and dinner, and only then by reservation. Patterson had eaten there once a few years ago with her father and Aunt Margaret. She hadn't paid for a cent of the meal, and she wouldn't have been able to afford it if she'd tried.

Rachette stepped up next to Patterson. "You like that guy?" he asked.

She frowned. "What?"

"That guy, Scott? I'm just asking. It looked like you might have been a little into him. He seemed to be into you."

She looked at Rachette for a few seconds and then shook her head. "Whatever, I don't know. He seems like a nice guy, I guess."

Rachette huffed and looked ahead.

"What?"

"He's married."

Patterson felt her stomach drop. "What?"

"Yep. Married. Has two kids."

Patterson looked over at him again. Rachette was staring at the snow and shaking his head.

"You're full of shit," Patterson said.

"I'm serious," he said. "Ask Wilson."

Wilson looked over with wide eyes. "I have no clue. I just met the guy."

"Well, he is," Rachette said.

Patterson shook her head and looked forward, feeling the heat rise in her cheeks. Then she slowed a bit and glared at Rachette's back. She felt like an idiot for letting herself swoon like a high-school girl so quickly, and now a bigger idiot that Rachette had seen through her so cleanly.

She guessed she had to be grateful to Rachette, though. Her

partner had her back, and now she knew, sooner rather than later, that Scott was a scumbag, before he had become some full-blown romantic fantasy.

The doors to the Antler Creek Lodge were at least fifteen feet tall, and both of them looked like one solid piece of wood, each with a rack of antlers burnt into them. They were behemoths, Patterson thought, but they swiveled easily as Rachette pulled them open.

Inside, a hostess podium stood underneath an enormous elk-antler chandelier suspended from the ceiling with a heavy-gauge rusted chain. Beyond that was a vast room filled with round and square tables, each draped with a white tablecloth and topped with understated fresh floral and candle centerpieces.

Thick logs spanned the A-framed ceiling, and on the far wall were floor-to-ceiling windows offering a panoramic view from Williams Pass to the south to the town of Rocky Points below, Cave Creek Canyon far to the north, and the snow-covered peaks of the continental divide behind all of it.

Soft jazz played through invisible speakers, and the air smelled like spices and roasting meat.

"Ah, hello, Officers," a man said. He turned away from one of the tables with a hand flourish and walked toward them. He was medium height and heavy-set, dressed in a white button-up shirt and black slacks pulled high on his torso.

Identical attire to their victim, Patterson noticed.

"You the manager?" Rachette asked, and shook the man's hand.

"Yes, sir, I am."

"I'm Deputy Rachette. These are Deputies Wilson and Patterson."

"Welcome to Antler Creek. I'm Terrence," he replied in a

sing-song tone. "It's nice to meet you. I have to admit, I've been wondering what's going on ever since you called."

"We need to ask you a few questions about Stephanie Lang. Is she one of your employees?" Patterson said.

Rachette glanced at Patterson and then back to Terrence. "It's part of an investigation we're conducting."

Terrence nodded, and his slicked-back hair didn't move a millimeter. "Okay."

"What time did she leave last night?" Rachette asked.

"Oh dear," Terrence said, allowing his voice to take on a more-pronounced effeminate quality. "Come with me." He stormed off with a deep, hip-swaying walk toward two swivel doors that had submarine portholes, bashing through with stiff arms.

Rachette jogged to catch them before they swung shut, and Patterson and Wilson followed, looking at one another. They all stopped, almost barreling into Terrence, who was standing just inside the door, pressing his finger against a sheet of paper taped to the wall.

"Hmmm," he said. "She left ... with the first cuts. So about ten-thirty?" He looked up at the ceiling for a few seconds. "Yeah, probably about then."

"Isn't that a little late for the first cut?" Patterson said, thinking about a summer job she'd had waiting tables for a restaurant in Aspen.

"Normally, yes," Terrence said, "but last night was not normal now, was it?" Terrence zigzagged his neck a few times and then stared at Patterson.

"No," she said, "I guess not."

"Those people stayed way too long for the type of weather we were having. It was like they *wanted* to be stranded here overnight. They don't even know how lucky they were."

"Have you ever been stranded here?" Patterson asked, her curiosity piqued.

He narrowed his eyes. "No."

Rachette crossed his arms and looked between them. "Did you see her leave?"

"Pssh, I had plenty of other stuff going on."

"Who else was let off work at the same time?" Patterson asked.

Terrence twisted toward the sheet of paper again and pointed at the list. "All these with the number one next to them. Nine people."

Patterson pulled out her notebook and started writing down the names. "Can we please get their phone numbers also?" she asked.

Terrence kept his eyes on Patterson and put his finger on the sheet of paper underneath. It was a roster of the employees, with phone numbers next to the names.

"Thanks," she said.

"Just write down the men," Rachette said.

Patterson ignored him. Just because the text message had said she was with two men didn't necessarily mean that she'd left the restaurant with them.

"How many servers were working last night?" she asked.

"All those you see right there," Terrence said.

Patterson stopped writing on the third name and sighed. "Can we please take this schedule?"

Terrence shrugged. "I don't see why not."

Patterson pulled the sheet off the wall and folded it. "So what was the process last night for the servers? Did each server have a section? Or certain tasks?"

"They each had a specific section to keep track of. Within

each section, some were in charge of drinks only, while the others took care of the food and everything else."

"And which section was Stephanie in?" she asked.

Terrence rolled his eyes. "You're killing me. Do you mind telling me what's going on?" His attitude was pure sass, but somehow he used a light, sincere tone of voice that came across as friendly.

"It's just a part of an investigation," Rachette said quickly. "Now, please, the section?"

Terrence turned and walked away at full speed again, clicking on the tile floor and swerving his ample body between a few cooks who were preparing things on the stainless-steel counters.

They followed him, this time in less of a rush.

Terrence stopped at a door at the end of the kitchen and inserted a key. Pushing open the door and flipping on an interior light, he started whistling a vibrato melody and dug through a mess of papers on a desk. Then he picked up a sheet, stepped out, and slammed the door behind him.

"Here you go," he said.

Rachette took it and Wilson and Patterson gathered to look. It was an overhead diagram of the dining hall, and every seat was labeled with a name written on a line next to it. It only took a few seconds for Patterson to spot Wolf's name, seated next to Sheriff Harold Burton.

Terrence poked his finger on the sheet on the opposite side of the room from Wolf's table. "She was in section two, drinks. These two tables."

There were six people on a table, so twelve people in total. All in all, a heck of a lot of people Stephanie could have left with, and a heck of a lot of people to interview.

"Are there any servers from last night here now?" Patterson asked, slightly dejected.

Terrence shook his head with a sympathetic look. "Not for another couple of hours. Sorry."

Wilson cleared his throat. "How do you guys get down from the mountain at night?"

Terrence looked up at Wilson and leaned back, as if startled that the man could talk. "Same way you guys just got up here. The gondola."

"Thank you," Patterson said, and she turned and left the kitchen.

She heard Rachette and Wilson wrap up the interview as she pushed through the swivel doors and into the dining room.

"Hey, wait up!" Rachette said.

Wilson and Rachette jingled and thumped up behind her, catching up to Patterson as she went out the front door and back into the glare of the afternoon sun.

"What's the hurry?" Rachette asked.

"We've got a funeral to go to in an hour," Patterson said, not breaking stride.

They walked in silence toward the parked snow cat.

Scott Reed sat on one of the snow tracks with his elbows on his knees, taking in the sun with an upturned face. He spotted them coming when he heard the crunching footsteps and smiled.

"You guys ready to get back—"

"Do you know who Stephanie Lang is?" Patterson asked, stopping in front of Scott.

Scott stood up and pulled his coat down. "Yeah, she works here."

Scott gestured to the lodge behind them, and as he pointed

with his left index finger, Patterson realized he wasn't wearing gloves. Neither was he wearing a wedding ring.

"Everybody knows her," he said with a small chuckle.

Patterson narrowed her eyes, wondering what the hell that was supposed to mean. They kept hearing about Stephanie's promiscuity. Was Scott saying he knew her in that way? Giving a little nudge-nudge, wink-wink to Rachette and Wilson? This guy with his dreamy green eyes oozed scum to her now.

"Did you see her last night?" she asked.

"Yeah." He nodded and put on his gloves. "I took her over to the gondola, just like half of the rest of the people here. We had two cats going last night but, yeah, I remember taking her. She left early. The snow had just started."

"Was she with anyone?" Patterson asked.

"Like, what do you mean, with someone? I remember ... there were probably like seven or eight other people on the cat, and a ski patrolman sitting up front with me."

"Do you remember if she was conversing with two men?" Rachette asked. "Like she was leaving with them."

Scott raised his eyebrows and looked to be starting a grin, and then looked at Patterson's serious expression and scrunched his face in thought. A light went on, and he closed his eyes and nodded. "Yeah, she was. She was with a guy."

"One man?" Rachette asked.

Scott nodded.

"How do you know they were together?" Patterson asked.

"I remember them cuddling and laughing, trying to keep warm against the blowing snow as they got into the cat. And then they sat just behind me and to the right, and I remember watching them kind of groping each other."

"They were kissing?" Patterson asked.

"No. Just acting super friendly, you know? All smiles

and,"—he shook his head—"I don't know, just all up against each other." Scott pantomimed cuddling up next to a person, and then looked down at Patterson.

Patterson stared with half-closed eyes. "Can you describe the man?"

Scott swallowed, flicked a look at Rachette and Wilson, and cleared his throat. "No, sorry."

"Are you sure?" Rachette said.

He shook his head. "I'm sorry. No, I can't remember what he looked like. I shuttled so many people last night, and everyone was bundled up, and there was blowing snow ... I'd just be making stuff up if I gave you any sort of description."

Patterson stepped past Scott and got into the snow cat. Before she could stop herself, the words were already out of her mouth. "We wouldn't want you making stuff up," she said as she sat down on the rear bench.

"Uhh." Rachette looked at Patterson and then Scott. "I guess we're ready to hit it. I'll sit up front with you."

They bounced and swayed in silence on the short ride back to the gondola.

When they stopped, Patterson jumped out and walked to the front of the cat.

Scott met her halfway with an outstretched hand and a smile.

"Who was the gondola operator last night?" she asked, giving a quick and lifeless shake, not bothering to take off her glove.

"It was ... Victor. Victor Peterhaus."

She took off her glove and pulled out her notebook. "Can you spell that?"

He did.

"Do you have his number?" she asked.

He did and pulled out his cell phone and gave it to her.

"Thanks," she said, and walked into the gondola terminal, and into the first vacant gondola.

A few seconds later Rachette and Wilson came in, wobbling the car as they sat breathlessly, a wary look of concern on their faces. And zipped lips.

CHAPTER 9

AFTER SENDING Rachette and Patterson up to the mountain, Wolf drove up the road to check on the crime scene once again. They were clicking pictures, writing notes, and bagging evidence. Satisfied that Lorber, Blank, and the four deputies were processing the scene with expert efficiency and didn't need any help from him, Wolf turned his truck around and headed back down into town.

On the way he called Sarah. When it went to voicemail, he hung up and dialed Jack.

"Hello?" Jack said, his voice cracking, like it did so often these days.

"Hey man, what's going on?"

Wolf heard nothing. The connection was shoddy, as it was so often in the area.

"Can you hear me?"

"Yeah." Jack's voice was an old, scratched record.

"Hey, how's it going?"

"Good. How are you?" A flutter of wind hit his phone mic, and Wolf realized that Jack was probably on the mountain.

"You riding today?" Wolf asked, careful to use Jack's proper term for skiing.

"Yeah, I'm on the lift. It dumped huge. It's so epic."

Wolf nodded, picturing his son on the ski lift, his legs, lanky after a growth spurt that had hit him painfully that past few months, dangling with wide skis designed for deep-powder days, long hair poking out from under his cap, probably wearing way too little clothing for how cold it was.

"Hey, you know where your mom is today?"

"... center ... someone."

"What? You're breaking up."

"She's at the ... nity center, said she had to meet someone. To talk. I think she was meeting Chris Wakefield."

"Oh, really?" The community center. The old bank building. The two were synonymous. "Okay, thanks."

"She didn't say, but she gave me this big talk about suicide this morning, and then she said she had to go talk to someone who was having a hard time today. So I put two and two together."

Wolf nodded, wondering who Jack was sitting next to on the ski lift, divulging all this information in a voice just below a shout.

"Yeah, okay. Listen, we'll talk later." Wolf hung up.

At the bottom of the road, he stopped at the stop sign and took a right. Another block up, he slowed to a stop at the four-way, which, for Highway 734, was the only stop sign on Main Street for miles in either direction. He paused, looking at the signs and the freshly plowed roads extending in four directions.

Another truck crunched to a stop on Main and puffed patiently, waiting for Wolf to make his move. Wolf waved the driver on. He was thinking about Deputy Baine, Baine's nemesis, the helicopter pilot Matt Cooper, and the traffic stop the previous night.

As he drove on, he passed bundled people milling around outside the Edelweiss Bakery, a Bobcat mini-loader that was clearing off the sidewalk, and Greg's John Deere, still scooping and swiveling, building the ridge of snow in the center of the street.

Wolf's truck rocked and slid as he pulled into the half-plowed parking lot of the community center. Three vehicles were lined up, all parked along the front of the building—Sarah's Toyota 4Runner, an older-model silver Toyota pickup, and a Ford SUV that was billowing exhaust.

Wolf parked, and the Ford backed out and then drove away. He shut off his SUV and watched the truck leave. At the wheel was Chris Wakefield, the teenage son of Greg Wakefield, the mayor of Rocky Points, and Jen Wakefield, the woman who was to be buried later today after a closed-casket ceremony.

Wolf knew this would probably be one of the worst days of Chris's life, having to bury his mother. Maybe second worse only to two days prior when Chris had found out the news. It was no surprise that he was seeking comfort from Sarah.

Wolf stepped out of his truck and gave a somber wave, and Chris's hand rose and fell with a vague gesture as he peeled away.

Wolf walked over the softly packed snow and pulled open the door.

The community center in town was an old bank from the early 1900s, so it was commonly, and cleverly, referred to as the "old bank building" by the residents in town. Despite the name, there was no indication inside that it had ever been an old bank. There were no teller counters, no vaults, and no toiling employees with green visors scribbling in ledgers.

Instead, it had been renovated with short carpet and buzzing fluorescent lights, separating walls faced with cheap wood paneling, and plastic furniture that had probably been ten years old when it was brought in twenty years previously. Plain wood frames displayed old black-and-white pictures of Main Street on one wall. On another was a row of color headshots of the employees, with brass-engraved nameplates below. Each face looked too bright and washed out, but somehow, despite the flash burning into her face like an atom-bomb detonation, Sarah still looked good in her picture hung at the end of the line.

Nobody was inside the narrow room at the front, so he walked into the hallway and made his way back to the big room where the meetings were usually held, and where Sarah was most likely to be.

The wood under the carpet creaked, a clock ticked on the hallway wall, and the lights hummed overhead. As he approached, he heard nothing from the big room, so he was startled when he walked in and saw two faces staring at him, not just Sarah.

"Oh, hi," Wolf said.

Kevin Ash sat on a plastic chair in front of Sarah. The young man looked away from Wolf and stared at the floor. His eyes were red and his cheeks wet.

Sarah sat a few feet away, and there was a vacant chair next to her, apparently where Chris Wakefield had just been sitting. She looked up at Wolf and raised her eyebrows.

"Uh, sorry." Wolf backed out of the room. "I'll just wait up front. I was hoping to get a word with you, Sarah."

"Okay," she said quietly. "It will be a few minutes."

"No problem," Wolf said, and walked back down the hall and into the front room.

No more than a minute later, he heard the squeaking of footsteps coming down the hall and then Kevin came out with Sarah close behind.

Kevin's cheeks were dry, but he stared at the floor with a drooping mouth. His blond facial hair was a few days grown, and he had straw-colored hair peeking out from his black winter hat with a Rocky Points Ski Patrol patch sewn to the front of it. Despite his scraggly appearance, he looked strong, healthy, and fit from spending so much time on the mountain.

Since Wolf had interviewed Kevin Ash for what had ultimately become Patterson's position, they hadn't exactly been on speaking terms in the few times Wolf had seen him around town. Last summer, Wolf had dismissed the county council chairman's son as a terrible candidate for a sheriff's deputy—an assessment he still stood by—and that had hurt him. Wolf knew Kevin worked for the ski patrol now, and it was proving a much better fit.

"Hi Kevin," Wolf said.

"Hi," he said, avoiding eye contact.

"Not up at the mountain today? I would have thought Duke would be working everyone to the bone with this dump we had last night."

Kevin looked at Wolf for the first time, and Wolf thought he saw real hatred simmering inside his blue eyes.

"I took a personal day today," he said, and then walked away toward the door.

Wolf's mind was cranking. Was Kevin upset because he'd somehow just heard about Stephanie Lang? If so, how?

"Hey, Kevin," Wolf said.

Kevin stopped and looked up at Wolf with drooping eyelids, like he was about to be reprimanded by the school principal.

"Do you know Stephanie Lang?" Wolf asked, being careful with his verb tense.

"Yeah, she's in the group with us."

Wolf was surprised. "Oh, you're in Sarah's group?"

"Yeah, so what?"

"Nothing," Wolf said eyeing him. Then he realized it was clear that Kevin didn't know about Stephanie. Something else was upsetting him, and Wolf's line of questioning needed to stop.

Kevin lifted his hands and then dropped them at his sides.

"Sorry, I was just wondering," Wolf said.

Kevin shook his head and zipped up his coat. Without another word, he walked out, got in his truck, fired it up, and drove away.

Sarah was looking at him with wide eyes. "What the hell was that?"

"I don't know," he said. "We need to talk."

She parted her lips and squinted. "What the hell? You just start interrogating him like that, and then stop?"

"Sarah, we need to talk."

She sighed and walked down the hall to the big room.

He followed close behind. When they reached the main meeting room, he sat in the cheap plastic and metal chair Kevin had been sitting in. It was still warm.

Sarah shook her head and sat down across from Wolf. "Chris's mother killing herself has put a lot of strain on these kids."

Wolf sat quietly, watching Sarah pull her aspen-bark blonde hair behind her ear. She wasn't wearing makeup today, which was a look Wolf liked on her. It showed her beauty as God had given it, which was ample. Her face was darkly tanned on the lower half, goggle-eyed from skiing the past few weeks in the sun. Her blue sweater was snug against her body, accentuating the perfect bulges on her chest and athletic arms. Her jeans were old and frayed, taut against her slim legs. Underneath a tear in her jeans Wolf could see the fabric sheen of long underwear, a staple piece of clothing for winters in Rocky Points.

"What's up?" she said, finally meeting his eyes with her fiery blues.

Wolf took a deep breath and let it out.

"That's not good," she said, raising her eyebrows.

"No, it's not," he said. "We found a dead body this morning."

Sarah sat rock still and closed her eyes.

"It was Stephanie Lang," Wolf said. "That's why I was asking Kevin about her. I thought you guys might have been talking about her for some reason."

A tear dripped down her cheek and she sniffed. Her lips parted and quivered. "What happened?"

"She was killed. Murdered. We're looking for two men who might have been with her. You saw her last night, right? At the party?"

Sarah wiped her eyes and looked at him. "Yeah."

"Did you happen to see her leave? Or looking like she was going to leave with someone?"

Sarah looked through the wall behind Wolf, and then clenched her eyes tightly.

Wolf leaned forward and put a hand on her knee. "I'm sorry."

"It's my worst nightmare for her come true."

"What do you mean?"

"She used to do drugs a lot. Then she quit, but she … she was still an addict. Sex."

Wolf put his elbows on his knees.

"I was real worried about her, going around with all these strange men."

"So she told you about these men?" He sat up straight. "Talked about it in the group here?"

"Well, yes and no. She broke down once and told the whole group about it, and she stayed after once and told me about a man. A man who had roughed her up a bit. She was a little freaked out."

"When was this?"

Sarah stood, walked to a table near the window, and retrieved a tissue. "It was a long time ago. Like months. And ever since that night, she's never told me much. She kind of just goes through,"—she shook her head—"went through the motions at these meetings. I knew she was still out doing her thing with men, though. I've seen her. Even the other night at the party, she was, just … slutty. I hate to use that word, but she was just so confused, and she latched onto men, let them do whatever they wanted. It seemed like the worse she brought out in men, the better for her or something."

"You said the other night at the party." Wolf stood up. "What do you mean?"

Sarah blew her nose. "Charlie Ash's party. The whole thing was catered by Antler Creek and she was there."

"And she was with specific men that night?" he asked.

"No, not really. I just mean it was the way she was acting. Grabbing arms, rubbing lower backs, and pressing her boobs." Sarah sucked in a breath and looked up at the ceiling, and then shook her head.

"What?"

"Nothing."

Wolf stared at her.

Sarah rolled her eyes. "She did come over to our table last night, and she said hi to me, and then ..."

Wolf waited, then said, "She's dead, Sarah. Strangled. We believe two men are responsible. If you know anything, I need to know."

"All right. Well, I remember that when she came over to our table, she leaned down to talk to Klammer's assistant, like talk in his ear, and he kind of pulled her down by the arm and whispered something back. It was close, and it was a long whisper, so I remember thinking that maybe they knew each other from earlier. I remember that she was blushing when she stood back up. But she"—she shook her head—"she never came back. Never talked to him again. It was nothing. He was probably just asking for a fork and tried to hit on her or something."

"And what's this guy's name?"

Sarah slumped her shoulders. "Oh, come on, David. You can't ... don't go roughing this guy up and telling him I told you anything. If Klammer Corp gets the contract, and they're pissed at me, and they don't choose Margaret's firm to sell the units—"

"Relax." Wolf stepped close and rubbed her shoulders, a gesture he didn't realize would be so intimate until he was suddenly doing it.

She looked up at him with sad eyes. She smelled like memories of days making love in bed.

He dropped his hands.

"Jonas Prock," she said. "That's his name. Just, be discreet."

Wolf nodded and looked down at her. "Are you sure about the drugs? I mean with Stephanie. She was off them for sure?"

Sarah nodded. "I'm sure. She stopped. I can spot those things better than most. Why?"

"We searched her room, and she had twelve hundred dollars in her drawer. All crisp hundreds, straight from the bank."

"Well, could have been a big tip. Or she cashed a check." But Sarah was staring through Wolf again. "Or ..."

"Or what?"

"Or she was selling herself." Sarah sighed and another tear fell down her cheek. She stepped forward and gave him a hug, putting her ear on his chest. Then she shook with sobs.

He returned her embrace, and the butt of his pistol dug into his hip.

"What kind of world are we raising Jack in?" she asked.

Wolf stroked her head.

After what seemed to be a full minute, the hug seemed to turn from comforting one another to the beginnings of something else, and Sarah pressed into him even harder; then, just as abruptly, she pulled away and looked down at the floor.

"We have to talk one of these days, okay?" she said.

"Yeah," Wolf said. "Okay."

She sniffed and looked at her watch. "Shit, I have to go to the office before the funeral. I'll see you up there."

Wolf nodded and pulled down the waist of his jacket. "What about Jack?"

"He's coming to the office and we'll go from there. I have his suit and everything in the truck."

Sarah shut off the lights as they walked out of the room.

"Was Kevin Ash at his father's party the other night?" Wolf asked as they walked down the hall.

"No. Why?"

Wolf didn't answer. "And Chris Wakefield today? You were talking about his mother's suicide with him and Kevin?"

"Kevin and Chris are pretty good friends, and Kevin's been

helping Chris since his mother's death. Kevin's mom died a couple of years ago, so this is bringing up a lot of sad memories for him, too. It's a whole mess. I feel so bad for these kids. This news about Stephanie's going to be devastating."

Wolf stopped. "Kevin's mom died? In Tahoe?"

Sarah turned around, then narrowed her eyes. "Yeah. Before they moved here. Why? What?"

"How did she die?" Wolf asked.

Sarah fluttered her eyelids. "I … he doesn't like to talk about it, but I think a bad car crash. I don't push him." She tilted her head. "And, David, you need to use a little compassion here. Pull back from the cop routine a tad with these kids, okay?"

Wolf nodded. "Sorry. I'm just wondering is all, I guess. Just trying to figure out what the hell is happening around here, and I'm not sure where all the lines are drawn yet."

CHAPTER 10

"I'LL TAKE two eggs over easy, bacon, and hash browns. Wheat toast." Charlie Ash looked up at the waitress. "I'm still feeling like breakfast." He gave her a dismissive smile and looked out the window before she could chat him up anymore.

"Sh-should I wait for your two other guests to arrive?"

The cowbell on the door jangled, and Ash watched the two men he'd been waiting for enter through the front entrance. They stomped their feet and looked around. Ash raised a hand and waved them over.

He looked up at the waitress. "You can put my order in. These guys won't be eating lunch with me." Ash put his menu down and stacked the other two on top.

She nodded and picked them up with a small hesitation, then left. She did have a great ass. No wonder that heli-pilot Cooper was all hot and bothered about her. Too bad she was a simple moron who couldn't be taken out in public, like ninety percent of the rest of this town.

Elias Klammer walked in front of his bodyguard, or assistant, or whatever he was, all the while staring at Ash. Ash ignored what was surely meant to be a threatening glare and looked out the window at the trees piled with crumbling snow.

"Charlie," the man said, sliding into the booth across from him. *Chawley* it sounded like with his ridiculous accent.

Ash did not answer, and he shook his head when that freaking smell hit his nostrils. No matter how many times he smelled it, the cologne these two Austrians chose to wear was offensive to his nose every time. It was like Polo cologne mixed with ground beef.

"Jesus, you guys bathe in cologne before you leave the hotel?"

Klammer relaxed his eyes and looked out the window. The bigger, younger guy known as Prock, *more like Prick*, sneered and put an elbow on the table. He clenched his fist and stared at Ash.

"Give me a break," Ash said, rolling his eyes, careful not to give the underling any satisfaction by looking him in the eye.

The waitress came back up to the table.

"What did I say?" Ash raised his voice a few decibels. "They're okay, thanks."

She popped her eyebrows and leaned back on her heels, and then scurried away.

Klammer kept quiet and motionless while his assistant took off his leather gloves, tucked them into his hat and set the hat on the table.

"We are paying you a large amount of money to get what we want," Prock said in his thick Austrian accent, not even knowing how comically similar he looked and sounded to a younger Arnold Schwarzenegger. "And it is obvious we are not going to get it."

Ash glared at Klammer and pressed his lips together. "Why is your thug talking to me right now?"

Prock slapped the table, clanking the knife and fork in front of Ash and spilling some coffee over the edge of his mug. Ash looked down at the sloshing liquid and waited for the sudden silence in the restaurant to ramp back up to a murmur.

"Okay." Ash smiled easily at the big guy. "Now that you have everyone's attention ... I'm sorry, did you have something to say?"

Klammer's lip curled in a self-satisfied smile. This rich man liked to stay back in the shadows and watch his hired muscle work. He looked like he was sitting front row at the arena, watching his prized fighter.

"Like I was saying." Prock leaned forward.

Prock was an imposing man, Ash had to give him that. His thick, fur-lined jacket was unzipped, making him look huge, taking up more than half of the booth across the table. But Ash knew it wasn't the coat creating an illusion; the man was chiseled like a sculpture of Zeus underneath. Ash had marveled at the man's physique when they'd met on Thursday night. Had to be two hundred and twenty-five pounds of solid muscle.

And if the man's muscles weren't sphincter-clenching enough, then his eyes would do the trick. They were the color of dead grass. The whites were like milk, at times giving the illusion that he had only tiny obsidian circles inside those eyeballs. He used them well at the moment, as if he was staring into the fear-center of Ash's brain.

"We want that contract," Prock said. "And we have paid you to get the votes."

"Why are you spelling this out for me? You think—"

"It is obvious those votes we are paying you for are not there. The Hitchens woman had her nose up Irwin's ass all last night at the party, and Mayor Wakefield is clear about his intention to vote for Irwin as well. Another thing that is clear is that nobody likes you."

Prock stared, letting his last jab sink in.

"Listen—"

"How you became chairman of this county council is mind-boggling. Despite your position, your influence is none. Laughable. So you can see why we are confused as to why you are even calling this meeting. You should be running." The big Austrian's eyes narrowed. "You should be hiding."

The waitress came over, clanked a plate of food in front of Ash, and walked away without a word.

Ash looked up at her ass again and blinked. He picked up his fork and pulled the bed of hash browns on top of his eggs, and then started mashing them together.

"I'm glad you two are taking this tone with me because it makes the next thing I have to say that much more enjoyable." Ash took a fork-full of hash browns and eggs and put it in his mouth, and then took a bite of crispy bacon.

Klammer licked his lips as he watched Ash eat, and Ash smiled. Dangling things in front of people when they were desperate for them was his favorite pastime.

"As of two nights ago"—he set down his fork—"I have sealed the votes for your company. What you saw last night at the gala meant nothing; what you think you know about the inner workings of the seven members of the council is *nothing!*" Ash slapped the table and hissed the last word, hushing the dining room into silence once again.

Prock looked around the room with indifference and then to his boss sitting next to him.

"And how have you done that?" Klammer finally spoke up.

Ash swiped his hair back to the side and took a sip of

coffee. "That's for me to know and for you to reap the benefits from. That is, if you pay me the necessary price." Ash took a bite of his food, and then looked up to see if the hook had set.

Prock's eyes were wide open in either a murderous or amused glare, Ash couldn't tell.

"What are you talking about?" Klammer leaned forward and pointed his finger at Ash. "We've already paid you five hundred thousand dollars. For nothing."

Ash looked around the room. Satisfied that nobody was watching or bending an ear their way, he leaned forward. "The price has doubled."

The two men sat back and mumbled expletives in their foreign tongue.

Prock turned to Klammer and started chattering in German, and Klammer held up a hand.

Klammer stared at Ash, searching his eyes. "This plan of yours, it wouldn't have anything to do with the demise of the mayor's wife, would it?"

Ash dropped his fork and wiped his mouth. After another glance to make sure no one was listening, he lowered his voice and said, "What? The mayor's wife was diagnosed with a rare, progressive form of MS a year ago. Unfortunately, treatment had little effect, and she suffered neurological symptoms. She—"

"Yes," Klammer said. "I've heard about her disease from the mayor himself."

Klammer narrowed his lids and relaxed them, searching deeper into Ash's eyes.

Ash picked up his fork and took another bite. "Five hundred more, or I can ease up on my plan and let Irwin have the votes. I'll be fine either way, gentlemen. You can rest assured of that. Have a good flight back to Austria."

Ash took a bite of bacon. A bite of eggs. A sip of coffee.

Klammer's upper lip rose and fell, then he looked resigned as he signaled for his man to leave.

"I'll be in touch," Ash said, taking another bite.

Prock picked up his hat and gloves from the table, his freaky eyes boring into him as he did so.

The hook was set.

The leather booth creaked as they left.

CHAPTER 11

IT WAS one o'clock and Wolf was starving, so he drove into the parking lot of the Sunnyside Café. He'd be able to grab a bite in under an hour and still have plenty of time to prepare for the funeral at two-thirty, and he needed some time to sit and think.

As he parked the SUV, he was startled to see the Austrian he'd been talking about with Sarah come out of the door, followed closely by a shorter, older man.

They walked away from Wolf, both dressed in puffy coats with fur flowing out of the necklines. *Jonas Prock,* Sarah had told him. Followed by his boss. What had Sarah called him? *Clam, Calm,* or something?

Wolf sat and watched as they climbed into their Toyota Land Cruiser with rental plates and drove away. Though he couldn't see their eyes behind their mirrored sunglasses, they looked to be extremely upset, hissing words to one another with clenched jaws, steam shooting out of their tight lips.

He put on his hat and got out, watching the vehicle drive up Main toward the south, toward the mountain, where they were probably staying at one of the more expensive resorts in the ski base village. It would be easy enough to find out.

The hinges squeaked and a cowbell clanged as he stepped inside the Sunnyside, and heads turned and nodded in greeting.

Wolf nodded back and surveyed the room.

Charlie Ash sat in the corner, glaring at him over his wire-rimmed glasses for a second and then concentrating on a cup of coffee.

On a hunch, Wolf approached the table and sat down. Wolf wore jeans over thick long underwear, but he could still feel that the seat was warm and stretched out.

Ash said nothing to Wolf, just put down his fork on his empty plate and sipped his coffee.

Wolf said nothing back, just took off his hat and threw it next to him. He raked his fingers through his hair and beard.

"Hi, Sheriff," Laura Reese said with a smile as she stopped at the table.

"Hi, Laura," Wolf said.

"Need a menu?"

"No thanks. I'll take a barbecue bacon burger, medium, fries, Coke."

"You got it." She ignored Ash as she set a check on the table and took his plate.

Ash gave her a fake smile with squinted eyes and watched her go. "Great ass on that girl."

Wolf took off his coat and put it next to him, then looked at Ash. He was dressed in a black suit, white shirt, and dark-blue tie. His face was shiny, closely shaved. His thin lips smacked and his tongue picked pieces of food out of his teeth while his tiny gray eyes behind the gold wire frames looked everywhere but at Wolf. His ash-gray hair was a little out of place, not quite covering his bald spot on top, which made him look like he'd just been smacked in the face with an open hand. Or maybe Wolf was just fantasizing.

"I take it you're going to the funeral today?" he asked.

Ash nodded and sipped his coffee. "Tough business about Jen."

Wolf nodded and looked out the window, then glanced back at Ash.

Ash pushed a crumb with his fingernail, and then he placed his palm on the table. "Well, see you up there." He grabbed his coat and began sliding out of the booth.

"How are the Austrians liking town?" Wolf asked.

Ash stopped short of getting up and gave Wolf an appraising look. He parted his lips and then closed them. "They'll know one way or the other in two weeks, when the council votes on the bids. Just like I told them." Ash stood up.

"They couldn't crack Charlie Ash? Looks like they didn't try very hard. Didn't even pay for lunch."

Ash picked up the check from the table. "A nine-dollar breakfast at Sunnyside? Gonna cost a lot more than that." He winked. "Oh, hey, you have fun at the gala last night? Wait, were you there?"

Wolf smiled. Last night Ash had come to their table, schmoozing with the Sluice County and neighboring Byron County officials, one hand on Commissioner Heller's shoulder, the other on ex-Sheriff Burton's, asking questions of each person, careful to use their name and the names of their children when applicable, telling a witty joke that was just edgy enough without being dirty, all the while pointedly ignoring Wolf without so much as a glance.

"It was fun," Wolf said.

Ash slid back into the booth and put both palms on the table. "What did you think about the whole thing?"

Wolf blinked, not taking whatever bait he was laying out.

"About the two counties merging," Ash said.

Laura came over and gave Wolf his Coke.

"Thanks."

"You're welcome," she said, walking away.

"I think it's going to be great for both counties. You know the shit we have to go through to get money from the state right now? They hate the fact that we're still appointing government officials here in Sluice. If we want Rocky Points to be the next Vail or Aspen, which is just inevitable really, the whole government system needs to be restructured. We need to grow up. Join the twenty-first century. I think it's a perfect idea to merge Sluice and Byron counties. It'll open up appropriations funds with both the state and federal governments. Both counties are going to benefit. And the biggest benefactor? That's gonna be Rocky Points. I'm telling you, we're going to boom. This place is gonna be on steroids."

Ash looked at Wolf expectantly.

Wolf took a sip of his Coke. "I heard the talk last night, Charlie."

"Oh, really? You don't seem too interested in the idea."

Wolf looked out the window and back at Ash. "I'm well aware of what you're getting at. And it's my understanding that, along with the sheriff, all county council positions would become electable positions as well."

"You're right," he said, leaning forward, eyes bright. "No more appointments. It's going to be great. Elections are my bread and butter, always have been. It's equal parts art and science when it comes to inserting a desired someone into an elected office. Doesn't matter how entrenched someone is in a position of power, with the right approach and campaign, you can send them packing. In some cases, ruin their entire career, their reputation, wreck their chances of ever having one again.

"I would know, I've won four elections and served in four different government positions and on five different election committees over the years."

Ash looked out the window and took a deep breath, looking like he was reminiscing about the good old days, or looking forward to the new. Then he slid out of the booth and walked away.

Laura placed Wolf's food on the table. "You all set?"

"No," Wolf said.

"What do you need?"

He looked up at her. "Sorry, yes. I'm all set."

CHAPTER 12

WOLF STOOD in line with Sarah and Jack. There were seven people ahead of them, and then six, so they shuffled on the marble floor to keep the line moving.

"What did she look like?" Jack whispered.

"Jack," Sarah gasped.

Wolf gave him a disappointed look, and looked back up the line.

"Sorry, I'm just wondering. Closed casket?"

"Enough," Sarah said with a warning glare that lowered Jack's gaze to the floor.

Thanks to Jack's question, now Wolf couldn't help but think about Jen Wakefield's head. When he'd arrived at the Wakefield's house on Friday, he'd seen the damage done first hand. Whether or not it was something Jen had been aware of when she'd pulled the trigger, the gun had been loaded with a bullet designed to rip as it passed through flesh, and it had been messy.

As they stepped forward again, Wolf ignored the chatter around him and concentrated on the front of the line. Charlie and Kevin Ash had just reached the mayor and his son.

Charlie was first, grasping Chris's hand with both of his and giving a somber nod, along with what looked to be some heartfelt words. *Hang in there, kid. If you need anything, let me know.*

Next came Kevin, who hugged Chris, and Chris hugged him back like a good friend does when they're comforting each other in the worst of times. When they parted, Charlie and Mayor Wakefield came back into view behind them. Wolf saw the mayor whispering something into Ash's ear, and Wolf could have sworn he saw bared teeth.

Ash pulled away, raked a hand through his hair, and walked away slowly, not turning around as he slowed to wait for Kevin.

Kevin gave the mayor a hug and a somber word or two and walked after his father. Then they disappeared out the door.

"I'm so sorry," Wolf said, shaking Chris's hand. Chris looked up at Wolf and nodded, and then Wolf shuffled to Mayor Wakefield. "I'm so sorry, Greg."

The mayor's eyes were heavy and red. He looked hopeless and helpless, completely devastated.

Wolf nodded and had begun to turn away when the mayor's hand reached and grabbed his arm. Wolf looked back and met Wakefield's gaze.

"Thank you, David." Mayor Wakefield was wide-eyed and leaning toward him, as if pleading. He moved his lips like he wanted to say something, to beg for something, and Wolf wondered whether he was about to say, "Shoot me!" But then Wakefield relaxed, nodded, and turned away to Sarah and shook her hand.

Wolf shuffled away quietly, slipping on his winter jacket over his formal four-button coat, and watched Wakefield greet

Sarah and Jack. He was back to calm, collected, going through the motions once again.

Sarah grabbed Wolf by the arm and looked up. "You okay?"

Wolf nodded. "Yeah, let's go."

They walked out the door together, almost as if they were a happy, normal family.

The front of the chapel was in shadow, but the white peaks across the valley reflected brightly back at them, making Wolf squint and Jack sneeze as they walked down the steps.

"It's freezing," Jack said, jumping down the stairs and moving ahead of them.

"What was that in there?" Sarah asked quietly.

"I have no idea. Just … everyone grieves differently, I guess." Wolf failed to believe his own words.

"You want to walk and see your dad and John?" Sarah asked.

He shook his head and saw that Rachette, Patterson, Wilson, Baine, Yates, and a few other deputies were standing down in the parking lot making idle conversation.

"I'll see you guys later, okay?" Wolf said. He gave Jack a quick hug and kissed Sarah on the cheek, which almost turned into an awkward side-mouth kiss because she turned toward him and backed away at the last second.

Wolf left with what felt like gracelessness, beelining his way toward the deputies.

As he drew near, there was sudden commotion as the whole circle of uniforms turned toward a man who was passing them by, and Wolf realized it was Matt Cooper, the helicopter pilot on the mountain.

Cooper's chin was stuck out, saying something as he walked by, and it didn't look like *Hi, how's it going?*

Baine lunged at him without a second's hesitation, and then all hell broke loose.

Wolf sprinted through the packed snow as fast as he could in leather loafers. When he reached the group, he saw a haymaker fly from Baine, and heard the solid slap of fist on face. Then Cooper erupted into a flurry of flailing arms, which sent the other deputies darting in like a pride of lions on a wounded zebra.

There was no clear hole into the altercation behind writhing bodies, so Wolf tried to stop, but slipped on his dress shoes and landed on his ass with a spine-jarring thud. He gritted his teeth and got up, and then started ripping people aside and pushing himself ahead. A few seconds later he was next to the fight, and things quieted as everyone began backing away—everyone but Baine, who was still butting against Cooper, keeping him close with one hand as his other elbow flew backward, landing blow after blow.

Wolf gripped Baine's hair and pulled.

Baine squealed with mouth open to the sky and let go of Cooper.

Wolf let Baine drop to the ground and then took Cooper down onto his back much faster than gravity alone would have done the job.

Cooper squirmed and gasped, unable to take a breath for a few seconds, and then his lungs finally whistled, filling with air.

"Get the hell out of here," Wolf said, gripping his neck, inches from Cooper's face.

Cooper nodded with wide eyes.

Wolf let Cooper up and he left without looking back.

"Sorry, sir," said Baine. "He was talkin'—"

"Everyone to the sit room, now!" Wolf walked past Baine.

Nobody dared speak as Wolf weaved his way through the deputies and out into the parking lot, and nobody made a sound when he slipped on a sheet of slick snow, narrowly avoiding landing on his ass again.

CHAPTER 13

WOLF LEANED against the wall of the situation room, feeling the tender ache on his tailbone.

Patterson stood at the front, scribbling on the whiteboard, because out of all the deputies in the department, it turned out that she had the most consistently legible handwriting.

"Urine," Lorber's voice blared from the laptop computer set in the center of the table, and Patterson wrote down the word. "Nothing underneath her fingernails, other than chicken DNA," he added.

Fluorescent lights buzzed overhead, reflecting off the darkened windows. Outside, a half-moon hung over the silhouetted peaks.

"What can you tell us about the X on her forehead?" Wolf asked.

"Ah," Lorber said. "It wasn't made with the lipstick in her purse. So either it was another one she had in her purse and he took it when he got done, or"—he paused for effect—"he brought his own lipstick to the party."

Wolf watched as Patterson wrote on the board. Then he

looked at the deputies around the table and settled his eyes on Baine for the third time of the meeting.

Baine was Wolf's age, but still squirmed like a little kid under his gaze. "What's up?" Baine finally asked.

"Where did you pull over Matt Cooper last night?"

"At the four-way stop on Main. Why?"

"Was he on Main or Third?" Wolf asked.

"Main, going south. Rolled through the stop sign."

"Time?"

"11:30ish?"

"Gotta be more sure than that."

Baine looked up at the ceiling and then nodded. "Yeah, it was like 11:40. I remember. I looked over at Beer Goggles when I was driving just before that and looked at the time. I remember wondering when they were going to close up with the weather."

"And how about the guy with Cooper. Who was he?" Wolf asked.

"I ... I don't know. I know he had a winter hat on, and a thick coat. Black. I remember that."

"A fur coat? Fur coming out of the collar?" Wolf asked.

Baine looked at Wolf, and then sagged his shoulders. "I don't think so, but I was busy with Cooper, and he was givin' me shit. I didn't have time to shine my light in the car for too long. I remember the guy was clean-shaven, and dressed well. Definitely a black coat." Baine looked up at Wolf and sucked in his breath. "And he sat back all cool like. I remember that."

Wolf nodded. "Okay."

Patterson scrunched her face. "So where does that put us?"

"Nowhere," Wolf said.

"It's two men in the vicinity, driving away from the scene

where we found a dead body," Baine said pointedly. "One of em' was Cooper. I say we bring in Cooper."

None of the other deputies looked at him.

"What we have is a strangled girl," Wolf said. "With an X written on her forehead for unknown reasons."

"If the killer brought his own lipstick, sounds pretty premeditated," Rachette said.

"Could have been a female killer," Patterson said.

"Hand size and damage to the neck suggest a man," Lorber's voice chimed out of the speakers.

Wolf paced in front of the whiteboard. "Okay, a man with his own lipstick or ... not. An X on the forehead. Strangled. And we have a text message from our vic that says she was catching a ride home with two men. We have a witness on the mountain that she was with one man when she left Antler Creek. We also have a stack of hundreds in her room. Crisp. Fresh. Successive serial numbers. Like the kind taken out of a bound stack gotten at a bank. Why? Drugs? Prostitution?

"Then we have the two men you pulled over." He looked at Baine. "We know the identity of one of them, our resident helicopter pilot, Mr. Matt Cooper—a person you've pulled over five times in the last two weeks and wrestled in the parking lot of a funeral ceremony an hour and a half ago. We don't have any evidence that Cooper left with Stephanie Lang. These two tidbits make me a little wary of bringing him in for questioning, a move that just might send his boss over the edge, making him pull the helicopter off the mountain for good, and sending a shitstorm our way."

Baine sat back and glanced around the room, and once again no one looked at him. The man was poison.

Wolf looked at Rachette. "We need to talk to the gondola operator from last night. See what he says. Still no luck?"

"Still haven't gotten hold of him," Patterson said.

When Wolf stared at her, she pulled out her phone and stood up. She tapped the screen, put it to her ear and walked to the windows. She stared outside and left a cordial voicemail asking for Victor Peterhaus, the gondola employee in question, to call her back at the "very earliest possible convenience."

Wolf pulled back a chair and sat down, wincing and leaning on one butt cheek as the pain punched his tailbone.

"If I'm no longer needed, I'm going to go get drunk," Lorber said.

The deputies chuckled, and Wolf smiled despite the pain and their abysmal progress so far.

"All right," Wolf said. "Talk to you later."

A sploosh sound came from the computer.

"Patterson," Wolf said.

"Yes, sir."

"Get on this computer and find a picture of a man named Jonas Prock. Please."

Patterson got up, pulled the computer in front of her and sat back down. She typed a few words. "Ummm," she said, staring at the screen.

"What's the company name these Austrians are a part of?" Wolf asked the room.

"Klammer Corp," Yates said, and everyone looked at him. Yates shrugged and looked at everyone like they were idiots for not knowing.

Wolf leaned forward and pain shot through his butt again, so he stood back up. "Klammer. That was his boss's name," Wolf remembered out loud.

"Okay, I'm not getting anything," Patterson said, tapping the keys.

Wolf bent down and looked, and everyone else positioned themselves to see.

"I've got plenty of pictures of Klammer, but none of Jonas Prock."

They watched as Patterson tapped the keys and shook her head.

"Are you Googling his name?" Rachette asked.

"What am I, an idiot?"

Wilson, Yates, and Baine smirked.

"What about a car-rental company?" Rachette asked. "Did they rent a car?"

Wolf nodded. "I saw it was a rental. A Toyota Land Cruiser. Didn't see which company, though."

"Can't be many companies who rent those out," Yates said.

"Why are we talking about this Prock guy, anyway?" Rachette asked.

"Sarah mentioned him today," Wolf said. "Prock was sitting at her table at the gala, and she remembers that Stephanie came over to the table, and he whispered something in her ear, brought her down real close. And Stephanie was blushing when she stood back up, and then she left." Wolf shrugged. "That's what Sarah said."

"Sarah knew Stephanie?" Wilson asked.

Wolf nodded. "She was in Sarah's counseling group on Mondays and Thursdays."

The room went quiet.

"This Prock guy,"—Rachette squinted one eye—"you think he was the one who left with Stephanie?"

"He whispered in Stephanie's ear at the gala," Wolf said. "It's thin, but it's something."

Patterson looked up from the computer. "So you're saying Prock left with Lang, and then they hooked up with Cooper?"

Wolf shrugged again. "Cooper had a passenger when Baine pulled him over."

"But Cooper is the helicopter pilot for Irwin," Wilson said. "It's Irwin's helicopter."

They all sat silent.

"And Prock works for Klammer. So," Patterson said slowly, "why would Irwin's employee be hanging out with Klammer's employee? Aren't these two firms arch-rivals at the moment? Competing for that huge condo contract?"

More silence. Patterson pecked the keyboard a few more times, and clicked her tongue. "There's nothing online. No pictures of Prock. How are we going to ID him as the guy who left with Lang with no picture? Can you call Kristen Luke? See if she has it in a database?"

Wolf looked at Patterson, thinking it was an idea.

"We've gotta bring in Cooper, I'm tellin' ya," Baine said. "You put me in Interrogation One with him, I'll find out who was with him last night."

Wolf looked at the clock on the wall—4:55 p.m. He looked out the windows at the darkening sky, now twinkling with stars, and then the tired faces in the room. They'd had a long, action-packed day, and it was gearing up to be another big one tomorrow.

"All right, Baine, you're coming with me. Otherwise, let's pick up on this tomorrow. I want everyone to get some good rest." Wolf looked at the three deputies that were fresh in the station for the night shift. "Be diligent out there tonight. See you all at oh-seven-hundred tomorrow."

Wolf watched everyone stand up and leave the room, all except Baine, who looked at Wolf and scratched his head.

On the way out, someone said something about getting a beer, and someone else talked about food.

Wolf licked his lips.

"What's going on?" Rachette asked, staying behind. "You guys going to talk to Cooper now? Do you need help?"

Wolf shook his head. "Don't worry about it. Don't drink too much tonight and see you tomorrow."

"Me? Drink?" Rachette turned and left.

...

After a quick phone call to Sarah, and another promise that he wouldn't mention her name, Wolf learned the location where Prock and Klammer were staying in town. Ten minutes later, Wolf and Baine were driving there.

Wolf turned onto Main and started heading south toward the resort; then, when they were a block out of town, he turned up Edelweiss Road heading west.

Baine turned to him. "Sir, I'm sorry about today. I really am."

"So tell me what's going on with this guy, Cooper. Why the vendetta?" he asked, already suspecting he knew the answer.

"I don't know," Baine said. "Cooper's just one of those guys, you know? I can tell he's up to no good, all the time."

Wolf flipped on his brights for a better view of the dark stretch of forested road. "Laura?" he asked.

Baine sighed and looked over at him, then back out the passenger window.

"Yeah, something like that. He's always in the Sunnyside hittin' on her, and I heard he was slappin' her ass the other day. I just ..."

Wolf looked over at Baine. He was swallowing and shaking his head, staring out into the dark. He was heartsick, Wolf could tell. He knew the symptoms.

"And you think she might be egging him on?" Wolf asked.

Baine said nothing.

"Well, here's what you're going to do," Wolf said. "You're going to talk to Laura about the whole thing, and stop with this Cooper crap. That's the only thing that's going to resolve your problems, and it stops us looking like a squad of thugs."

Baine held up a hand and nodded. "What are we doing up here, anyways?"

Wolf pulled up to an address and slowed, then turned into the driveway. "We'll see soon enough."

CHAPTER 14

WOLF STEPPED up to the door and pushed the bell. The frosted glass on the front door of Klammer's rental property glowed red and yellow from the lights inside. It looked like someone was there, but whether or not they were going to answer was a toss-up. In Wolf's experience, many people could sit ten feet from a door and stonewall someone knocking for hours.

Thankfully, Wolf saw movement.

"Man, it's freezing again tonight." Baine tucked his chin inside his coat.

Wolf watched the bobbing shadow behind the glass get closer, and then the porch light flipped on.

The door opened a slice, then wider, and a squinting face emerged. "May I help you?" It was Klammer, the man Wolf had yet to meet but had seen around for weeks now.

"Mr. Klammer?" Wolf asked.

"Yes?"

"My name is Sheriff Wolf, and this is Deputy Baine. We're with the Sluice County Sheriff's Department. May we have a word with you?"

"Yes, yes," he said. "Come inside, why don't you? It's freezing outside."

Wolf nodded gratefully and stepped in, Baine on his heels.

"Nice to meet you, Sheriff Wolf. I have heard a lot about you," he said with a smile, shaking Wolf's hand.

Klammer was dressed in a white dress shirt and tie, slacks and black shoes glossed to a mirror. He smelled like a fresh spritz of cologne, and his short gray hair had perfect comb marks in it like rake lines in white sand.

Klammer walked through an expensively furnished living room and into a modern kitchen. "It's not the same cold as Austria out there. Austria is more brutal, I can assure you. Can I make you two some coffee? Or something more interesting? A Scotch perhaps?"

Wolf smiled. "No, thanks. On duty. We're fine."

Klammer's smile was disarming, like he and Wolf were long-lost friends. "Please, what can I do for you?"

"Is your assistant staying in this house as well?" Wolf asked.

Klammer nodded. "Yes, why?"

"May I speak with him for a moment?"

"What about?" Klammer asked.

Wolf returned the disarming smile. "It's about something we talked about last night at the gala. I saw him—"

"Yes?"

Wolf turned at the deep voice. Jonas Prock stood just outside the kitchen. He was dressed similarly to Klammer, though he filled out his clothing with more muscles. He buttoned a cuff and looked up at Wolf. "What was it that we were talking about last night, Mr. ..."

"Wolf. Sheriff Wolf."

Prock walked in, and the bright kitchen lit up his eyes.

Wolf watched Prock's pupils narrow to pinpoints, making his entire eyeball look off-white with just a speck of black. A memory of Stephanie Lang's dead eyes surfaced, reminding Wolf exactly why he was there.

"We'd like to speak to you in private for a minute," Wolf said.

Prock stared at Wolf, as if considering the question, and then looked at Klammer. Neither of them moved a facial muscle but, still, it looked like a thought had passed between them.

Klammer sniffed and then coughed. "Well, I have to finish getting ready, anyway. Nice to meet you two. I trust I'll see you around town." Klammer walked back toward the front door and disappeared up the carpeted stairway.

Wolf pulled out his cell phone and tapped the screen a few times. "Mr. Prock, do you know a woman named Stephanie Lang?"

Prock stared at Wolf, and then he shook his head once, almost imperceptibly.

Wolf nodded, glaring into those canary-yellow eyes. "How about Matt Cooper? Do you know that name?"

Prock tilted his head, looked up at the ceiling, and then closed his eyes, as if starting to meditate. His lower lip stuck out and wrapped over the upper, then pulled down. He tilted his head side to side, as if flaunting his infinite patience.

Somewhere, an electronic device beeped, probably plugged into a wall nearby. The man smelled peculiar, Wolf thought as he watched Prock play his game. It was cologne, but heavy on the musk, almost animal-like.

Prock finally looked back at Wolf and shook his head again. Again, it was almost imperceptible.

Wolf glanced at Baine.

Baine stood stiffly, looking between the two men and then cleared his throat. "You were with Matt Cooper last night," Baine said to Prock. "I pulled you two over on Main Street."

Prock looked over at the stairway, then back to Baine.

"Yeah," Baine said looking at Wolf now. "It was him. I'm sure of it."

Wolf looked back at Prock, and Prock glanced again at the stairwell. Wolf held up his phone and snapped a photo. "You don't mind if I take a picture of you, do you?"

Prock flinched at the flash, turning his head a fraction, and then exhaled and relaxed, fixing his yellows on Wolf with undisguised menace.

"Thanks for your time, Mr. Prock," Wolf said, returning the glare. "We'll be in touch if we have any more questions." Wolf motioned for Baine to lead the way, and they let themselves out the front door. Before Wolf closed the door, he saw Klammer looking down on them from the top of the steps. Wolf stepped out and let the door click shut.

The outside light flicked off, leaving them to navigate the steps in darkness.

"You sure it was Prock with Cooper last night?" Wolf asked.

"Yep. He was doing that same frickin' thing—closing his eyes, head back, that whole lip thing. It hit me like a ton of bricks when he did that. I never did see his eyes last night, which I would have easily recognized, but when I saw that move he just did … hundred percent, Sheriff."

Wolf climbed in the SUV. The dash clock said 5:49.

"Where to now, sir?" Baine asked. "Cooper's finally?"

Wolf shook his head. "We've proven that Cooper and Prock were together last night, and nothing else."

Baine scoffed and looked out the window. "So what now?"

"So let's get some rest, and get this picture in front of the lift op and snow-cat driver tomorrow, and see if Prock left with our vic last night. I'm beat."

Baine yawned. "You got that right. Could still use a beer, though. Drop me off at Beer Goggles?"

"Sure."

"Headed home?" Baine asked.

Wolf shrugged, noncommittally.

Wolf drove back into town, dropped Baine off at the Beer Goggles Bar and Grill to meet up with Rachette and the rest of the off-duty crew that liked to drink, which was most of them, and then went back to the station.

He walked through the squad room, down the hall, and into his office. His stomach growled, but his body was heavy and sluggish, and the need for rest was an overwhelming drive. He hadn't slept a second the night before, thinking about Jen Wakefield's hollowed-out, dripping head, and it had caught up to him.

He took off all his winter gear and hung it on the coat rack, then pushed his boots up next to the radiator. Next he took off his belt, bent down and opened an oak cabinet on the wall. He pulled out his sleeping bag stuff-sack. With a flourish, he stretched out the nylon sack and got inside.

Despite his bruised tailbone, the hard carpet felt like a memory-foam bed. In a matter of seconds he was asleep.

CHAPTER 15

WOLF OPENED his eyes with the vision of an eight-year-old Sri Lankan boy in his crosshairs branded in his mind. Wolf had come to suspect that what was once a recurring nightmare now only showed up when danger was close. It was Wolf's subconscious telling him to be careful. Or at least, that's what he liked to think. Otherwise, it was just an uncontrollable memory that tormented him whenever it felt like it, and Wolf didn't do well with giving up control like that.

Slashes of light streamed through the blinds of his office, painting the wall pale yellow in the otherwise pitch-dark room. The clock ticked but he couldn't see it, so he checked the glowing dials of his watch—10:05 p.m. He'd been asleep for about three and a half hours, he calculated.

He rolled to his back and once again felt the bruise on his tailbone.

"Shit," he whispered, and stood up.

His stomach churned air, but he was screwed on food. Nothing would be open this late on a Sunday night, not even the chain fast food joints.

Flipping on the light, he stretched his arms over his head and padded out into the hall in his socks.

There was tapping of a keyboard coming from the now dimly lit squad room.

Wolf poked his head around the corner and squinted.

Deputy Sergeant Canton looked up and smiled. "Howdy, sir."

"Hi, how are you Stew?" Wolf asked.

"Can't complain."

Wolf opened the small refrigerator and saw three packs of string cheese. Vaguely remembering that they had been put in before Christmas, he skipped over them and pulled out the vegetable drawer, which to Wolf's knowledge had never once held a vegetable. Two Newcastle beers sloshed in their bottles, leftover from another night he'd stayed in the office the week before. Wolf looked up at Canton, who was back to typing on the keys. He pulled out one of the beers, walked back to his office, and shut the door.

He shut off the light switch and pulled up the blinds all the way, letting in the soft glow from outside. The moon hung above the resort, illuminating the slopes to the pallid color of dead skin. A row of brightly lit snow cats crawled down the middle of the mountain and, even though miles away, their roar was audible through the window.

Wolf pulled a bottle opener from his drawer and popped the beer. He took a long pull and put his feet up on the windowsill. The cold glass sucked out heat through his socks.

Across the street, a pair of headlights illuminated the Hitching Post Realty building, and then a car bobbed into the parking lot and pulled next to a parked car. It was Sarah's 4Runner parking next to Margaret's car.

Wolf watched with interest as the interior cab light popped

on and Margaret stepped out into the lot. She closed the door with a thump, waved to Sarah and then walked past her own car and all the way to the office door, weaving a little as she looked down and fumbled with her keys. She turned and yelled something back to Sarah, which was a murmur to Wolf, and then Sarah pulled out and left.

The big window of the storefront office lit up, and Margaret walked around inside, marching here and there; then she stooped to dig through a desk drawer.

Wolf took another swig and put the beer down. After another second of hesitation, he got up, grabbed his jacket and hat, slipped on his boots, and was out the door.

Canton looked startled to see Wolf stepping fast through the squad room, pulling on his gear.

"I'll be right back," Wolf said with a dismissive wave.

Outside was biting cold, and his face seemed to solidify after five steps into the parking lot. The laces of his boots slapped around as he walked faster, seeing that Margaret had shut off the interior light and was coming out of the building.

"Margaret!" Wolf called.

Margaret peered into the night and saw Wolf jogging across the street.

"David!" she called back, mimicking Wolf's tone.

She finished twisting the key and walked to her car, concentrating on the ground as she stepped off the curb.

"Hey, whatcha doing?" Wolf asked.

"Just headed home."

"You been drinking?" Wolf asked.

She rolled her eyes then opened the rear door and dropped a folder in the back seat. "I've had one."

Wolf smiled and slowed to a stop.

"Okay, two," she said. "What? Look, I've gotta go. I'll be careful. It's freezing ass out here."

Wolf looked at her for another few seconds, and she sagged in defeat. She pulled open the back door of her car and took out the folder, shut the door, and then walked toward Wolf.

Wolf let her pass and then caught up.

She looked down at his flipping shoelaces. "What the hell? You sleeping in your office again?"

Wolf looked down and didn't answer.

"Oh, honey, you have got to get back with Sarah."

They walked in silence for a beat, and Wolf saw her glance at him a few times.

"Sorry," she said. "I've been drinking."

Wolf shook his head. He pushed the button on his keys and the lights flashed on his SUV. "Hop in."

A few minutes later they were cruising up Fourth Street headed east.

"So, out with her tonight?" Wolf asked, keeping his eyes on the road. The buildings thinned and the pines thickened as they climbed in altitude.

"Yeah, we were out with Ted and his assistant," she said.

"Ted Irwin?" Wolf asked.

"Yep."

Wolf flipped on the brights, and the passing forest lit up.

"So, you're out to dinner with Irwin, and Ash is out to lunch with this Klammer guy."

Margaret stared at Wolf for a second. "So what?"

Wolf shrugged, and they drove in silence for a while.

"I'll tell you what I told Klammer"—she turned in her chair —"and what I told Irwin. Whoever is awarded the contract for those condos, their next move had better be to hire my firm to sell them. And if they don't believe me, take a look at what happened to Beaver Run before we came in, and then how quickly they sold when we took over the listings. Then take a look at the Fish Creek Complex. Then take a look at our sales over the last two years compared to any other firm. We wipe the floor with them!"

Wolf held up a hand. "Okay, okay."

"Well ..." she shook her head and stared out the window. "You're saying these guys are trying to sell me, like I'm buyin' or something. I'm selling these guys. You better believe that, Jack." She pointed out toward the trees. "Besides, Ted and I are old friends. We grew up two years apart in high school in Aspen. I was just keeping the schmooze up, introducing him to my new top agent." She glanced at Wolf.

Wolf smiled. "Okay. Sorry. I didn't mean to insinuate that you were doing shady business with Ted Irwin. Ash, however? Wouldn't put it past him."

Margaret looked at Wolf and then out the window. "Ah, I don't know. I don't think it would make a difference even if he was."

"What do you mean? Irwin's already a lock on winning the contract?"

She shrugged. "Probably. At least, I think I'll vote for him. And I think Wakefield's going to. Ash seems keen on Klammer's proposal, but it's too ... Tyrolean for my taste. It's all mountain-flower wood carvings, and makes you wanna have a Weiner Schnitzel and yodel while wearing lederhosen. Nyeh."

Wolf smiled. "And the rest of the council?"

"I think they're the same way. In the end, they usually go with what the mayor thinks, and like I said, he likes Irwin's proposal. Another thing, Irwin's company is from Colorado. Not some multinational conglomerate from Europe. How would it help the local economy if we brought in a bunch of engineers and big wigs from Austria?"

A pool of light ahead marked the first property on this stretch of road where houses were large and spaced well apart. Margaret's was still a mile or so up. As they passed the first house, another light came into view ahead, and they both knew it was Mayor Wakefield's house they were approaching.

"Jesus, he was bent up today," she said.

"Yeah. Not an easy thing, I'm sure. Burying your wife."

They both kept silent and looked down the driveway as they passed. Almost every light was blazing inside, but Wolf saw no movement in the windows.

Margaret cleared her throat and looked Wolf up and down. "Seriously, though, what are you doing sleeping in the office? I've seen your light on late a lot. What's the matter? Don't like the rebuild?"

Margaret was alluding to the explosion at his house a couple of summers ago, when a man had filled his kitchen to the brim with propane, and then ignited it, nearly killing Wolf's son in the process. A trillion splinters of wood, tile, and appliances was all that was left of the kitchen, and the rest of the house had been a charred mess after the fire department had finally stopped the blaze.

It was only this fall that the renovations had been finished. Up to that point, Wolf had been camping out in a corner of the remaining structure for months on end. Truthfully, now that it was done, Wolf felt like the memories had been gutted out of the place and he was living in a generic shell of a home.

It wasn't that he didn't *like* the rebuild. He would be an idiot if he didn't like the brand-new kitchen, appliances, carpet, windows that sealed out the icy wind, and all the perks that came with a big insurance check and great friends in the construction industry. But it was … lonely, he guessed. Even with Jack staying there a few nights a week, he found that they often piled in the car and drove away from the quiet house to have their fun, either going to eat in town or out into the woods to shoot or fish.

Margaret was staring at Wolf. "You do need to talk to Sarah."

"We've done that, many times."

Margaret looked back out the window. "Come on. She broke up with Mark because Mark was sick of her talking about you all the time. Sick of Jack and Sarah talking about you, and what you were doing that day, and when you were going to come over, and when you were going to pull your head out of your ass and throw Mark out and ask your ex-wife to marry you again and then live happily ever after in your brand-new house on your family's ranch house."

Wolf kept his eyes on the road.

"Okay, maybe I made that last part up," she said. "But it sure makes sense to me."

"She's hiding something," Wolf said.

Margaret turned to him. "What?"

"To answer your question, I'm staying in the office because we've got a case going on, and I'm gonna have to be back in the morning, so it doesn't make sense to … whatever. Listen, do you know a girl named Stephanie Lang?"

She frowned, thinking. "No. Why? Who's that?"

"A waitress at the Antler Creek Lodge. She was killed last night."

"Jesus, is that what Sarah was talking about?"

Wolf shrugged.

"She told me something had happened, and she didn't want to talk about it. What did happen?"

Wolf exhaled. "We found her strangled on the side of the road this morning. A truck plowed her up."

"Oh my God," Margaret said. "Oh my ..."

After another half-mile, Wolf slowed down and pulled into Margaret's driveway, which was lit up by a halogen lamp mounted on a pine tree. Her wood-paneled house was large, brightly lit, and looking behind the house Wolf could see a sliver of lights from the town far below.

Her husband Harry came to the window and looked out. His eyes opened wide, and he disappeared. Then the front door opened and he stepped out onto the porch in his socks. He squinted, peering into the windshield of Wolf's SUV and held up his hands.

Margaret leaned forward and gave him the OK sign, then waved him back inside.

Harry flipped his hand, went back in and shut the door.

"Strangled?" Margaret asked. "Do you know who did it?"

Wolf shook his head. "Not yet. But I'm starting to wonder if you guys and your land grab have anything to do with it."

"Why's that? And it's not a land grab. The town owns the land. We're just trying to figure out the best use for it."

Wolf nodded. "You were at Charlie Ash's party the other night, right?"

"Yeah, why?"

"Antler Creek catered that party, too?"

Margaret sucked in her breath. "Yes, they did. And she was there?"

Wolf nodded.

"Oh geez. Who do you think did it?"

"That's the big question. I might come talk to you tomorrow, show you a couple of photos." Wolf turned to her. "You remember what happened to Chet Rentworth five years ago?"

Margaret looked down and nodded.

"What happened to him?" Wolf persisted.

"He ran his car into a tree and died because he was drunk driving."

"Just because I love you doesn't mean I won't lock you up next time. So quit it."

"I'm sorry."

"See you later," said Wolf.

Margaret got out of the car and walked to her front door.

CHAPTER 16

WOLF WOKE EARLY the next morning on the floor of his office. After a shower in the locker room, a half pot of coffee, and donning a fresh set of clothing he kept in his locker as standard procedure, he headed up to the ski resort with Rachette and Patterson, but not before stopping at the Sunnyside for three breakfast burritos to go—Patterson and Rachette didn't eat.

Ski lifts at Rocky Points Ski Resort officially opened at 8:30 a.m. and it was a Monday morning, so when Wolf and his two deputies parked at 7:45, they did so in the front row. And when they walked to the gondola, only a few skiers waddled about near the lift ticket windows. Otherwise, it was going to be what locals would call an *epic powder day*—free from the weekend crowd, and with so much snow having dropped over the weekend that there would still be plenty of untouched powder stashes if one knew where to look.

The sky was once again bright blue, but the air outside felt like they stood in a furnace compared to the day before. The dash computer had said twenty-nine degrees this morning, and it would get well above freezing today according to the forecast.

"Thank God for this weather," Rachette said, looking around and rubbing his hands together. "I'm sure it was good skiing and all yesterday, but way too cold for my taste. Couldn't have paid me enough to put skis on."

"Pussy," Patterson said without hesitation.

Rachette mumbled something and Wolf smiled, but only because he was walking in front and neither of them could see him do it.

The gondola terminal, a large building made of tall windows and black painted steel, stood a short distance up the slope from the main lodge of the resort. It was humming as the line of empty cars hanging on a braided cable zipped in and out.

Wolf followed a lane of orange ropes and stepped inside, where he saw two men dressed in resort gear, cradling steaming cups of coffee.

The electric engine whined, twisting the big wheel in the center of the building. Five or six cars with doors wide open proceeded around it at a slow walking pace before being whisked away again up the mountain.

It was much warmer inside the terminal and Wolf pulled off both gloves. "Victor Peterhaus?" he asked.

The nearer of the two turned and looked, and then stood straight, clearly surprised to see three sheriff's deputies entering. "Yes? I'm Victor." He was foreign, Wolf realized.

"I'm Sheriff Wolf. These are Deputies Rachette and Patterson. We have a few questions about Saturday night."

Peterhaus looked concerned. "Okay … am I in trouble for something?" *South African, that was the accent.*

Wolf shook his head. "No, we just want to know if you saw

someone in particular come out of the gondolas. You were working the base here on Saturday night, right?"

Peterhaus looked relieved and also embarrassed, probably from letting his guilty conscience show so easily. "Yes, I was here until we closed down after midnight."

"Do you know a woman named Stephanie Lang?" Wolf asked.

Peterhaus nodded. "Yeah. Works at the restaurant. We're decent friends."

Wolf pulled out a glossy printout picture of Prock and held it up. "Was this man with her on Saturday night?"

Peterhaus squinted and leaned forward, like he wasn't wearing his prescription glasses and had left his contacts at home. "Yes."

Wolf raised his eyebrows. "You're sure?"

He nodded and stepped back. "Yes, that guy was definitely with her. I remember him. He's got crazy eyes, you see that? Stephanie introduced me to him. Jonas or something. He's from Austria. We talked about it for a while—I'd worked there one winter, in the Dolomites. Well, it was Italy, but the Austrian speaking part, so close enough."

"Did you see anyone else with them? Did she say they were meeting someone else?" Wolf asked.

"No, they just said they were going back to Stephanie's and they left out the door." Peterhaus pointed behind them, and they all turned to look outside. All they saw was the complex of buildings at the base.

Wolf shoved the picture back in his coat. "You know where Matt Cooper is?"

Peterhaus turned back to the other lift operator. "Is Cooper up here yet?"

The other lift operator stepped forward. "Yeah, I saw him fly up earlier. Right before you got here."

Peterhaus nodded to Wolf.

"He flies up?" Rachette asked.

The other lift operator pointed past the gondola cars. "He parks the helicopter out there at night, a few hundred yards away, over in the trees. It's insane, how he flies straight down into that tight spot every day. He just flew it out of there a little while ago. You guys just missed him. Usually shows up pretty early, and he flies it up to the ... helicopter pad or landing zone or whatever you call it. Wasn't here this weekend, though. Too much snow. Avalanche danger over on the heli-runs."

Wolf nodded and stepped toward an open gondola. "Thanks. You don't mind if we head up, do you?" Wolf asked.

The two operators shrugged. "Go ahead. All yours."

They stepped inside and sat, and the doors clacked shut, cutting out the loud industrial sounds outside. After another few seconds they whipped up the side of the slope on the bouncing cable, and the base complex came into view below them, getting smaller by the second.

For a few minutes they sat in silence, all eyes glued to the bright peaks and landscape below. Corduroy groomers and steep powder-buried runs slid by beneath them.

Wolf stared down, picking lines he would ski now, and then picking lines he would have skied fifteen years ago. Patterson and Rachette seemed to be doing the same thing, though Rachette with much more trepidation than Patterson.

"How's the skiing coming?" Wolf asked, pulling off his hat. It was getting warm inside the heated car.

"Not bad, if I do say so myself," Rachette said, nodding to Patterson.

Patterson glanced at Rachette. "Yeah, not bad," she said with little enthusiasm.

Rachette gripped the bench when they bounced over the rollers on the lift towers.

Patterson looked nervous as well, but not about the movements of the gondola car. It was something personal that bothered her, Wolf decided.

At the top of the mountain the gondola swung into the upper terminal, slowed to a crawl, and the door split open.

Rachette was out first, all but diving out the door, and Wolf followed Patterson out.

Wolf looked at the clock mounted above the lift operator's office—8:20.

Bob Duke, the head of ski patrol, was outside laughing with Scott Reed—both men whom Wolf had known for a number of years as fellow residents in town.

Duke turned to them. "Hey, there they are."

Wolf smiled and shook his hand, and then Scott's.

...

Patterson watched Wolf smile at Scott Reed and give him a hearty handshake, as if they'd known each other for years.

"How's it going, Dave?" Scott said.

"Not bad. You?" Wolf said.

Patterson kept back, shook Duke's hand, and then Scott's only because it would have caused a scene if she hadn't.

Scott's hand was warm and big, just like she remembered it. But now his touch sent shivers of revulsion up and down her spine, and his genuine smile seemed to magnify the effect.

She decided that for the remainder of her time with these two men she'd keep her sunglasses on.

She followed in silence, taking in the vast view as she always did, and once again she peered at Aspen Mountain and wondered what her family was up to this morning. With the amount of snow dropped Saturday night, her dad would probably be playing hooky from work and hitting the slopes until lunch, along with the rest of Aspen.

They walked toward Scott's cat waiting on the freshly groomed snow.

Patterson took up the rear, and then sped up at the end and slipped into the back hold of the cat before anyone else. Bob Duke took shotgun and Wolf and Rachette sat back with Patterson.

Wolf was eyeing her suspiciously, but she ignored him and looked out the rear window.

"We need to speak to Matt Cooper," Wolf said.

"I know. I can't get him on the radio right now." Duke shook his head. "Probably has his flight headphones on. We'll just drive over there."

The cat vibrated and the diesel engine sputtered loudly, but Wolf continued his conversation with the men in front.

Patterson leaned forward and looked out the windshield, ignoring Scott's green eyes glancing at her in the rearview mirror. The bright-red helicopter she'd seen many times this year—either on the top of the ridge where it sat now or thumping in the sky as it flew back and forth between peaks—sat on the far end of the ridgeline past the Antler Creek Lodge. It hadn't been there yesterday. Probably hadn't been the best business for helicopter rides when perfect powder had been right here on the mountain for no extra cost.

"How's Hillary?" Wolf asked Scott, leaning toward the front.

"Oh, I split with her last year. Geez, I haven't talked to you in that long?"

Patterson kept her gaze out the windshield, ignoring the urge to look over at Rachette.

"Yeah, I guess it's been a little hectic for me. I haven't been out much," Wolf said.

"Well, I heard about the whole deal you and Jack went through last summer, and what Deputy Rachette here did, getting shot and all." Scott shook his head. "Wow."

Patterson finally sat back and looked across the hold at Rachette.

Rachette glanced at her and then leaned forward to speak over Wolf's shoulder. It would have made more sense to perhaps mouth the word *sorry*—to apologize for making your partner look like an idiot for being interested in a married man, a man who'd in fact split up from his wife so it wasn't as awkward as her partner had made it out to be, but that wasn't Rachette's style.

The pieces fell into place, though, and she was seeing Scott Reed in a whole new light. Scott didn't wear a wedding ring for a good reason.

She looked in the rearview mirror and locked eyes with him for a few seconds, then looked out the windshield again. Now she felt bad for being so cold toward the man, when he'd been so clearly interested in getting to know her.

Could she date someone with two kids, though? She barely thought of herself as a grownup as it was. And how old were the kids? Given Scott's youthful looks, she couldn't picture them being much older than five or six. Then again, he could have been a teenager when he'd had his kids, and then they'd be almost her age. Two kids? Could she do it?

One more time she looked at Scott's face in the bouncing mirror, and once again they locked eyes. *Probably,* she thought as she marveled at his green eyes for the tenth time.

CHAPTER 17

CHARLIE ASH PARKED his Range Rover and stepped out into yet another cloudless morning. He shut the door and wiped off his wet fingers on his pants, and then stepped along the driveway to the house that he could describe only as a Frank Lloyd Wright rip-off. Ash could think of many better ways to wipe your ass with a few million dollars than to erect a piece of crap like this.

The gutters plunked and trickled, and the snow under his boots was turning to slush. Branches sagged, and a small stream had already started forming along the road on the drive up. The day was unseasonably warm for late February, and he loved it. It reminded Ash of Tahoe, where the warm temperatures often melted the snow just as fast as it dropped. *Thank God.* Breathing through his mouth so that his boogers wouldn't freeze was becoming unbearable. Humans weren't meant to endure cold temperatures like they'd been having. At least *he* wasn't meant for it. In fact, he'd already vowed to himself that when the Klammer payment went through it would go toward a country-club membership and winter house in Scottsdale.

As he stepped onto the porch and pushed the doorbell, he longed for the days of Lake Tahoe once again, with his lake house, his boat, his Treasurer position in city government and people lining up for favors. Those were the heydays, when he was like the godfather, before things pushed him and Kevin east. That was when he had been on top. That was when everything he'd touched turned to gold, and when everyone had respected him for the savvy businessman he was. Until his wife went and fucked it all up.

The door clicked and opened, and a white lady dressed in sweatpants stood in the opening. She held a feather duster and some headphones hung from the neck of her sweatshirt.

"Hello, Mr. Ash," she said.

"Hello," Ash said, excluding her name, because he neither knew nor cared what it was.

She smiled at him for a second, like he was going to say something else, like her name or something.

"The mayor!" he yelled, satisfied at the way she jumped and opened the door wide.

"Yes, sorry. Come in, he's in his office," she said.

Ash walked past her and across the little rug without wiping his feet, and then onto the hardwood floors and down the hall. Over the squeaking of his boots he was pretty certain he'd heard the woman call him an asshole under her breath. Maybe one day he could figure out how to make her regret that.

He stopped at the closed door to Wakefield's home office and stepped onto the carpeted alcove. He turned the knob and walked inside, not bothering to knock.

Wakefield was already staring straight at Ash as he entered. His eyes were red-rimmed, and he sat board stiff with both palms on the top of his mahogany desk. He wore a wrinkled long-sleeved polo shirt. There were no lights on, just the half-closed blinds letting in too little sunlight. It was silent as a vault.

Ash looked around and closed the door behind him. He noticed that the computer on Wakefield's desk wasn't turned on, and there was nothing in front of him. Ash took off his jacket and hung it in the corner on the coat rack that was made of old skis, and noticed Wakefield tracking him with his unblinking gaze.

Ash walked to the desk and sat down. He sighed, sat back, and crossed his legs. "You wanted to speak to me?"

"She's fucking dead?" Wakefield blurted.

Ash popped his eyebrows and stared at Wakefield for a few seconds. *Was he drunk? Had he been staring at the wall, drinking all night?*

"Yes," Ash said slowly. "As I said before, I was so sorry to hear about your wife."

Wakefield narrowed his eyes and leaned forward. "What?"

Ash stared at Wakefield. The man was unstable. Ash couldn't tell what this was. Was Wakefield acting like he didn't know his wife had offed herself until now? Had he forgotten the reason for her suicide? How far off his rocker had he gone?

"I'm sorry,"—he sat motionless—"you're confusing me."

"You don't know?" Wakefield asked.

Ash kept silent.

Wakefield stood up from his chair and leaned forward, pressing his hands into the desktop. He studied Ash with comical intensity, like Ash was a half-opaque ghost sitting in his midst.

Ash felt his skin crawling, and decided now was a good time to leave. He began to stand up.

"Stephanie Lang," Wakefield said.

Ash froze. "What?"

Wakefield stared at him for another second and then sat down. "You're serious!" He yelled, and then exploded into laughter.

Ash held up a hand and looked back at the closed door. "What are you talking about?"

Wakefield stopped laughing and wiped his eyes. "Stephanie Lang is dead. A plow dug her up out of the snow yesterday morning."

Ash sat back down.

Wakefield closed his eyes and his leather seat creaked as he sat back.

Ash looked around, thinking. Then he stood and walked to the office door and opened it. Poking his head outside, he was startled to see the housekeeper a few feet away, wiping water footprints off the floor with a rag. She had white headphones jammed in her ears.

She looked up and sucked in a breath, then pulled out a headphone. "Can I help you, sir?"

Ash glared at her and closed the door. He walked back to the desk and sat down again.

"What the hell are you doing to me, Charlie?"

Ash sat forward. "First of all, quiet down. Second of all, I don't know anything about this. This is news to me."

Wakefield stared. "So you strangle her, and then make it look like I did it? What's next for good old Mayor Wakefield in your plan? Somehow the X is supposed to lead the cops to me or something?"

"The ex?" Ash squinted and shook his head. "Ex-what? What the hell are you talking about. I … she was strangled?"

"You're a good actor, Charlie. I'll give you that."

Ash stood up to think. "Who the hell?" he murmured to himself.

Wakefield leaned an elbow on the arm of his chair, all false amusement drained from his face. "You really don't know who did this?"

Ash ignored him and walked to the coat rack. "I've gotta go."

"Where are you going?" Wakefield asked. "Who the hell did this? Do we have to be worried? Was the X a signal to us? You're telling me this is just a coincidence that she's been killed?"

Ash put on his coat and then stopped, narrowing his eyes. "For the last time, what do you mean, *the ex*? Who are you talking about?"

"There was an X drawn on her forehead." Wakefield put his index finger to his forehead and crossed two lines.

Ash's face dropped. His pulse raced and his skin crawled, itching as sweat leaked out of every pore on his body.

"I have to go," he said, and walked to the door. He opened it and hurried out, and then almost stepped on the maid. Twisting in mid-stride to miss her, he slipped on a wet spot and fell hard, planting his elbow onto the wood floor. Pain exploded through his arm, paralyzing him. "Ah!"

"Oh my God, I'm sorry, Mr. Ash!" the maid said.

Ash got to his knees and bent over, gripping his elbow, grunting through gritted teeth.

"I'm sorry," she said again, placing a hand on his shoulder.

Ash slapped it off and stood up, and then made his way carefully down the hallway and out the front door. He climbed into his car and pressed a number on his phone. It rang six times and went to voicemail.

"Shit," he breathed, and then he dialed another number. When it went to voicemail after one ring, he knew his call had been screened, and then he knew exactly what was going on. He was in trouble.

CHAPTER 18

"A Bell 212 Twin Huey," Duke yelled back to them. "Can hold twelve passengers."

Wolf nodded, looking out the window of the snow cat as they pulled up next to the helicopter. He'd been in one while in the army; it had been painted camo, whereas this one was a glossy red with a yellow stripe, and had metal meshed baskets the size of coffins on each skid for ski gear.

The rotors were twisting lazily as if it was powering down.

"When does he do the first flights of the day?" Wolf asked.

"On a busy day, he'll start flying at about nine a.m., get done in the early afternoon before the light gets too bad," Duke said.

Wolf leaned forward and peered out the window. "Stop the cat!"

Scott twisted. "Why? What's going on?"

"Stop!"

Scott stopped the cat on a dime, and Patterson slid into her side on the bench, catching herself before toppling onto the floor.

"What's up?" Duke asked.

Wolf looked at Patterson and Rachette and then leaned up between Scott and Duke. "Stay here."

Wolf stepped out of the snow cat; his boot sank up to his knee in the wind-crusted powder. He stepped back up onto the hardened snow and looked around.

"What the hell?" Rachette whispered, now seeing what Wolf had a few seconds ago.

The rotor blades whipped by overhead and the engine whined at a steady low pitch. If it idled any slower, Wolf thought, it would have been shut off.

They faced east, and the morning sun blazed through the glass-enclosed cockpit of the whirring aircraft, illuminating it like a light bulb. On the window nearest them, a splash of glowing crimson painted the window, and a red X had been scrawled through it.

Wolf took out his pistol and walked to the aircraft, peering through the red-tainted glass at the figure inside. A man was slumped motionless in between the two cockpit seats.

The whooshing rotor overhead stirred the air, but other-wise the wind on top of the mountain was dead calm, and it smelled like jet fuel and the faintest hint of gunpowder.

Beyond the helicopter, there was a drop-off into Brecker Bowl, the terrain that had been bombed yesterday morning, sending a mountain of snow down onto the highway far below.

To the south—their right—was Williams Pass, and to the north the ridgeline they stood on continued all the way to Antler Creek Lodge, which sat in the distance reflecting the sun off its windows. Below was Rocky Points, the vast open valley beyond it to the north, and Cave Creek Canyon over thirty miles away. It was all a majestic view, but the grisly sight on the window hooked their eyeballs and reeled them closer.

Wolf noticed that the blood spatter was on the inside of the window, and the red X was scrawled on the outside. It was drawn with an oily red paint, or lipstick, just like the mark on Stephanie Lang's forehead.

The movement of the rotor blades gave Wolf the sense that the shooting had happened mere seconds ago. Of course, the engine could have been idling for quite a while.

He stepped up next to the window and looked in at the slumped body, and then looked down at the snow. There were two sets of prints.

"That Cooper?" Rachette asked, coming up behind Wolf.

"I don't know," Wolf admitted.

Wolf popped open the door and studied the man. He was wearing lace up hiking boots and ski pants. Wolf looked back down at the prints. One set matched the man's boots; the other appeared to have been made by ski boots, presumably the killer's.

A wallet bulged inside the man's ski pants. Wolf dug inside and pulled it out. His action moved the body just that little bit, which unleashed a fecal smell that was stirred by the rotor wash.

"Oh," Rachette said covering his nose.

Wolf opened the wallet and looked inside. The ID said Matthew Cooper. The picture showed Cooper tanned with a shaved head, smiling wide with a malicious looking grin.

Wolf handed it to Rachette. "Looks like it's Cooper."

Wolf looked down and traced the ski-boot prints to the front of the helicopter and then over to a spot where someone had clearly put on a pair of skis.

Wolf tracked the path of the twin ski tracks from where he was standing—over the edge, down to the left, and then off to the right to a ridge that ran away from them and down. Along the ridge was an orange rope marking the ski-area boundary—out of bounds to the right—and the ski tracks slalomed next to it and went out of sight over a small rise.

"He's dead," Patterson said, walking up behind Wolf. "He's still warm."

Wolf looked at her, then walked over to the ski cat and stopped.

Scott turned off the engine and opened the door. "Is that Cooper's blood?" he asked with wide eyes.

Wolf nodded. "Afraid so," he said, looking into the vehicle at Duke's feet, and then to the pair of skies in one of the slots on the side of the cat. "Duke, what size feet are you?"

Duke looked down and then up at Wolf. "Ten and a half? Eleven?"

Wolf cringed, and then climbed into the back of the cat. "I need to borrow your boots and skis … and poles and goggles."

Duke nodded and climbed into the back of the cat, sat down and took off his boots.

Wolf took off his Sorels and scooted them to Duke. "Trade ya."

It took a few seconds and a lot of toe cramming, but Wolf packed his feet into Bob Duke's warm, sweaty ski boots. Then he put on the mirrored-lens ski goggles; the terrain outside darkened and popped—the optics making it much easier to see gradation and depressions in the otherwise blazing white snow.

"Good thing you have fat feet, Bob," Wolf said.

Bob didn't respond. He was staring out, probably at the red smear on the helicopter window.

Wolf buckled the boots on as loose as he could and stepped outside. His feet mashed painfully into the front of the boots, the nails breaking the skin on their neighboring toes. He pulled out the Rossignol skis and clicked into the bindings, strapped on the poles, and skated over to the front of the helicopter.

Rachette held up his hands. "What are we supposed to do?"

"Secure the scene," Wolf said. "Call Lorber and get him up here."

Wolf skied up to the edge of the cirque and looked down. He saw a tiny car driving on the highway far below; then he focused closer and back to the fresh ski tracks that disappeared over the rise.

"What if the tracks go out of bounds?" Patterson asked.

Wolf thought about it. "Get someone to drive up the pass right now—whoever's closest—and tell them to wait for me. If they see a skier, make sure they know he's armed and dangerous. Tell them to not engage until backup arrives."

"Where do they wait?" Patterson asked.

"At the slide zone," Wolf said.

"Okay."

Wolf let go of a pole and let it dangle from his wrist, and then took off his glove. He pulled off his radio and twisted the dial, then pushed the button and held it to his lips. "Check," he said, his voice was clearly audible from Patterson and Rachette's radios. He put the radio into his jacket pocket and then felt the pistol on his holster underneath. While mentally rehearsing how he might pull the gun out to use it—drop pole, glove off, jacket up, pistol out—he jumped over the edge and landed on the steep snow with chattering skis.

CHAPTER 19

IN SPITE of how much snow the resort had gotten over the past forty-eight hours, the terrain under Wolf was hard and unforgiving because most of the powder from the bowl had slid to the bottom of the valley the day before.

The skis scraped on the ice as he cut to his right. When he reached the rope, he slowed to a stop and looked up. Rachette and Patterson were watching him. They waved, and Wolf raised a pole in return. Then he turned to look down the slope.

There was a clear crack where the snow had slid yesterday. To the left it was ice; to the right, fluffy powder with one set of tracks down it. He looked left across the expanse of the bowl and up to Antler Creek Lodge on the ridge, and marveled at the huge amount of snow that had to have cleaved and dropped.

Wolf studied the tracks. When he had been in his midtwenties, Wolf and this skier would have been good companions on the mountain. The tracks were long and symmetrical, turning the same arc on the left as the right, with a lot of distance in between. They were the tracks of an expert skier flying down the mountain at speeds most people weren't comfortable with—speed Wolf was no longer comfortable with now that he was pushing forty.

Wolf pointed Duke's skis down and entered into the powder. It came up to his knees, and the deep snow helped him check his speed with each turn. The wind blew on his face and was loud in his ears. He bounced up in between turns and sank deep as the wide skis carved through the snow.

He continued down with a steady rhythm, still marveling at the aggressive distance between the turn tracks he followed. The man he followed was competent on skis for sure, but Wolf thought that they were the tracks of someone running with nothing to lose. Maybe death didn't even matter to this person. If Wolf caught up with him, he had no doubt the man would be dangerous.

The rope ahead turned to the left, steering skiers back toward the flat zone at the base of the bowl, and then onward to the left and to the rest of the Rocky Points Ski Resort beyond. The tracks, however, ducked the rope and veered right.

Wolf stopped at the point where the tracks went under. His breathing was labored; his legs ached, already a little wobbly and slow. The helicopter was gone, out of view beyond the tracks he and his prey had left.

He stood sucking wind and following the tracks below with his eyes. They continued for another five or so turns, then abruptly turned right and then straightened, into a swath of dense forest, then they came out the other side into a powder field.

Wolf sucked in a breath and squinted. In the middle of the powder field the tracks led to a dark figure huddled in the snow. It was clearly a man, but any more detail than that was impossible to discern.

He pointed his skis down, gathered some speed, and then cut right. When he reached the tracks of the other skier, his velocity increased once more.

Had Wolf been seen?

The person was out of sight now, and all Wolf could see were the tracks that led into the dense copse of trees ahead.

As he entered the forest, he swerved back and forth, keeping on the narrow snake of depressed snow, not daring to deviate from the tracks an inch and risk slamming into a tree or stopping altogether.

He was going fast on the tracks, much faster than the man in front of him had gone, having less friction underneath him, and a few times he crashed through small branches, narrowly avoiding smashing straight into thick trunks by fabric-ripping margins.

The tracks were crazy lines, snaking downhill and gaining speed where Wolf would have chosen to keep skating across. Just when the trees got so tight that Wolf was certain a collision was imminent, they abruptly thinned out, and Wolf could see the man no more than a hundred yards ahead of him.

As Wolf came out into the open, he kept his eyes glued ahead and began the process of pulling his gun as fast as he could. He took his right pole and tucked it under his other arm, then yanked his glove off and shoved it into his jacket pocket, pulled up the bottom edge of his jacket and lifted the pistol out of its holster. All this he did in the span of a few seconds, and all of it, along with his approach, had still gone unnoticed by the figure in front of him.

The person was either unaware of Wolf's presence, or waiting for Wolf to get nearer for an easier shot. There was no telling from this distance, but Wolf wouldn't have to wait much longer to find out.

A downed tree that had been uncovered lay just ahead, and Wolf realized at the last second that he needed to jump to get up on top of it, or risk putting the skis under it and clothes-lining himself in the shins. So he jumped, and when he came down his skis thwacked on the log, and the noise startled the man ahead into motion.

And it was impressive motion.

Immediately he was up and charging straight down the steep glade to the left, this time not turning at all.

Wolf watched him go, trying to take in some of his charac-teristics. All that stood out for Wolf was the red hat. It was bright red, the red of the helicopter that sat on top of the mountain. Otherwise, the man was a blurry cloud of powder flying down the mountain at high speed.

Wolf turned his skis down and cut over. He was traveling painfully slow, the distance between them spreading by the second. But then Wolf realized exactly where they were, and knew things might turn in his favor in a matter of seconds because the man was headed straight for a line of cliffs.

The slope seemed to disappear ahead, like they were skiing on the side of a massive barrel, and the edge kept rolling under. Wolf knew that when the edge finally did come, it was a fifty-foot drop at the lowest point, and upwards of eighty feet at the highest. The man looked like he knew this terrain, and if he didn't want to plummet off the edge of the world he would have to turn one way or the other soon, losing valuable speed.

Wolf let the ski pole that was tucked under his arm drop, and he made some long turns, still grasping his pistol in his now numb right hand.

As the terrain steepened, his turns did little to check his

speed. More disturbing still, the man ahead was gaining speed.

Options raced through Wolf's mind. He knew that young crazy people jumped off these cliffs all the time, given the right conditions and enough cameras to capture it. These were definitely the right conditions. But he also knew that young crazy people jumped with the aid of spotters, making sure their lines were right so they didn't land in trees or on rocks and die.

The man in front of him was gone. No more cloud of powder. Nothing.

Wolf's final thought was of the long, kamikaze tracks higher up the mountain, and then he balked. He dropped the gun, turned ninety degrees to his right, and slid on his side, digging the edges of his skis in, and his right hand into the powder. The terrain steepened, and then steepened some more, and then all he could see was the tops of trees on the distant valley floor below, and a gentle slope to the highway, where an impossibly tiny car drove on the curvy road.

Wolf slid down, all his efforts to halt his progress for nothing, and just when he thought he was going over the edge, he stopped in the thick snow. Before he'd finished taking a breath of relief, the entire mountain started moving downward.

His stomach lurched as he slid, and then he twisted to his belly and swam with his arms, and when that didn't stop him he dug his hands down as hard as he could. His gloveless right hand was a numb stump, his left catching no purchase on anything. Everything was sliding down, him with it, and it was futile, like a man trying to swim up a waterfall.

Just as he was about to turn back around and make a leap for it so he might clear any rocks jutting from the cliffs below, his hands gripped a jagged outcrop beneath the snow. He grabbed with all his might, hugging the hook of a rock, and felt the snow slough over his head and back, burrowing deep into his jacket, pulling him like a fat man hanging onto his shoulders, suffocating him. And then just as quickly as it had started, the slide passed and his body was light again.

Wolf flexed his arms and shoulders and shook his head back and forth, flinging the cold snow off his skin. His goggles were caked with powder so he stared at pure darkness, but there was no way he was going to let go of the rock with either arm to wipe them off.

He needed a foothold. He picked up his right leg and felt the ski flop around, heard it scraping against bare rock. With a grunt, he kicked his rear binding and heard the released ski tumble down the rocks for a long time and then a whack as it landed far below. Then he kicked the other ski off and jabbed the toe of his right boot into solid rock, and realized he had no foothold.

After what seemed like a minute of grunting, staring at a sliver of light that seeped through his blocked goggles, his legs floundering beneath him, he found purchase and stood on the tiptoes of the boots. Only then did he dare take a second to reach up and rip off his goggles with one hand.

A wave of dread hit him when he looked up and saw near vertical rock and dirt for at least twenty feet above him. There were few depressions to dig his hands into, and with clunky ski boots, footholds would be wobbly and tentative at best.

He looked down. His feet appeared to be standing on air. Then he scanned right and left, and knew he was clinging to one of the highest points in the line of cliffs.

Movement below caught his eye and he did a double take.

Red Hat was skiing slowly toward the road, looking up at Wolf with interest as he took wide turns. The man was moving fine. Not injured in the least, or hiding it well if he was.

"Yee-haw!" the man yelled from below, waving a pole. Then he gained some speed, slalomed through the forest, and stopped at the side of the highway.

Wolf's foot slipped an inch, so he pulled himself up into a bent-elbow position and felt around for new, more stable footholds. For agonizing seconds there was nothing. He was scraping on a sheer, almost-vertical rock face.

He pulled his right leg up and pressed a knee into the rock under his belly, and then wondered just what the hell he was doing as he felt even less stable than before.

As he lowered his body back down to the original precarious position he'd been in, he studied the ground above him and picked the line he was going to climb. It was going to happen. He was going to make it. And ...

The rock underneath his hands let out a sickening crack and shifted down, and then the chunk of granite dropped toward his legs.

He pushed off his toes and kicked his legs back in time to avoid the crushing force of the rock, which would have certainly shattered his leg bones to splinters. As he brought his legs back in, the toes of his boots smacked against the cliff and bounced; now he was dropping.

With all his might, he twisted his body around, pushing his hands against the rock to help him. Then he brought his legs up in a squat, bent forward, and kicked into the side of the cliff as hard as he could. The boots slapped and gripped for an instant, and then he jumped out head first and looked down.

"Oh sh ..." Wolf whispered as the air rushed against his face, building to a deafening roar.

The initial shock of dropping eighty feet onto solid ground left him as he realized that his rotation was going to land him smack dab on his head if he didn't do something about it.

It isn't solid ground, his mind screamed through the terror. It was a pile of slough on top of a huge amount of snow from the last storm, which made his landing even more important. In the event he survived, landing headfirst would be a sure way to suffocate shortly thereafter.

The air was howling now, rippling clothing against his body as he accelerated more and more.

He tucked into a ball and willed his body to spin forward in a front flip. It didn't seem be working fast enough, as the rocks slid by a few feet from his face. He was still upside down.

Then, somehow, the wind caught his body, pushing him so that he was now looking at blue sky. And then he landed.

He barked involuntarily as he slammed back first into the snow—or maybe he hadn't. It was so instantaneous that it was impossible to register the events in his mind. One instant he felt the cement-hard blow of the landing, and the next he stared up at the steep walls of a narrow impact crater.

It was peaceful. A few clumps of snow crumbled off the edge above, widening the oval of blue sky even more. Relief turned to panic immediately as he tried to suck in a breath and couldn't. The wind was knocked out of him. He tried to struggle but couldn't against the snow, which only filled him with more dread.

Finally, with a long whistle, a breath entered his lungs. His vision tunneled as he sucked a cold lump of snow into his throat, causing him to cough out the little oxygen his body had managed to inhale.

The pain in his chest was agonizing, and then everything went black.

CHAPTER 20

BEEPING AND SQUAWKING VOICES. A body slumped in an office chair. A woman stuck her tongue out at him. A man yelled at him to get down. He raised the rifle and shot.

Wolf opened his eyes.

The oval of blue looked the same as it had … *when*? He heard the muffled beep of his radio and squawking voices, and he thought he heard his name.

His breathing was calm and normal. He coughed, clearing his lungs of moisture, and realized there had been no pain as he'd done so.

He steeled himself and took stock of his body. No stabbing sensation. No tingling ache of broken bones anywhere. He moved his left hand, and then tried his right and felt nothing. Then he remembered he'd lost his glove. He flexed his right arm, pulled it free from the heavy snow, and extended it out in front of him. His hand was covered with snow and stuck in a writing position. He brought it to his mouth and breathed on it, feeling nothing. He bit it, and felt nothing. He decided to forget about it and wriggled his left arm, and with a grunt he heaved it out of the cement next to him.

For a few moments he tried to sit up, but his body didn't budge, weighed down by the hundreds of pounds of snow pressing on him. Or was it that his back was broken and he was unable to move? Panic slashed at him, but he closed his eyes and took a calming breath.

No, he decided, feeling his feet wiggle in the compact ski boots, then his knee flex, then his thighs, his butt, his back, his shoulders, and his neck. He was fine. It was just that he was buried, and needed to dig himself out. So he began moving snow with teeth-gritting determination.

It took him at least thirty minutes to extricate himself. He parted the snow on his chest, sat up, and then freed his legs. Then it was a matter of crawling up and out of the five-foot hole. "... Wolf? Sheriff Wolf?" The radio sat in a small impact crater a few feet away.

"Wolf!" Rachette yelled into the radio, like he was calling a lost dog as he marched down the street.

Wolf bent down and picked it up. "Yeah, I'm here."

He took a step and sank all the way up to his crotch in the snow, and then realized he still had a whole mess of a problem ahead of him.

"Are you all right? We've been calling you for thirty minutes. Patterson is coming after you."

Wolf shook his head. "Patterson, do you copy?"

There was no response.

"Patterson!" Wolf said, afraid she was going to go over the cliffs next.

"Down here," she said. "I'm to your left, down near the road. I had to skirt the cliffs. I'm heading up your way."

Wolf waved. He looked around and saw a bright-orange sliver in the snow. It was the base of one of Bob Duke's skies poking out.

"Just hang tight," he said. "It's too deep. I found a ski."

Wolf dug it out and put it on, then trundled down the remaining hillside to the road to meet Patterson.

"I thought you were buried in an avalanche or something." Patterson was speaking fast. "I followed your tracks, and saw them end at a slide, and then that cliff." She looked up. "Oh my God. Look how high that was."

Wolf didn't bother looking as he slid down a steep bank and landed on the hard packed powder next to the road.

"How did you get skis?" Wolf asked.

"Scott got a ski patrol to bring some up for me on a snow-mobile." She took a deep breath. "We were pretty worried."

"Well, thanks," Wolf said. "Who's waiting on the highway?"

"Wilson is at the slide zone," she said.

"Wilson, do you copy?"

"Yes, sir, I'm on my way up now, let me know ..." Wilson drove around the corner at that moment. "Aha, there you guys are."

"Sir," Patterson said. "Your hand."

Wolf nodded. "I know. I need heat."

Patterson took off her glove and held it out, then took it back and shook her head. "Sorry, probably wouldn't fit you, now would it? Did you hear the radio chatter about the shooting at the top of the pass?"

Wolf's heart sank. "No. When?"

"Someone just called in about a shooting on top of the pass. Nobody's hurt, but a man was shot at, and his snowmobile was taken."

...

At 11:15 that morning, Wolf stood on the shoulder of Highway 734 on the top of Williams Pass, and it was clear that Matt Cooper's murderer had gotten away, using the mountains surrounding Rocky Points Resort, ingenuity, and a psychotic disposition to his advantage.

Apparently, Red Hat had hitched a ride up the pass, picked up by an unknown vehicle. It was customary practice for a driver of a truck with an open bed to stop if a skier came out of the woods and needed a lift back up to his or her car parked on the top of the pass.

When he'd arrived on top, however, he hadn't had a car parked there. Instead, he'd flashed his pistol at a man who'd just finished unloading a snowmobile off the back of his truck. A shot in the air had been enough to coax the man to start the machine and give it to the gun-wielding lunatic, who then took off up the western slope at the top of the pass.

They didn't know what Red Hat had done next, but after staring up the slope a few minutes, Wolf had a pretty good guess: When Red Hat had gotten to a specific point, he'd ditched the snowmobile, donned his skis, and skied down a grooved trail that meandered through the trees worn smooth by a group of ski-resort poachers the day before. Then he'd ducked a rope back into the resort—a well-known move that had got many into the back side of the resort, where tickets on the slower, two-seater lifts were not scanned.

If he was right, then it looked like a perfect getaway with local knowledge helping him pull it off.

"What now?" Patterson asked. "We have to get up there and check out where he went with that snowmobile. Should I call Ritchie?" She meant Brad Ritchie, a man with search and rescue who could bring more snowmobiles.

"Sure," Wolf said. "Have Yates and Wilson go up—they're

best on the sleds. I think they're going to find he ditched the snowmobile and skied back into the resort."

Patterson looked up.

Wolf walked toward the nearest SUV, flexing his right hand underneath the glove. After ten minutes in front of the car heater, the numbness had subsided, and had now been replaced with tingling and burning.

"Okay, so what now?" she asked, coming after him.

"We follow through with what we started today," Wolf said, climbing into Wilson's vehicle. "We talk to Jonas Prock."

"Am I coming with you?" Patterson asked, watching with interest as Wolf commandeered Wilson's SUV.

"No," he said.

"So what am I doing?"

"You're going with Baine to pick up Prock," he said, pointing over at Wilson and Baine, who stood off alongside the road.

"Okay, and—"

"I'm going to go lay down." Wolf shut the door and started the car, exhaling as the heat blasted his frigid, wet feet.

CHAPTER 21

The cold shadows of the mountains had already passed over the station outside when Wolf opened his eyes. His office was darkened and his ticking clock said 3:05 when he woke up on his office carpet.

His boots, the ones he'd taken off and given to Bob Duke at the top of the mountain, stood inside his closed door. He sat down on a chair and pulled them on, wincing from a sharp pain that traveled up his back. After a few seconds of bending forward, the pain ebbed away, but it left him wide-eyed and wondering if he'd pinched a nerve.

After tying his boots and successfully standing up without falling over, he walked into the squad room.

Rachette got up from the edge of Wilson's desk. "Interrogation room one."

Wolf looked at him. "Interrogation room one?"

"Prock. We picked him up and he's in there."

Wolf frowned. "How long's he been here? How long have I been asleep?"

"I was just about to wake you up. I figured you needed the rest." Rachette pointed down the hall. "Besides, he's only been in there a few minutes. We couldn't find him for hours. Apparently he was skiing." Rachette arched his eyebrows, as if the piece of information explained everything.

Wolf smoothed his hair. "Where's Patterson?"

"She's in the lab, checking out a USB drive that we found on Cooper."

Wolf squinted and shook his head. "He had a USB drive on him?"

Rachette nodded. "And when I say on him, I mean on him. It was just balanced on his shoulder. We didn't notice it until later, when you'd already skied down the mountain."

Wolf nodded, and then stood thinking, trying to get his bearings on the present moment. "And what else?"

"Lorber came and took Cooper off the mountain."

"And the X written on the window of the cockpit?" Wolf asked.

"Looks like it was lipstick, matching what we found on Stephanie Lang's forehead."

"Any usable prints inside or outside the cockpit?"

Rachette upturned his hands. "Lorber's on it."

The door to Tammy's reception office clicked and she poked her head out. "Sheriff."

"Yeah?"

Her eyebrows arched. "We have someone out here who insists on seeing you. A Mr. Klammer?"

Wolf sighed and nodded, and then walked to the superheated reception room.

"Ah, Sheriff Wolf," Klammer said, standing in front of the windows. "I wanted to know if I could come in and be a part of this ... inquiry."

Wolf shook his head. "Sorry, Mr. Klammer, we need to speak to Mr. Prock alone."

"Shall I call our lawyers?" Klammer asked with slow deliberate pronunciation.

Wolf considered the plural use of the word lawyer, and turned to Rachette who was behind him. "Please have someone get Mr. Klammer a drink. We'll talk soon, Mr. Klammer."

Rachette nodded.

"And then get back here," Wolf said as he walked away.

Wolf continued through the squad room, into the hallway, and past his office. Then he entered a closed door.

Observation room one was a small box with a one-way mirror window into the interrogation room beyond. Wolf stopped and took a moment to study Jonas Prock.

Prock sat under a pool of yellow light with his legs crossed and his coat across his lap. Looking around with a steady gaze, he was cocked sideways, leaning one arm on the wooden table, tapping out a rhythm with his finger.

"Jesus," Rachette said as he came inside. "This guy's kind of creepy. Didn't say a single word at all when we arrested him, and hasn't said a single word since. Here." Rachette held out a cup of coffee and a manila folder.

Wolf took the folder, peeked inside, and then took the coffee. "Thanks."

Wolf went inside with Rachette in tow. He sat down and set the folder on the table, and Rachette stood against the wall behind Prock.

Prock raised his eyebrows and looked over his shoulder, and then his lip curled and he shook his head.

Wolf leaned forward and opened the folder. Inside was a glossy photo of Stephanie Lang, an employee headshot photo taken at Antler Creek Lodge. She was smiling wide, a happy grin, as if she was friends with whoever was behind the camera.

Prock flicked a glance at it and kept his face expressionless.

"What can you tell me about this woman?" Wolf asked.

Prock didn't move.

Wolf looked at him for a few seconds. "We have two witnesses who say you were with this woman on Saturday night after the gala."

"I was?"

"According to two people on different parts of the mountain, yes, you were."

Prock closed his eyes and took a deep breath, like he was going to start meditating right there. When he finally opened them back up, he stared at the wall beyond Wolf.

Wolf tapped on the table.

Prock did a double take at the new picture Wolf had substituted with the last.

The photo was a close-up of Stephanie Lang's frozen corpse. Wolf watched as Prock took the whole picture in—the iced-over eyes, the frozen tongue sticking out, the torn-open flesh, the frozen meat underneath. Then, to Wolf's surprise, Prock's tough act vanished for an instant.

"I'll repeat," Wolf said, sensing the weakness in Prock's façade, "we have two witnesses who say you were with this woman after the gala on Saturday night. This picture"—Wolf tapped it—"was taken Sunday morning."

Prock stared at the photo, then looked away and closed his eyes. He scratched his neck with shaky fingers, an unconscious gesture of vulnerability. An unconscious gesture to his neck.

"Did you strangle Stephanie?" Wolf asked quietly.

Prock looked up. "What? No." He mumbled something in German.

Wolf took a sip of his coffee and set it down. "We know you and Matt Cooper were with Stephanie last night. So why don't you tell me what happened? Was it Cooper? Did he do it? Did he hold her down while you did it?"

Prock gripped his head with both hands and rubbed. "Ahhh ... no. We did not do this."

"Then tell me what happened," Wolf said in an even tone.

Prock pulled his hands away from his head and looked up at Wolf with wet eyes. "I didn't kill that girl." His voice was barely a whisper.

There was a firm knock on the door and then it opened.

Patterson stuck her head inside. "Sir, sorry. I need to speak to you."

Wolf turned and raised his eyebrows in response.

"It can't wait, sir," she said.

Wolf shut the folder slowly, then scraped his chair back. Without a word, he and Rachette left the room.

"What's up?" Wolf asked when the door clicked shut.

"There's a movie on the USB we found in the cockpit ... on Matt Cooper ... and you have to see it." She left the room and waved for them to follow.

They went into the squad room to Wilson's desk. He was bent close to the computer screen, and then he looked up and scooted back.

Patterson sat down in a chair and wheeled it close to the desk, then gripped the mouse. She clicked on a media player and tracked the movie playing on it to a position she wanted.

Wolf knitted his brow when he saw two people crawling all over each other on the screen, moving at light speed as Patterson found her desired mark.

"Whoa," Rachette said.

Finally, she clicked and sat back, letting the movie play.

Wolf leaned forward.

"Mayor Wakefield," Rachette said.

The image on the computer screen was of the interior of a vehicle, recorded with a fish-eye lens and at an angle that suggested it was mounted on the rearview mirror. It was a sharp picture, tinged green with a night-vision setting, and both the passenger and driver's seats were in the frame.

Mayor Wakefield was driving the car, dressed in a thick dress coat with a suit and tie beneath. He drove without giving much attention to the road. Instead he was swiveling left and right, looking in the side-view mirrors, and shifting to press his face to the glass, as if seeking something in the blackness of the night surrounding him.

What he was searching for became clear a few seconds later. The camera jerked as he stopped the car, and then he smiled, looking out the passenger window into the night. He bent over and pulled on the handle. The cab flashed green for a second as the picture became overexposed by the interior light. When it adjusted back to normal, a woman was sitting in the passenger seat. She leaned over and kissed him, and he kissed her back with passion, twisting in his seat and fondling her breast. After a few more seconds they parted and looked around out the windows as if making sure they weren't being watched.

"Stephanie Lang," Rachette said.

It was her. She had a mischievous look, groping at Wakefield's crotch with her left hand as she looked out the passenger window.

Lights streamed past the rear of the car. As they dimmed and receded into the distance, she leaned into his lap and stayed there for good.

"Okay," Wolf said. "So this is a sex tape of Mayor Wakefield and Stephanie Lang. It's definitely a development, but why are you pulling us out of the interrogation?"

Patterson held up a finger and then grabbed the mouse. She clicked on the bar below and pulled the marker to later in the movie. In the split second it took her to scroll through the whole movie, the screen showed snippets of the frames. Though hard to register exactly what was being seen, it was clear enough that Lang and Wakefield were naked, having intercourse, and in multiple positions for the next several minutes.

"Wow," Rachette said. "Got busy."

Wolf kept his eyes on the screen and waited while Patterson slowed just before the end of the movie.

"See here?" It was the same shot, but now the vehicle cab was empty.

"Okay," Wolf said.

"Wait for it," Patterson said. "Five more seconds."

Five seconds later, the picture flashed green again. After another few, it darkened and then bounced and jiggled. For a while a palm was all they could see, then an arm, and then, after a few seconds of swirling images, a face with glowing eyes took up the whole picture.

Patterson clicked the mouse, freezing the movie.

Wolf leaned forward. "Matt Cooper."

"The movie stops a second after this picture," she said. "You can't tell who starts the recording at the beginning, but it's unmistakable at the end. Matt Cooper."

"What about prints on the USB?" Wolf asked. "Did you find any?" He glanced at the USB inserted in the PC tower.

"That's ... not the original USB," Patterson said, following his eyes. "The original is in the lab. I didn't find any prints on it, but there is definitely blood, and it does *not* match our pilot Matt Cooper. I've sent what I have to Lorber's office, and when he gets back there I'll talk to him about it."

"Blood not matching Cooper's?" Rachette asked. "That's what we like to call in the business, a clue if I've ever heard of one."

Patterson pointedly ignored her partner.

"Keep me posted on that," Wolf said.

Wilson shook his head at the screen and pushed his chair back. "There's no way to know when the recording was made. There's no time and date stamp on it. No meta data."

"I would say it was made Thursday night after Charlie Ash's party," Wolf said. "You can see Cooper's valet uniform. That's how he got in his car and planted the camera at the beginning. He could have gone into town and made a copy of the key during the party to come back and retrieve the video camera later."

"Rascal's Hardware," Wilson said, referring to the only place in town that made keys. "I'm pretty sure they're open until nine p.m. on weeknights."

"And the mayor went somewhere and picked up Stephanie after the party?" Rachette asked.

"Antler Creek catered it," Wolf said. "She was at the party. They must have planned a rendezvous that night."

Patterson looked up, skepticism etching her face. "And Cooper knew all this was going to happen?"

"Looks that way," Wolf said as he left the room.

...

Wolf sat back down in front of Prock while Rachette took his position against the wall. Prock's demeanor was night and day from earlier. What was once a cool gaze was now the look of a cornered animal, his eye movements quick and urgent.

"I didn't kill Stephanie," he said.

Wolf kept silent.

"I swear." Prock put his elbows on the table and pressed his hands together. "We were just taking her home, and we dropped her off."

Wolf held up a hand. "Let's start with how you know Cooper. You're from Austria, he's from Aspen. More importantly, he works for Irwin, you for Klammer. How is it that you end up hanging out with an employee of the firm you're competing against for a multi-million-dollar contract? Does Klammer know?"

Prock sat back and exhaled. "No, I was ... it's complicated."

"Try me. Your life depends on it."

Prock shook his head and blinked. "We were working together for the last few weeks."

"In what capacity?" Wolf asked.

"I was approached by Irwin Construction Corporation a few months ago. They offered me a deal: I keep them abreast of progress, and they give me compensation."

"A double agent."

Prock nodded in his almost-imperceptible way.

"Progress?" Wolf asked. "About what?"

Prock held up his palms. "About our progress of winning the bid for an important contract."

"And how was progress going?" Wolf asked.

Prock looked at Wolf for a second, considering his answer. "Touch and go."

Wolf nodded. "Saturday night, at the gala. You licked Stephanie's earlobe. How did you know her?"

Prock frowned. "I didn't lick her earlobe."

"Whatever, you were flirting with her, and it was clear to a number of people at your table. How did you know her?"

"From the party last week."

"Charlie Ash's party?" Wolf asked.

"Yeah." Prock shifted in the seat. "Could I have a glass of water?"

"Not yet," Wolf said. "The party?"

Prock sat back again and exhaled. "Cooper introduced me, and we hit it off. We got together in one of the rooms for a few minutes."

"And then what?"

"And then nothing," Prock said. "We didn't see each other again that night."

Wolf shook his head and looked back at Rachette.

"She disappeared," Prock said quickly. "I never saw her again until Saturday night, at the gala, when she came to our table. We talked that night, and she agreed to hang out after she got off work."

"So you met her after her shift," Wolf said. "Then you two went down the mountain together?"

"Yes."

"And then you hooked up with Matt Cooper?" Wolf shook his head and sat back, looking at the ceiling. "I don't get it. Why wouldn't you take your own car? A cab? One of the shuttles that comes to the roundabout at the bottom of the gondola?"

Prock rolled his eyes and put the side of his hand on the table. "I couldn't take the company car, and we didn't want to take a shuttle or a—"

"So Cooper not only flies skiers in helicopters, but he's fine with giving couples rides to wherever they want to go have sex? He's just a nice guy like that?"

Prock stared at Wolf for a second and lowered his eyes to the table.

Wolf watched Prock's skin grow hot, like he was either furious or embarrassed. Wolf couldn't tell which.

"Why involve Cooper in your little sex adventure?" Wolf asked. "You're not making any sense. Start telling me the truth."

Prock glared up at Wolf. "That was the point. I wanted Matt Cooper involved in the sex adventure."

Wolf felt his own face flush. "Oh." Wolf took a deep breath and stretched his neck. "So you and Cooper?"

"Yes. That is why we got along so well when we met." Prock stared at Wolf with drooping eyelids, as if waiting for the judgmental remarks to come.

"So then what?" Wolf asked.

"I called Cooper to pick us up. He was at the bar in the village, picked us up, and we drove up to Stephanie's house."

"But you didn't get there, did you?" Rachette said.

Wolf looked up at Rachette and then back at Prock.

Prock leaned forward. "We dropped her off on the side of the road. She wanted us to"—he opened his eyes wide and held up a finger—"there was someone behind us that night. We passed another truck."

Rachette blew out of his nose, and Prock twisted in his seat.

"Why would you drop her off late at night in the middle of a major storm?" Wolf asked. "It was snowing like mad. It had been for hours."

"Stephanie and Cooper. They were fighting the whole way up the road. I couldn't stop them. He was being vulgar, and she was definitely upset. I tried to tell both of them to stop, but they just kept shouting. She was screaming for him to let her out of the car, and wouldn't listen to either one of us. So he stopped and she got out." Prock waved a hand.

"What was the argument about?" Wolf asked.

Prock squinted and shook his head. "He was treating her like a ... prostitute, how do you call it?"

"A prostitute," Rachette said.

Prock nodded. "He was calling her names and insulting her, and she didn't like it. I think they had a history, a fight before or something."

Wolf leaned forward. "Tell me exactly what they were saying."

Prock rolled a palm up. "I don't know ... he said that she had to do us both, and he wasn't going to pay her the cost, as if she had a price or something. It was ... it was bad."

"And what was her cost?" Wolf asked. "What was her going rate?"

Prock swallowed and looked at Wolf. "What? What kind of a question is that? What's wrong with you? I told you—"

"You said Cooper was talking about a cost. What was the cost he was talking about? Do you remember a specific number?" Wolf asked.

"I don't know." Prock huffed.

"Was it twelve hundred dollars?" Wolf asked. "Was it one thousand two hundred dollars?"

Prock's face dropped. "Yes," he said carefully. "It was."

Wolf sat back and ran a hand through his hair.

"How did you know about that?" Prock narrowed his eyes.

"What happened next, after you dropped her off? Did Cooper tell you about the sex tape?"

Prock straightened. "What sex tape?"

"You didn't press him about what had just happened?"

Wolf asked. "Didn't you want to know what the whole argument was about?"

"I did. I asked him. But we ended up arguing. He was calling her a whore again, and telling me to forget her. I was telling him to go back and pick her up, and he refused to. He said the truck behind us would pick her up and not to worry. I figured he was right."

"It was a truck following you? What kind was it?" Wolf asked.

Prock looked up in thought. "I think it was an SUV."

"Was it a truck or SUV?" Rachette asked.

"I don't know."

"What color?" Wolf asked.

"It was snowing hard. The headlights were in our eyes."

"Did you see it pick up Stephanie?" Rachette asked.

"No. I didn't. We were gone. We left."

Wolf studied his face and decided the man was telling the truth.

"And that was it about the argument between Cooper and Stephanie?" Wolf asked. "No more bringing up the topic?"

Prock shrugged and glared at Wolf. "We didn't have much time to talk about it anymore because an asshole cop pulled us over. Gave Matt a drunk-driving test out in the snow."

Wolf took a deep breath and crossed his legs. The room was cold, the air somehow penetrating the windowless room through unseen cracks. Just like his office.

Wolf changed direction. "What were you and Klammer talking to Charlie Ash about the other day? At the Sunnyside Café."

Prock's face transformed to cool and untouchable in the span of a few breaths. "The pursuit of the contract. Of course."

"Specifically?" Wolf asked.

Prock shrugged. "Just business."

"Maybe I'll go talk to Klammer," Wolf said. "Let him know about your dealings with Irwin's company."

Prock shrugged again. "I was going to tell him anyway. After all, it was the kind of thing I'm paid for. It was a strategic move, taking the job offered to me by Irwin, and it was something I couldn't tell Klammer about at the time, in order to work both sides effectively."

Wolf smiled. "Because you believe Klammer is going to come out on top."

Prock stared at the wall in response.

"What were you doing this morning between seven and nine a.m.?" Wolf asked.

Prock's eyebrows pulled together. "I was waking up, then eating breakfast with Mr. Klammer. Why?"

"Where were you eating?" Wolf asked.

"The Sunnyside," Prock said. "Unfortunately. Such terrible cuisine in this country."

Wolf got up and walked to the door. Rachette followed.

"Hey, I want to—"

Prock's voice was muffled as the door closed.

Patterson and Wilson were on the other side of the door in the observation room.

"Well?" Rachette asked. "Did this guy do it or what?"

Wolf turned and watched Prock through the glass.

Prock got up off his chair and began pacing, staring at the floor and mumbling to himself in his native tongue.

"Let him go," Wolf said. "Make it clear to Klammer that we want both of them to stay in town, though. Let's put surveillance on them."

"But shouldn't we check on his alibi for this morning first?" Patterson asked. "I can call the Sunnyside."

Wolf walked out of the room and into the hallway. "Okay, go ahead. But I think we're looking for someone else."

"Don't most Austrians come out of the womb with skis on?" Rachette asked. "You sure that wasn't him this morning?"

Wolf shook his head. "Prock could be a world-cup skier, but that doesn't change the fact that it was a local who gave us the slip this morning. Whoever that was knew the backcountry too well." Wolf looked at Wilson. "Let me guess, the snowmobile tracks went up to Poacher's Trail, where it was found ditched."

Wilson nodded.

"That's how he escaped. Went right back to the mountain, blended in with the Monday-morning resort skiers. Didn't need to scan a lift ticket at any of those back side lifts. Prock wouldn't have known that move."

"He could have learned about that trick over the last couple weeks he's been in town," Patterson said.

They stood in silence for a beat, and then Wolf nodded. "Of course you're right. Confirm his alibi at Sunnyside. And keep me posted about the blood on that USB."

Patterson nodded and went to the squad room with Wilson on her heels, leaving Wolf and Rachette.

"Who do you want to put on tailing Klammer and Prock?" Rachette asked following Wolf into his office.

"I don't know. It doesn't need to be covert or anything. Just plant a deputy on their ass."

"Where are you going?" Rachette asked. "Can I come?"

Wolf turned around and found Rachette a few inches away. "What's going on?"

Rachette shrugged. "Nothing. Can I come?"

"What did you do?"

"What do you mean?"

"Why are you desperate to hang out with me, and why is your partner mad and not speaking to you?"

Rachette blinked, pretending to be confused.

Wolf walked past him out into the hallway.

"Where are you going?" Rachette asked again.

"The mayor's. Talk to you soon."

Wolf stopped at Wilson's desk on his way through the squad room, pulled the USB out of the computer, and pushed through the doors into the cauldron that was reception.

Klammer was in the waiting room and stood up from his chair. His face was red and his sleeves were rolled up, but he stared at Wolf with a bored expression, as if he were perfectly content with playing the waiting game.

"Prock will be out in a minute," Wolf said walking past.

Klammer parted his lips and inhaled, preparing to say something.

Wolf left through the front door before any words escaped the man's mouth. His patience with the backroom games these people were playing had long since evaporated.

CHAPTER 22

DURING THE WINTER months of Rocky Points, and anywhere else in the mountains for that matter, the sun could disappear early in the day, depending on where you were in the valley. Darkness could begin at two in the afternoon in spots, or even earlier. Snow and ice could cling in these places for almost three quarters of the year.

Wolf considered himself lucky that his ranch house was situated in such a way that light bathed the property until later in the afternoon, but the department headquarters building was one of those places that went into shade at about two-thirty in the afternoon in winter.

Mayor Wakefield's property, high up on the western-facing slopes overlooking the town from the east side, didn't have that problem. It took advantage of all the sunlight the day could offer at any time of year.

As he drove up the snow-packed road toward Wakefield's, Wolf squinted as the day's final rays of sun knifed through the pine trees, cutting into the edges of his vision. KBUD was playing an old Widespread Panic tune that reminded Wolf of his high-school days—back when he would have been coming home this time of the evening after an afternoon of skiing with his brother, John, or his best friend, Nate Watson.

Wolf chugged some water out of a half-frozen bottle and felt it douse his empty stomach, realizing he still needed to sit down and eat for a straight hour or so.

As he got closer to Wakefield's, he thought about his brother again, and how he had died. John had been murdered, made to look like he had killed himself. Had Wolf missed something the other day with Jen Wakefield? It had looked like a cut-and-dried suicide, but if the same thing had happened today, after two murders in town, maybe he would have scrutinized the scene more thoroughly.

He lowered the volume of the music and turned into Wakefield's driveway. He raised a hand to block the setting sun and pulled in next to Chris Wakefield's Ford truck.

Wolf got out and walked to the ornate wood door and rang the bell. It chimed inside, and a few seconds later Chris Wakefield opened it up.

"Oh, hi Sheriff," he said. "Can I help you?" Chris was fully dressed with his coat and boots on, looking like he was ready to leave.

"I came to speak to your father."

Chris stepped aside. "Dad! Sheriff Wolf is here!"

Chris Wakefield was in his late teens, almost Wolf's height and, if Wolf wasn't mistaken, rumored to be a very good skier. He watched Chris closely, scrutinizing him for signs of nursing injury from hurling himself off a sixty foot cliff earlier in the day.

"Yeah, okay, let him in!" Mayor Wakefield said from somewhere inside.

Chris turned back to Wolf and opened the door wider.

Wolf stomped the snow off his boots and stepped inside. It

was warm, and bright as a sunset in the entryway, with the sun streaming in through the huge windows of the next room straight ahead.

"Well," Chris said, nodding at Wolf, "I'll see you later." He stepped out the door and pulled it shut, leaving Wolf on the carpet inside the foyer.

It smelled like toasted bread, and Wolf heard a plate clank in the distance and then muffled footsteps.

Mayor Wakefield walked around the corner wearing a sweatshirt, sweatpants, and socks, a stark contrast to the usual suit and tie in which most Rocky Points residents were accustomed to seeing the mayor dressed. He wiped his hands on the already dirty-looking sweatshirt and walked to Wolf. "Sheriff, what can I do for you?"

Wolf shook the mayor's warm and greasy grip. "I just wanted to speak to you about a few things."

"Sure." Wakefield looked down at himself. "I, uh, wasn't expecting company. Please, come in."

Wolf wiped his feet on the carpet and then followed Wakefield into the living room.

"Please, sit." Wakefield walked to the windows and pushed a discreet button on the wall. A window blind hummed and lowered with a continuous swish, blocking out the bright rays one foot at a time.

Wolf sat on the edge of a square leather footrest.

"There," Wakefield said when the blind was fully down. Then he sat on a leather chair across the coffee table from Wolf. It groaned and so did Wakefield. "What's up?"

The grandfather clock in the corner clunked and then started chiming—big echoing tubes of metal being pounded by mallets. Wolf saw that it was five o'clock, and rather than raise his voice over the noise he waited. They were going to be covering some tough subject matter.

His gaze was inevitably drawn past Wakefield, and to the open room across the hall that they used as a family den. There were shelves with books, an expensive globe on a floor mount, and other elegant office furniture.

Wolf stared at the wooden table with the black office chair pulled up to it—a *different* black office chair. That's where Wakefield had found his wife last week, and that's where Wolf had seen Jen Wakefield's lifeless body sagging off the chair with a blown-out skull that Wolf had heard dripping on the floor hours after her death.

"Tough to look at, isn't it?" Wakefield said, snapping Wolf out of his daydream. The clock was silent now.

Wolf sucked in a breath and looked the other way toward the kitchen. There was a big wooden table with an open laptop computer perched on top.

"Could I please borrow that computer?" Wolf asked.

Wakefield looked at Wolf for a second and then got up.

Wolf watched the man pad down the hardwood hall and go into the kitchen. Wakefield unplugged the computer, picked it up and walked back, stopping to switch on some lights. The sun had dipped behind the peaks.

"Here," Wakefield said, and put it on the coffee table in front of Wolf.

Wolf pulled the USB out of his jacket pocket, inserted it, and pulled up the movie.

Wakefield feigned interest across from Wolf, but he was fidgeting and clearing his throat too much to fool anyone.

Wolf pushed play, moved the tracker to the middle of the movie, and then turned up the volume and twisted the laptop toward Wakefield.

Sounds of frenzied sex bellowed out of the computer speakers, and Wakefield looked horrified, but not surprised. He bent forward and shut the computer with a thud.

"What the hell is going on?" Wolf asked. "You know damn well we found this girl murdered Saturday night."

Wakefield stared through the coffee table.

"This movie was recorded Thursday night, after Charlie Ash's party, am I right?"

Wakefield nodded.

Wolf let the big clock tick a few times. "Did you pay this girl to sleep with you?"

Wakefield looked aghast. "No."

They stared at one another for a few seconds, and Wakefield blinked first.

Wolf's phone vibrated in his jeans, and he reached through the fabric and pushed a side button to forward it to voicemail.

"Where were you on Saturday night?" Wolf asked.

Wakefield popped his eyes wide open. "You don't think I killed this girl, do you?"

"Where were you?" Wolf asked again.

"I was here, getting shit-faced on Scotch. Like I've been doing since ..."

Wolf sat forward on the couch, elbows on knees. His cell phone vibrated again, and then again. Wolf stood up and pulled it out. The screen said one missed call, one voicemail, and one text message.

Just then another text message flashed on the screen. It said, *Call me, now! Important!*

It was from Patterson.

Wolf held up the phone. "I have to make a call."

Wakefield flicked a wrist.

Wolf dialed the number and Patterson picked up halfway through the first ring.

"Sir."

"Yeah?"

"Lorber matched the blood on the USB."

"And?"

"It's Jen Wakefield's blood." Wolf looked at Wakefield.

"Sir?" Patterson said in the earpiece.

"Thanks," Wolf said. "Is that all?"

"Yeah. Do you need—"

Wolf hung up and put the phone back in his pocket.

Wakefield raised his gaze and Wolf looked past him to the wooden table in the den. It was getting almost too dark to see inside the room, but something still caught Wolf's eye. His boots squeaked on the hardwood floor as he stepped around the couches and across the hall. He stopped at the entryway and flicked on the light.

Wakefield walked up silently behind Wolf.

The office chair was different, understandably a new model to replace the one Jen Wakefield had died in, and just as understandably there was a rug underneath it that hadn't been there days before. It was a carpeted room, and the rug under the chair would have been put there to cover the stain, at least until they got around to re-carpeting the whole space.

Wakefield watched Wolf with a wary expression. His chest was heaving, nose whistling with rapid breaths.

Wolf pulled the chair aside. Then he bent down, crawled under the table, and yanked a computer charger out of the wall.

"What's going on?" Wakefield's voice cracked.

Wolf climbed out from under the table with the charger in

hand. He held it up and studied it for a second, and then held it by his side.

"Did your housekeeper clean up in here?" Wolf asked.

Wakefield swallowed and shook his head. "We had a company come in and do the cleanup."

"Hollow point bullets," Wolf said. "Supposed to stay in the body, do as much damage as possible, and cause less collateral damage to others. At least that's the argument, and that's why we use them in law enforcement." Wolf looked over at the table, and then down at the rug. "But the problem is, they do a lot of damage in the body. And if that damage comes out the other side? Well, it makes a real mess."

Wakefield clenched his eyes shut and shook his head.

Wolf held the end of the charger between his thumb and forefinger. "Tough to clean a mess like that, to the point where everything's completely gone. Pretty much impossible. You'll have to replace everything, repaint the walls, the ceiling. Replace the carpet."

Wakefield opened his eyes and stared at Wolf. A tear rolled down his cheek.

Wolf held out the wire in front of Wakefield. "See that? Blood. And it's here, all the way down the wire of the charger, until about here."

Wakefield stood quietly and let the tears flow.

"I thought it was weird when I came here that day, and you'd wiped the table. You played it off pretty well, like you were just going a little bit crazy, and had to get started cleaning up the mess. Couldn't stop yourself. Of course, now it all makes sense."

Wakefield stared at him.

"She was watching that sex tape when she killed herself, wasn't she?" Wolf asked.

Wakefield looked down, dripping tears onto the carpet as he moaned and shook. After at least a minute he swallowed, sniffed and looked up at Wolf, the same way he'd done in the chapel after his wife's funeral. *Shoot me.*

"Why don't you tell me what really happened," Wolf said.

Wakefield trudged back into the big room and Wolf followed. The peaks behind the window covering were black silhouettes against a midnight-blue sky.

"My wife wasn't supposed to see it," Wakefield said. "Ash went to my downtown office on Friday and dropped the USB on my desk with a cryptic note. On a fluke, Jen came looking for me in my office, to have lunch or something. She read the note and brought the USB stick home.

"When I got home from work, I heard the sex noises coming from the den. I thought it was Chris watching porn or something. When I got in the room, I ... I saw her. And I saw the video playing in front of her. She'd looped it, so it played over and over again. She wanted me to find her like that. God!" He shook his head and looked up. "I still thank God Chris didn't find her. She ... she hadn't been doing too well, psychologically, with the MS. It was eating at who she was. Making her ... hard edged. A completely different person."

Wakefield paused and flicked a glance at Wolf. "I saw the note. It was sitting right next to the computer. I panicked. I ... picked it up and I pulled the USB out of the computer. And then the damn window of the movie was still up on the screen, so I had to close it with my finger on the track pad, and before I knew it I was smearing my wife's blood all over the damn thing. So I just picked it up, cleaned it in the sink and then got to work cleaning the table. It was so dumb." He shook his head. "Every time I finally get to sleep I wake up thinking about what I did to her, and then what I did with her blood. I have to drink myself unconscious."

Wolf sat in silence, watching Wakefield's mind rip itself apart. "What did the note say?" Wolf asked.

"Huh?"

"The note."

"Klammer gets your vote, or else," Wakefield said. "From Charlie Ash."

"That's exactly what it said?"

"It's burned in my mind."

"It said, 'From Charlie Ash'?"

"Well, no, but it was him." Wakefield stared into nothing. "He hired Stephanie to seduce me. My wife wasn't at Charlie's party on Thursday night. She never went out anymore, not with her illness. She didn't like being in public, it was too hard for her."

Wakefield sat forward, picking his fingernail on the coffee table. "A couple of years ago, when I met Charlie Ash, when he moved to town from Tahoe, I'd been screwing around on my wife. And Charlie and I, we went out to a bar to have a drink, to get to know each other. You know, the state of the real-estate market, the political atmosphere. He was interested in getting involved in the county council.

"Anyway, this girl came up to me. This girl I'd been … seeing. She was young. She was out with her friends and came barging into the bar, and she came right up to me and started putting her hand on my face, and I brushed it away and got her to back off before anything too telling happened. But Charlie Ash knew." Wakefield smiled. "Ash knew, but he pretended like he hadn't noticed. I remember it like it was yesterday. She didn't give it away, and I acted pretty well, getting that girl out of there without making a scene. But he knew. I saw the gears churning in his head, and he just kind of ... pointedly forgot about it, never mentioned it. But I knew he knew, and I thought his ignoring it was ... I don't know, him being loyal to me or something. His silence saying he didn't care, he was going to be a good friend from now on, so just ... *forget it. I already have.*"

Wakefield squirmed in the chair. Scratched his cheek.

"So his little plan worked perfectly. He dangled a beautiful girl in front of me while my wife was home dying in her bed. And me, being the asshole that I am, I fell for it. I screwed her, and he videotaped it."

Wolf cleared his throat, and then stood up and walked over to a smaller window with a view. He looked down at the twinkling lights of the town and then at Wakefield's reflection in the glass. He was sitting board straight and staring at Wolf's back.

Wolf turned around. "That doesn't prove it was Charlie Ash who made that tape."

Wakefield snorted. "Oh, it was him. He came over and clarified things on Saturday, even after knowing my wife had just shot herself."

"And how did he clarify things?" Wolf asked.

"He came over and said that I must vote for Klammer's bid, and persuade everyone else I can to do the same. If I do that, I'll get money and the video stays private."

"And has he paid you any money?"

"No. I don't even want money."

"Where's that note?" Wolf asked.

"I burnt it before I called you." Wakefield looked down. "I was panicking."

"And the USB drive?" Wolf asked.

His face froze and he looked up. "Wait, the USB drive." He

looked over at the computer on the coffee table. "How did you get that?"

"We found Matt Cooper dead today. The USB was left on him. And your wife's blood was smudged on the drive."

Wakefield's mouth dropped open. "What? Cooper had the USB? The helicopter pilot? How?"

"Cooper didn't have the USB. He was killed, and the murderer left it for us to find."

Wakefield jumped up off the couch and walked out of the room.

"Hey!" Wolf called, putting his hand on his pistol. "Stop."

Wakefield stopped and then held up a hand. "Wait, I have to see something." Then he waved Wolf down the hall and started walking again.

Wolf caught up fast, keeping his hand on his gun.

Wakefield stepped through cones of light as he marched down the hall and then veered left into a dark cave of a room.

Wolf followed on his heels into the darkness, and then the space lit up with the sound of a switch. A mahogany desk was the centerpiece of a large room filled with patterned rugs, bronze statues, and dark-wood carvings. Shelves lined the walls with hundreds of books.

Wakefield stopped at the desk and reached for the top drawer.

"Stop, or I will shoot," Wolf said in a steady voice. He aimed his pistol at Wakefield's back.

"What?" Wakefield swiveled and thrust his hands in the air. "What are you doing?"

"Step away from the desk, now," Wolf said.

Wakefield did.

Wolf kept his eyes on Wakefield and opened the desk

drawer. Inside was a tray full of pens and pencils, a small calculator, a pad of graph paper, and a USB drive.

Wakefield bent closer and pointed in the drawer. "There," he said. "That's the USB I took out of the computer. I swear."

Wolf took out the USB and shut the drawer, then kicked the big leather office chair toward him. "Sit."

Wakefield sat down, keeping his arms in the air.

"You can put your arms down," Wolf said. He reached over and shuffled the mouse on the desk, and the desktop monitor came to life. Without speaking, he put the USB in, waited for it to be registered by the computer, and then clicked the folder on the desktop. The drive was blank. No files at all.

"Blank," Wolf said.

Wakefield stood up and walked over. "Shit. I ... Ash. It was Ash. He must have switched the drives on Saturday. When he came over."

"Sit down," Wolf said.

"I knew he was setting me up. I knew it yesterday when I talked to him."

"You talked to Ash yesterday?" Wolf asked.

Wakefield nodded. "Yeah. I had heard about Stephanie, and I called him to come over. I wanted to figure out what the hell was going on."

"And what did he say was going on?"

"He didn't. He played dumb about the whole thing. He actually kind of freaked out, tripped over the maid on the way out."

Wolf glared at Wakefield. "Freaking out about you?"

"What do you mean?"

"After Stephanie Lang seduced you, and Matt Cooper set up the video camera to record in your car, I'd be pretty pissed off if I were you."

Wakefield frowned. "Wait, Matt Cooper set up the camera? I didn't know that. How would I know that?"

Wolf looked hard into Wakefield's eyes. There was fear, confusion, regret, and a whole lot of hangover, but Wolf didn't think there was deception.

"What about Chris?" Wolf asked.

"What about him?"

"What was he doing on Saturday night?"

"You think my son killed Stephanie Lang?" Wakefield's voice was quiet, almost a whisper.

"Just answer the question, Mayor."

"He was … he went out. To a friend's. I don't really know. I was pretty drunk, and I just kind of let him do his thing."

Wolf stood up and gazed down the rows of books. "And this morning? What was he doing?"

"He was"—he shook his head—"sleeping here, then woke up and went into town for a while. I don't know what he was doing. He skipped school. Said he didn't want to go, and I didn't blame him."

"What time did he wake up and leave?" Wolf asked.

Wakefield thought for a moment. "Woke up at like eight. Left at about ten. Why?"

Wolf stared at Wakefield, still seeing truth in the man's eyes. "You're certain on those times?"

"Yes. Yes I am. What are you thinking?"

Wolf thought about Ash, and Irwin, and Klammer, and Prock, and Margaret Hitchens. Was *she* lying to him about something? Was she involved in her own form of corruption, lying about the listing contracts? What about Sarah? Was she getting involved too?

Wolf shook his head, snapping out of his thoughts. "I think

I need to get a shovel to start digging through the bullshit you guys are piling up in Town Hall."

Wakefield looked down at the floor.

Wolf walked out of the office, down the hall, and went outside, not bothering to shut the door to the house as he left.

Only after he'd driven a mile did he realize his jaw had been clamped shut since he'd left. The mayor hadn't killed Stephanie Lang or Matt Cooper. But what about Jen Wakefield's suicide? What was Wolf going to do about that? The mayor had covered up the full truth by removing the computer and cleaning the table, but what was that? An obstruction of justice? And had Wakefield really caused his wife's suicide by carrying out the adultery caught on tape? Or had it been Cooper's fault for setting up the camera? Or was it Ash, who allegedly set the whole thing up to blackmail the mayor? Or a rare form of multiple sclerosis attacking Jen Wakefield's brain?

The questions banged around in Wolf's head, giving him a headache.

Charlie Ash. Wolf's jaw clenched again as he thought about the man. He knew Charlie Ash was involved, but instinct was telling him to steer clear until he had his ducks in a row. But what ducks would those be? The phantom burnt note from Charlie Ash? There were no prints on the USB drive. Cooper was dead, and along with him the true reason why he'd set up the video camera to capture the mayor and Stephanie having sex.

And Wolf could have just been played by Wakefield, he couldn't forget that. He couldn't forget that Wakefield was a politician, and a damn good one at that. And many politicians got where they were by knowing how to lie through their teeth.

And the corruption. How should Wolf deal with it? Was there any real evidence, any wrongdoing that had occurred between the two construction firms and members of the county council? Any evidence of illegal payments to Charlie Ash, or any contracts breached by Prock as he acted as a double agent working for both firms?

Who gives a shit? Wolf wasn't a forensic accountant, and he wasn't a white-collar crime prosecutor. He was a detective, a small-town cop, and there were murders happening in his small town. He was going to find the killer. The strangler with a pistol. The psychotic skier with a tube of lipstick that had almost gotten Wolf killed. The rest could be sorted out later.

CHAPTER 23

ON A MONDAY NIGHT in the heart of winter, Rocky Points was dead. From Mayor Wakefield's house to Main Street, Wolf passed only one other vehicle. On the south side of town, there would be more action, as the younger crowd working at the mountain gathered for happy hour either at Beer Goggles or in the base village. That was a six-days-a-week inevitability for most ski bums. But on the northern edge of town, the roads were dark, most people snug at home, tending their wood stoves in front of the TV.

Wolf stopped at the grocery store and picked up a bag of fried chicken, some soda, chips, eggs, bacon, and bread, and then stopped at the liquor store for a six-pack of Newcastle, and decided he had enough supplies to head home.

As he drove down Main, he passed dark shops and a quietly sleeping Sunnyside Café. The station was lit up as usual, but he wasn't in the mood to go in. Just as he hadn't cared to return home the night before, he didn't care to return to work tonight.

Aside from the station and the Hitching Post Realty office,

one other building was conspicuously bright—the old bank. Six vehicles crammed the lot in front, including Sarah's 4Runner and Chris Wakefield's black Ford truck.

Wolf looked at his dash clock—6:17. Sarah's Monday-night meeting, he realized. He slowed and turned the wheel, bouncing off Main into the lot. There were no available plowed spots so he rammed the Explorer up the side of a snow bank next to an old truck he didn't recognize, yanked the parking brake, and climbed out.

A beat-up Chevy Blazer hummed a few cars over, spewing a thick cloud of exhaust. A light clicked on and the door opened.

"Nice park job, Sheriff." It was a female's voice.

Wolf walked over and peered inside, then smiled. "Oh, hi Jan. How are you?"

Jan Olson had been in Wolf's class in grade school, which meant he'd seen her just about every day of his life growing up. Back then she was skinny with long blonde hair and brown eyes. Now, after a baker's dozen years of heavy smoking and hard mountain living, Jan looked sickly thin and leathery, much older than a woman in her late thirties.

"Not bad. Not bad at all." She looked at him and winked. "What? You here for Sarah?"

"No, just a little business."

She nodded at the news and winked again.

Wolf sniffed in response. In eighth grade, he'd attended a party and twisted a glass bottle that had spun and landed on her. The rules of the game stated that they enter a closet for two minutes, and, just like Vegas, what happened in the closet, stayed in the closet. And what happened in the closet that night had traumatized him for at least a year.

Since that eighth-grade party, he'd been cornered by Jan Olson numerous times, and every social interaction with her usually ended with Wolf feeling violated.

"You waiting for Walter?" Wolf asked, talking about her teenaged son from an unknown father.

Jan pulled out a smoke and nodded.

"Well, see ya," Wolf said and walked away, pushing memories of sharp fingernails groping the bare skin of his crotch out of his mind.

He walked inside. The lights overhead seemed to hum louder tonight, as if working overtime at the end of the day. He pulled off his hat and unzipped his jacket, letting the dry warmth burrow into his underclothing.

The air smelled like pizza, and Wolf's mouth watered.

Just like the day before, no one sat at the desk in the narrow anteroom, but he heard the murmur of voices, and then laughter coming from around the corner and down the hall.

He stepped toward the hallway, stopping when the floorboards creaked, and then he shook his head and walked. He'd launched himself off a cliff today, there was a murderer on the loose, and most importantly he had a bag of fried chicken in the car and he was hungry as hell. He was going to crash this meeting—in and out—even if it meant upsetting Sarah.

Thinking this as he walked under the flickering tubes of light down the hall, he was surprised when he reached the doorway of the interior room and the people inside seemed to chat freely, as if his approach had been unnoticed. He stopped, his curiosity winning out over his hunger.

"… down the slope on his face," someone said.

The group laughed. They were loud and unreserved with one another, and Wolf suddenly felt like he was an intruder.

Wolf craned his neck a few inches to look in and saw the back half of Sarah.

"So," Sarah said, "you aren't going to go back to tele-marking anytime soon, I take it?"

"No, screw that," the same young man said. Wolf recognized the voice, but couldn't put a face or name to it.

There was a short silence.

"Okay," Sarah said, "let's talk about what's going on at home. Like always, you don't have to share, but I encourage you to. We've taken the pledge, and nothing leaves this room. Nothing leaves this group."

Wolf swallowed, feeling like a guy with his pants down looking in a window now.

"So let's start with—"

"Ahem," Wolf cleared his throat and knocked on the door-jamb. "Uh, sorry."

Sarah gave Wolf a facetious smile. Her eyes sparkled, and everyone else in the room seemed to have the same happy look.

Tonight she was dressed in a tight white shirt and shabby jeans. A simpler outfit she couldn't have worn; better looking she couldn't have been.

"Can I help you?" she asked.

Wolf twisted his hat in his hands and stepped inside. "Hey Chris, Todd, Lisa, Walter." Wolf made a pained face at a pimply girl in her late teens. "I'm sorry, I don't know you."

"I'm Bridget."

"Hi, I'm David Wolf. Sorry to break in here. I was just on my way by ..."

Sarah pushed her chair back and stood up.

"... and I need to talk to Chris."

Sarah looked over at Chris in surprise, and Chris looked up at Wolf.

"It'll be quick," Wolf said.

Chris stood up quietly.

Wolf ignored Sarah's suspicious frown and walked out of the room. Chris followed him down the hall and around the corner to the front room.

"Hi Chris. I just needed to ask you a few questions, and it couldn't wait."

"Okay," he said. "What's going on? Is this about my dad?"

Wolf narrowed his eyes. "Why would you ask that?"

Chris shrugged. "I don't know."

Wolf stared at him for a beat, trying to read him with no luck. "What were you doing Saturday night?"

Chris popped his eyebrows. "I ... was over at Walter's most of the night"—he pointed a thumb over his shoulder—"and then I just went home."

Wolf nodded. "What time? From when to when?"

"I don't know, like five to midnight?" Chris looked Wolf in the eye. "Why?"

"I just need to know." Wolf pointed out the window at Jan Olson's Chevy. "So if I were to ask Mrs. Olson right now, she'll say that you were there on Saturday night? All the way until midnight?"

Chris shrugged. "I don't know. Yeah. I don't know if she was asleep or not when I left."

Wolf stretched his neck and took a deep breath. "What about this morning? What were you doing?"

"I don't know, nothing?" He shrugged. "Just slept in and then came into town and had some food."

"Food where?"

"At Sunnyside."

Wolf straightened and glanced out the window. "Thanks. That's all."

"That's it?" Chris asked.

Wolf nodded and gave him a soft look. "Hey. I was … if you ever need anything, you let me know, okay?"

Chris looked at his feet and nodded. "Okay. Thanks."

Wolf watched him leave around the corner, and then he put on his hat and went back out into the parking lot.

Jan's Chevy was now puffing smoke from the cracked window as well as the exhaust pipe.

As Wolf neared, the door clicked open again.

"Change your mind?" she asked.

Wolf smiled and slowed to a stop. "I just needed to ask you a question."

"Shoot." She sucked a drag and propped her foot up on the inside of her door.

"Was Chris Wakefield at your house on Saturday night?"

She blew smoke out of her nose. "Yeah, why?"

"What time did he leave to go home?" Wolf asked.

"I don't know." She threw the cigarette on the ground toward Wolf.

Wolf stepped forward and squashed it with his boot.

"I think he left after midnight." She looked at the smoldering butt and smiled, as if satisfied that she'd made Wolf do something for her. "I remember hearing him leave. Remember him pulling out of the driveway, the lights blazin' in the window, waking me up."

"And it was after midnight? How do you know?"

"Because the man next to me said, 'What the hell is that kid doing with his goddamn lights on? It's after midnight.'" She curled her lip, stroked the inside of her knee, and stared at him with as much suggestiveness as she could muster.

Wolf nodded and looked back to the window of the building, for no other reason than to look away from Jan Olson.

"Thanks," he said.

"You're welcome," she said.

CHAPTER 24

WOLF SAT ON HIS BARCALOUNGER, leaned all the way back, socks off, and chewed the last bite of his fried chicken. The old speakers of his analog stereo played soft country music—some song about being laid back, blue jeans, an old truck, a back road, a cold beer, and skinny dipping. He sipped his second Newcastle, feeling the warm buzz soothe his body, and longed for an old beat-up truck and a warm summer night on a back-country road. With a woman.

He wiped his greasy fingers on his jeans, picked up his phone, and decided that since crawling inside the stereo was out of the question he'd do the next best thing. Besides, he needed to talk to someone. His mind was churning with ideas and dead-end thoughts.

Staring at the phone screen, he marveled at the twists of fate that had alphabetically placed the name Kristen Luke directly above Sarah Muller in his phone contacts.

He pushed the name and put the phone up to his ear.

"Hey, handsome," Luke said in a mock-throaty voice.

"Hi. How's it going?"

Luke fumbled the phone for a few seconds, and then came back on. "Oh, okay. Can't complain here."

"Am I catching you at a bad time?" he asked.

"No. I pushed pause on the remote."

Wolf chuckled. "Ah, an adventurous Monday night?"

"How do you know I'm not sitting here cuddling with a man?"

"Are you?" Wolf asked.

"No."

They sat in comfortable silence for a beat.

"You just calling to hear me breathe?" she asked.

"No, actually I need to run over a case with you."

"Okay," she said, clearly interested. "Have at it."

Wolf told her about the strangling of Stephanie Lang, the shooting of Matt Cooper, the red Xs found at both scenes made with the same lipstick, the chase that led to Wolf plummeting off a cliff, the sex tape, and Charlie Ash allegedly blackmailing the mayor in order to secure votes for a construction firm.

"Holy crap," she said. "I recommend bringing in the FBI on this. I can leave first thing in the morning and be there by breakfast."

"No, sit tight. Besides, I've already brought in the FBI. I'm talking to her now."

Luke huffed into the phone, clearly nonplussed.

Wolf took a long pull of his beer and set it down. "Well?"

"I'm thinking," she said.

Wolf waited.

"The X thing," she said.

"Yeah, the X thing. Does that ring any bells with you? You ever encountered another killer who left that mark?"

"No," she said. "I can't say I have."

Wolf finished his beer and walked to the kitchen.

"No doubt it's a message of some sort, but to whom?" she said. "Law enforcement? A particular person?"

Wolf flipped his beer bottle into a recycle box, dug into his brand-new refrigerator, and pulled out another.

"I've been thinking about that, too." Wolf popped off the cap with the opener and walked back to the chair.

"If it's not clear now why that X is showing up, then it's because you don't know the reason the killer is putting it there."

Wolf took a sip and smacked his lips. "That's a brilliant assessment. I'm glad I've brought the FBI in on this. Thanks, I'm—"

"Shut up, I'm serious. I mean … you have to start digging into the past of the killer, which means you have to dig into the past of everyone involved."

Wolf set down his beer and sat back with closed eyes. "Yeah."

They sat in silence.

"Sorry. I know I'm not much help. I'd be better if I came up there."

Wolf took another sip.

"How's Jack?" she asked.

"Good," Wolf said, still thinking about where to start the following morning. What was the next move? Maybe Lorber would wake up and find a crucial piece of forensic evidence that cracked the case. In the meantime, just like Luke had said, he had to start digging into the pasts of anyone and everyone he could think of involved—Stephanie Lang, Matt Cooper, Wakefield and his son, Charlie Ash and …

"—David? You there still?"

"What?" Wolf asked.

"I said, is Jack the *wettest* skier on the mountain up there, or what?" She chuckled, clearly proud of herself for using Jack's slang term in a sentence.

Wolf sat up. "That's it."

Luke went quiet. "What is? What did I say?"

Wolf leaned forward. "Look, I gotta call Jack. I'll talk to you later."

"I expect a briefing tomorrow," Luke said. "I'm not gonna be able to sleep tonight thinking about this. I'm serious, I'll come up and help. I'll bring a couple of good agents. You just say the word."

Wolf nodded. "All right. Thanks. I'll talk to you soon."

Wolf hung up and called Jack.

"Hey, Dad."

"Hey, I have a quick question for you."

Jack ignored him. "Where are you? At your house?"

"Yes, I am," Wolf said. "Uh … what are you doing? You at your mom's?" Which, ever since Sarah had broken up with Mark Wilson meant, *You at your grandparents' house*?

"Yeah," Jack said, and then he sounded like he was eating something.

"Listen, did you go skiing today?"

"Of course." He had quite a mouthful. "Went after school. It's sick up there right now."

Wolf knew he was talking to the right person. "Who are the best skiers in town?"

…

Wolf stared at the glowing computer screen perched on a fold-out plastic table. He twisted lazily in the pleather chair he'd picked up from the consignment store in town, which rounded out the furnishings of his home office.

It took him a second to find the webpage for the Lake Tahoe Police Department, and then another to scroll down and find the number.

Wolf twisted open the blinds and stared out the brand-new windows, thinking that they held the heat inside much better than the old ones. Outside, the pines were bathed in moonlight, their undersides pitch-black pools of shadow.

"Lake Tahoe Police Department," a bored-sounding man's voice said into the phone.

"Hi, this is Sheriff David Wolf of the Sluice County Sheriff's Department, in Colorado. I'd like to speak to Chief Gunnison."

"Sorry, he's gone home," the man said. "Is there a message?"

Wolf exhaled. "How about a cell number? I need to speak with him today. It's very important."

The man chuckled. "Sorry, Sheriff. I'm sure you understand that I'm not at liberty to—"

"Chief Gunnison has critical evidence that will help to expose a killer who's filling up our morgue with dead bodies. I need to talk to him now, not tomorrow."

"I wish I could help you, Sheriff."

Wolf took a deep breath. "What's your name?"

"Zack," he said.

"Zack? Listen, Zack, either you can give me his phone number, or I can call the Truckee FBI field office and have them send down an agent to get the information I need, and your department can foot the bill for the interstate invest—"

"Okay, okay. What did you say your name was?"

"Wolf. Sheriff David Wolf of Sluice County, Colorado."

"Okay. I'm *transferring* you to his cell phone," he said. "Will that work, sir?"

"If he answers that will work. If not, I'll call you back and I'll need to speak to someone else."

"Well, let's hope to God he answers."

The phone line clicked and then it began ringing.

"Hello?"

"Chief Gunnison?"

"What?" It was a demand, not a question.

"This is Sheriff David Wolf from Sluice County, Colorado."

"Oh, hi. What can I do for you?" Gunnison had a deep voice.

"I need to speak to you about a death that happened in your town two years ago."

"Uh, okay. Wait a minute." The phone rattled a little bit and Wolf could hear footsteps and then a door closing. "Who are we talking about here?" Gunnison asked.

"A woman named Cynthia Ash."

CHAPTER 25

CHARLIE ASH'S home was situated on a vast tract of flat land, smack in the middle of the valley floor six miles to the north and east of Rocky Points. The front of his house faced west toward a treeless meadow filled with flowers and cattle in the summer and herds of elk stomping through wind-crusted snow in the winter. A few neighbors populated the horizon, but so far away that on a night like this they were blobs of light rather than imposing structures.

The rear of his house facing east was a decent-size snow-covered lawn that butted up against a wall of virgin pine forest that extended for miles along the valley floor to the north and south.

Charlie Ash was worried about the rear.

He had been sitting in the pitch dark of his house for over two and a half hours now, ever since the sun had gone down. He wasn't going to be snuck up on. He wasn't going to be taken out.

Built to offer close to a three-hundred-and-sixty-degree view of his surrounding land, his home office had a semi-circular cluster of windows facing the west, and an identical yet opposite cluster facing the east. To see those final few degrees of view to the north and south, he had to press his face to the glass.

He was doing this now, feeling the cold window against his nose as he searched for movement outside.

The grounds surrounding his house were bright yellow, reflecting the halogen floodlights he'd turned on at sundown. Beyond them lay dark-blue snow and black forest.

Ash switched his pistol to his left hand and wiped the sweat off his palm, and then walked across his darkened office to the other set of windows—a movement he'd repeated at roughly ten-second intervals for the past two and a half hours.

An outside observer would have deemed the behavior ridiculous, but Ash knew what was coming. It was a sure thing. Only vigilance would protect him, and standing his ground when the time came.

His house was big and had five outside entrances. Two were vulnerable and all he could do was make sure he saw his intruder coming. Then it should be simple enough to make his way downstairs, take up position somewhere, and shoot.

He reached the rear windows and looked outside again. The darkness of the old-growth forest was absolute. No matter how hard he peered, details eluded him any further than fifty feet into the pillowed pine boughs.

Nine ... ten. He looked down, along the edges of the exterior walls of the house, seeing no footprints except the two elk tracks from earlier in the afternoon, and then he turned to walk again.

Oily lines of light reflected off his circular $120,000 Parnian desk in the center of the room. He ran his hand across the top of it as he walked by, feeling the small depressions of the exotic wood inlays. The small gesture gave him a reassuring sense of control. He was ready.

As he looked out into the dim night, panic hit him again, and he cursed himself for having not bought some night-vision binoculars at some earlier point in life. Then he could've seen everything happening in that meadow and out in those trees.

Nine ... ten.

He walked back and stopped at his desk this time. He pulled the plug on his crystal whiskey decanter, poured a couple of fingers in a glass, and then threw the liquor down his throat.

"Dah!" he said to the empty room as the liquid burned all the way down. He shook his head and jogged to the rear windows.

CHAPTER 26

WOLF LISTENED INTENTLY as Sheriff Gunnison finished recounting the details of Cynthia Ash's death.

"Looking at the physical evidence," Gunnison said, "the condition of the car and the way it'd tumbled into the forest, we figured her going one hundred and twenty miles per hour."

Wolf grunted in surprise.

"Yeah," Gunnison said. "There was no surviving a crash like that. Car disintegrated in seconds. Her body was torn and burnt to nothing recognizable."

Wolf walked back out into his living room and picked up the half beer sitting next to his chair and sipped it. "You get a BAC?"

"Did you just hear what I said?"

Wolf nodded. "I take that as a no."

"No." He chuckled without humor. "If she was driving under the influence when she crashed, we'll never know. It was bad."

"Did you suspect any foul play?" Wolf asked.

"What foul play?"

"I don't know, tampered brake lines?"

Gunnison chuckled again. "Nah, I don't think so. First of all, the car was too wrecked to check on something like that, and, yes, I did think about it. But here's my take. She was going one hundred twenty miles per hour". He paused. "That's just suicidal fast. She was blitzed, and that's all there was to it. If she was going slower and missed a turn, I'd think maybe brakes. But this was just a swerve into the trees on a straightaway."

Wolf stood thinking.

"You still there?" Gunnison asked.

"Yes. So what was the whole story?" Wolf asked.

"I just told you the whole story."

"No, I mean, what bar was she at?" Wolf asked. "Who was she with? What can you tell me about before the crash?"

"She was at a bar on the lake, called Swanson's. Just a local joint, kind of upscale. Wasn't with anyone. Came in by herself. I guess she was upset, cryin' with makeup all over her face. She'd had an argument with her ex-husband, went to the bar and started drinking."

"Wait a minute, ex-husband? Charlie and Cynthia Ash weren't married at this time?"

"Nope. Got divorced earlier that year as I recall." Gunnison sipped something and exhaled into the receiver.

"And that would be something you'd recall?" Wolf asked. "Them being divorced, I mean." He walked back into his office and flicked on the light, pulled out a pen and paper and sat down at the ready.

"Yeah, you know, small town and all. And Ash was a pretty prominent figure here. Treasurer of the city government. Why you so interested anyways? Whatchu got goin' on over there in the mountains of Colorado?"

"Charlie Ash lives in my town, now," Wolf said.

"Pretty nice guy, huh?"

Wolf couldn't tell if he was being sarcastic or not. "We've had two murders in town; I'm just looking into the Ashes. There may be a connection. I don't know yet."

"No shit? Two murders?" He whistled. "And you think they have to do with Cynthia Ash's car accident?"

Wolf took another sip of the beer and set it down, then figured it was time to come out with it. "Have you had any murders, unsolved or otherwise, with the killer painting a red X on or near the victim?"

"No," Gunnison said. "That's definitely not something that's happened around here."

"What about unsolveds at about the same time of Cynthia Ash's death?"

Gunnison let out an impatient sigh. "Look, I understand you've got a job to do, but I'm sittin' here smellin' steaks that just came in off the barbecue and they're getting colder by the second. I can send you an electronic copy of the entire file tomorrow morning, first thing."

Wolf didn't answer. The silence mounted for a few seconds and then Gunnison caved in.

"Ah, Jesus Christ." He huffed into the phone. "Okay ... unsolveds. Shit, you know how it is. Things get all mashed up over the years."

"Unsolveds?" Wolf asked. "Those stick in my brain for years. The specifics haunt me until the case is wrapped, and I'm talking about two years ago."

Gunnison sniffed and paused for another moment. "There was a woman beaten and strangled, but up the road in Truckee. Younger, mid-twenties. A real-estate agent. It was a Truckee county investigation in the end, but it was called in by a realtor from South Lake Tahoe, so we were in on the beginning of the case."

"And that was right about the same time as Cynthia Ash's death?"

"Yep. I remember we were still pickin' Cynthia and her car out of the forest, and we got the call about the murder."

"Can you give me a few details of the scene?" Wolf asked.

"I'm sure the Truckee Sheriff's Department could," he answered curtly.

"Listen, I just think things aren't done here, you know? This guy could be killing here in my town now, and he could be killing tonight."

"Jesus. Yeah, all right," Gunnison said. He slurped again and ice tinkled in a glass. "We brought the whole cavalry in there, but I was one of the first in. I saw her. She was laid out on her back, lyin' in a pool of blood. It looked like there was a lot of anger involved with the whole thing. Our coroner said she'd been strangled first, and then beaten with a blunt object on the head. So she was extra dead when this guy got through with her."

Wolf took fast notes.

"After a thorough search of the house, it looked like the killer entered through an unlocked window at the rear of the property. But the front door was also unlocked, because she'd done a 'walk-through', as they like to call it in the real-estate biz, and she'd left it that way. So we figure she walked in on a robbery in progress, and the guy had a psychotic streak and killed her."

"Any sign of sexual assault?" Wolf asked.

"None."

"And what was her name?"

"Mary. Mary ... Richardson?" He sighed. "Mary Richardson."

Wolf wrote down the name and circled it a few times. "What about the neighbors?"

"None of them saw anything. This is in an area where the houses are few and far between. Lots of money. Multimillions."

Wolf frowned. "And someone got in through an unlocked window? Pretty lax security on a multi-million-dollar house, no?"

"That was a whole thing. The house was for sale, and real-estate agents were coming in and out of there. We think one of them left it open. Nobody fessed up to doing it, of course."

"How about prints?" Wolf asked. "The murder weapon?"

"No prints on the body"—he sighed yet again, sounding impatient—"and no murder weapon found at the scene. Otherwise, clean as a whistle forensically. Large hand bruises on her neck, gloved hands—like I said, no prints. The blow marks to her head were on the left side of her face, the killer standing over her. Forensics said blood spatter was consistent with a right-handed male, and that was as far as we got. Since that narrowed it down to about fifty percent of the population, we ended up getting nowhere fast with this, and it just cooled over the past couple of years."

"What about other agents? Showings on the—"

"I'll send our file on Cynthia Ash tomorrow morning, Sheriff Wolf," Gunnison said with finality.

"Okay, thanks," Wolf said. "You got a contact I can talk to at Truckee Sheriff's Department?"

"Yeah, the sheriff."

The line clicked dead.

Wolf set his phone down next to the scribbled notes. He

stood up and walked into the family room, picked up his beer and brought it to his lips, then stopped short and set it back down. His body was heavy, felt bruised all over, and tacking on a hangover would make tomorrow unbearable.

He took a deep breath and stretched, sniffing his armpit. No deliberation needed—it was time for a shower. He walked to his bedroom and flicked on the light, then went into his bathroom and hit the switch there, too.

Pulling off his T-shirt, he cried out as a sharp pain stabbed deep in his lower back. It was the pinched nerve, or whatever the hell it was, and it was so painful that he collapsed to his hands and knees.

After an agonizing minute on the ground, stretching and twisting his torso into various positions, the pain finally subsided.

He opened his eyes and stood up, feeling faint as he did so, so he put his hands on the counter and stared in the mirror. He looked like a tired hobo, he thought. His brown eyes were bloodshot, half-closed with swollen eyelids, and his dark hair was sticking up like he'd just woken up from a nap against a brick wall.

Wolf felt the tickle of an idea that had been niggling at him, waiting in the dark to spring out into the light. He peered deeper, wondering what it was and just how long the feeling had been there. He willed his brain to unlock his subconscious.

What was it? Something in the details of Cynthia Ash's death? Details from Mary Richardson's unsolved murder? Some passing comment from Chief Gunnison of the Tahoe PD that he needed to make sense of? Some tenuous connection with Charlie Ash's past and the murders occurring now?

Of course, it was. It was all that.

He blinked and stood up, and then froze as adrenaline pulsed from his head to his feet.

No, it wasn't.

The feeling spawned from something he'd seen moments before but not registered. He was sure of it now, because he was staring at the reflection of a bright-red X scrawled across his bedroom window.

WOLF REACHED BACK and flipped the light switch, sending the bathroom into darkness. Then he reached out of the doorway and turned off the bedroom light.

He stood against the bathroom wall and stared at the reflection. The X looked black in the dim light, and it appeared to be on the outside of the window. He focused beyond it, into the night. There was no movement, no silhouette of a person in the trees.

His service pistol sat in its holster on a chair just inside his front door. He never locked that front door when he was at the house. Would he have noticed if someone had come inside? Surely a cold wave of air would have blown in the door and wafted over him. But he was unsure with most of his house being new construction. He hadn't spent enough time in the place to learn the subtle nuances.

One other gun was much nearer, a Walther PPK, next to his bed inside the top drawer of his nightstand. But it wasn't loaded. The clip was hidden in the lowest of the three drawers. Though Jack was well versed in firearm use, it had made Wolf feel safer to store his gun that way. He would need to move fast.

Forgetting the crippling pain that had brought him to his hands and knees a minute before, Wolf sprinted to the bed and jumped, landing in a roll and sliding off next to his nightstand. To his surprise there was no pain.

He kept his eyes on the doorway into the living room as he slid open the drawer and reached inside the unzipped case for the pistol. His hand closed around the small grip and he pulled it out, then he opened the bottom drawer.

For agonizing seconds, he felt vulnerable as he dug for the clip, like a deer frozen in semi-truck headlights as certain death barreled toward it. All the killer had to do was turn the corner and shoot him as he fumbled for ammunition. *Or stick his arm out from under the bed.*

Wolf rammed the clip home and racked the slide, and then bent to look under the bed.

Nothing.

He looked over at the window, now only a few feet away. The mark was clearly on the outside of the glass. He wasted no time walking to the bedroom doorway and peering out into the living room. His holster and pistol were undisturbed on the chair next to the front door.

He held his breath and strained to listen. Blood pounding in his ears and the twang of a Telecaster guitar coming from the speakers was all he heard.

He turned around and looked back out the window past the red mark of death. Still no movement.

Then he looked closely at the linoleum floor inside the front door. It was completely dry, save a small puddle of meltwater surrounding his boots underneath the wooden chair where his pistol sat. Since Wolf hadn't been home enough to shovel a path to his front door in the past few days, anyone entering would have tracked in snow with them. That left two options: either someone had been inside the entire time, or nobody was inside.

If they'd been inside the whole time, why wasn't he dead? He had given the killer ample opportunities—digging in the refrigerator, sitting as he mindlessly drank beer, pacing the house during distracting phone conversations.

There hadn't been any noticeable footprints outside when he'd arrived. That was something you noticed living alone and in the middle of nowhere—a strange set of footprints to your front door that disappeared inside. Had he left the kitchen door to the carport open? The thought raised his pulse.

First things first, he thought. Straight ahead of him was a hallway bathroom and his spare-bedroom door. He swept both rooms and found everything exactly like he'd left it—undisturbed and without murderers inside.

Keeping the pistol aimed in front of him, he walked through the family room. Looking outside was out of the question because all the blinds were closed and he hadn't bothered to open them when he'd gotten home.

That last thought stopped him in his tracks, and then he back-shelved it and continued to the kitchen. He twisted the knob. It was locked.

After another five minutes of checking every conceivable hiding spot in the house, Wolf walked back into his bedroom and over to the window.

The X looked to be lipstick, just like the others. It was scrawled in jagged, angry swipes, gone over a few times to make sure it was highly visible—even more so than the X written on the helicopter cockpit window.

He returned to his thought about the window shades.

They'd all been drawn when he'd gotten home, he was sure of it. All except one—this window right here.

Wolf remembered leaving the shade drawn up the other day. He'd pulled it in the morning, after his shower, and hadn't bothered to put it back down before he left for work. There was no rhyme or reason why he'd done this or why he remembered it now.

And now here was this mark.

He leaned against the window and checked the ground below. A set of deep, scraping footprints came in from the left, stopped under the window, then led back the way they'd come along the back of the house.

Wolf went into the family room, shut off the stereo, and began dressing. He buckled on his duty belt, and put on his jacket, boots, and hat. Gripping his Glock now, he slowly opened the door.

As he suspected, there was one set of footprints into the house—his.

He shut the door and went from room to room, switching off lights and peeking through the shades. After fifteen minutes of staring outside into the dark from every angle, he'd finally traced the complete route of the person's tracks. They'd gotten out of their vehicle at the front of the house, walked into the carport past his pickup truck, out the back to his bedroom window, and then returned all the way to the vehicle. And since the vehicle was no longer there, that meant they were gone.

Wolf unlocked the kitchen door and stepped out. The cold bit him with needle teeth so he buried his face down into the neck of his jacket. He stared at the footprints for another few seconds and went back inside.

He dialed Rachette on his cell phone.

"Hello?" Rachette said.

"Hey, it's me."

"What's up?"

"Listen, I'm at home and I just found a red X written on my window."

"What? I'll be right there. Have you called the station?" He clanked something in the background and breathed into the phone.

"Listen. Get to the mayor's as fast as you can and bring everyone. But nobody goes in until I get there."

"What? No way, I'm coming out—"

"I'm not in danger. The mayor is. Go now!"

CHAPTER 28

WOLF DROVE along the river and into town, flew down Main, took a right on Fourth and mashed the accelerator up the steepening road to Wakefield's house.

Wolf's heart was in his mouth because a frantic call had come over the radio a minute before. It had been Patterson calling for backup with high-pitched panic in her voice.

Wolf had been driving at the edge of crazy ever since.

The mayor's house was up ahead, easy enough to see as turret lights flashed everywhere in front of it. He began to slow early so he wouldn't slide into the forest when trying to make the turn.

At the last second he jammed the brakes as Rachette jumped in front of the hood.

Rachette stepped quickly to his window. "Hey!" His eyes were wide, pupils dilated.

"What's going on?" Wolf stopped the SUV and got out.

"He's inside," Rachette said, making his way toward the driveway. "Now. We got here and he was inside."

From the top of the driveway, Wolf could see an SCSD SUV parked sideways up ahead with roof lights twinkling. Nearest them, four deputies were lined up and leaning on the hood in crouched firing positions. In front of them were the trucks of Chris Wakefield and Kevin Ash, parked nose-in to the front porch, and beyond that the brightly lit front door.

They jogged down the driveway, and Patterson, Baine, Wilson and Yates turned with wide eyes.

"What's going on?" Wolf asked, crouching next to Yates.

Patterson came over behind Wolf. "Rachette and I went to the front porch, and Kevin Ash opened the door with a pistol aimed at our faces. He told us he wanted to talk to you, told us to back up, and then he slammed the door and locked it."

Wolf took a deep breath, feeling the cold air freeze the inside of his nostrils.

"I don't get what's going on," Patterson said. "Kevin's been doing this? Is Chris Wakefield involved, too?"

Wolf looked inside the big windows at the front of the house. There was no movement inside.

"Stay out here," Wolf said. "I don't want you guys coming in and startling him."

"You're going in there?" Rachette asked. "He's waving a pistol around and looks way over the edge."

"He won't kill me," Wolf said, hoping he was right.

Wolf stepped around the SUV and walked up to the porch. He put his ear to the cold wood and listened. Hearing no sounds, he knocked three times.

"Who is it?" a muffled voice screamed inside.

Wolf reached out, grabbed the handle and pushed his thumb down. The door opened an inch.

"It's Sheriff Wolf," he said through the crack.

"Are you alone?" the voice asked.

"Yes."

"Then come in."

Wolf put both hands in first, and then swung the door open with his forearms. Keeping his hands up high and visible, he entered, stopped the door with his foot and kicked it shut. Then he reached behind him and twisted the lock. It clicked home.

Kevin Ash was in the big room straight ahead. He lay on the floor, facing Wolf, his back against one of the big leather couches. His neck was cranked forward, and he was leaning on an elbow with one knee up. He held a pistol in his hand and rested it on his stomach, aiming at the floor beside him.

Wolf held up his left hand and reached for his pistol with his right. "I'm going to take off my gun and set it down right here," he said.

Kevin pointed his gun at Wolf and held it stock still. "Don't try anything."

Wolf slowly pulled out his pistol and set it on the bench next to him. He backed off from it and stepped further inside, keeping his hands high.

Kevin squinted one eye and lined Wolf up in his pistol sight, then twisted his lip a fraction. "You sure trust me, after what I did to your window."

Wolf shook his head and shrugged. "I knew you were just setting a diversion. And I know you aren't going to kill me. I know what happened. I know why you're doing this." Wolf lowered his hands.

Kevin opened his eye, keeping the gun pointed at Wolf.

"I know about your mother. I know how she died," Wolf said. "More importantly, I know why she died."

Kevin lowered his gun and sat up straighter against the back of the couch. He flitted a glance past Wolf's left shoulder.

Wolf looked to see why, and then took a sharp breath and shook his head.

Mayor Greg Wakefield sat inside the den, slumping heavily in the office chair. One side of his head was gone, blown out onto the table in front of him. The small desk lamp was on, covered in blood and brain. It cast a red light that silhouetted his body and reflected off the fluids everywhere. His arm was dangling off the armrest and a pistol was on the carpet beneath his limp hand.

"He didn't hesitate when I told him to do it," Kevin said. "Just lifted up the gun and bam." Kevin lifted the pistol to his own head and pantomimed.

Wolf stared at him, waiting until the gun dropped back down. "Where's Chris?"

"He's okay. I gave him a roofie. He's sleeping it off. So you think you figured it out?" Kevin sprang to life and stood up. "I thought I'd thrown you for a loop with making it look like I was coming after you." He nodded and walked away from Wolf toward the windows. "And don't think I've never thought about it. The way you treated me in that job interview last year."

"I just got off the phone with the police chief from Lake Tahoe," Wolf said, meeting Kevin's gaze in the reflection. "I know about your mother's car crash. She'd been drinking, so everyone thinks it was an accident how she drove into those trees. But I know what you and your father know. I know she killed herself."

Kevin turned and glared at Wolf.

The grandfather clock in the corner ticked as the brass pendulum swayed back and forth. Faint beeping and scratchy radio voices came from outside.

"Tell me about what happened," Wolf said.

Kevin shook his head. "You wouldn't—"

"Tell me about Mary Richardson."

"He killed her," Kevin said, his voice barely a whisper.

Wolf cocked his head. "Your father killed Mary Richardson?"

Kevin frowned. "No, my mom. She killed herself because of him, and he didn't give a shit." Spit flew out of his mouth.

Wolf kept as still as possible.

"He was screwing her." Kevin stared into the past. "Mary Richardson. She was an agent with my dad's real-estate company, and my mom found out. That's why they got a divorce in the first place.

"He made a little agreement with my mom—she agreed to keep quiet about the whole thing if he gave her a divorce and paid her well enough." A tear trickled off his cheek and hit the floor. "She was a good woman. It's not like she was black-mailing him or anything. She wouldn't do anything like that. She just needed to survive, you know?"

Wolf blinked and nodded, goading him to keep talking. There was a good fifteen feet between them now. With slow movements, Wolf stepped his right foot forward, then his left.

"And so they got the divorce." Kevin stared past Wolf. "But my dad did something, and ended up screwing her out of getting any money. I don't know how. Somehow he and his lawyer made her look bad, so she didn't get anything."

Kevin lowered his eyes.

"And then what?" Wolf asked, watching the stringy muscles on Kevin's forearm flex, the knuckle of his index finger white on the trigger.

Wolf took another step forward and then froze.

Kevin looked up, both eyes swimming with tears now. "Then my mom came over that night after dinner and was screaming at my dad. She just needed some money. She'd been staying at a friend's house … and a fucking motel. She didn't have anywhere to go. Her mom was dead. Her sister lived in London. There was nowhere for her to go. She was asking how he could do this to her."

Kevin swallowed and wiped his cheek with the palm of his gun hand, pointing the pistol at the ceiling.

"I was sitting on the steps listening, and I came down and watched them fight. And I never knew my dad was like that until then. Even after all those years of yelling at me when I sucked at baseball, or when I couldn't pass math ... still, he'd never acted like this.

"He was calling her a cunt, had her up against the wall, pinning her neck with his forearm." Kevin clenched his teeth and held up a shaking forearm in front of him. Then his face relaxed and he dropped his arm down. "I just watched. I just watched as my dad pinned her, dug through her purse and pulled out a stick of lipstick, and wrote an X on her forehead. He kept saying, 'You're my *ex*-wife and you don't get shit. You're my *ex*-wife.' And I just sat there ... I just watched her choke and stare at me, and I ..."—he shook his head—"I picked up a brass statue, and he heard me, and then he let her go. I was about to kill him, I swear to God. I wish I had ... none of this would have happened."

Kevin screwed his eyes shut and bared his teeth.

Wolf took another couple of steps forward and then cleared his throat. "So she killed herself that night. But only you and your dad knew it."

Kevin opened his eyes and nodded, wiping tears again, this time with the knuckles of his free hand. "Everybody else said it was an accident, but we both knew what'd happened. Nobody wanted to bring up the obvious question—*Do you think she just jerked the wheel?* But if they'd known about what my father had done to my mom ..."

Wolf exhaled. "So you went and killed Mary Richardson. The woman who split up your parents' marriage. You got back at your dad the only way you knew how. And he found out, so you guys came to Colorado. To escape any suspicion."

Kevin nodded and sniffed. "He helped me cover it up. Helped me stage it to look like it was a break-in. Then we kind of ran, to get away from what I'd done."

Wolf squinted. "So you killed her and then felt bad about it? Told your dad and he helped you cover it up?"

Kevin sagged. "No. He found me next to her. I'd already killed her. It's complicated and you wouldn't believe me anyway." He started to raise the pistol.

"Wait, Kevin. Listen. Just tell me about it. All of it."

Kevin glanced around the room and then looked embarrassed. "I've got a disease where I do stuff and don't remember it."

Wolf frowned. "Are you saying you don't remember doing any of these killings?"

Kevin shook his head. "Like I said, you wouldn't believe me. It doesn't matter anymore."

As Kevin shut his eyes and lifted the gun, pressing the muzzle into his temple, Wolf was hit with a realization that made him flinch like he'd just been punched in the nose.

Because Kevin Ash was holding the pistol with his left hand.

Wolf lunged forward as fast as he could and the gun flashed with a deafening boom.

CHAPTER 29

ASH STOOD at his office window, looking out at the twin headlights as they flickered through the edge of the forest and out
into the meadow. It was unmistakably a deputy cruiser—one
of those decked-out expensive models of SUV the Sheriff's
Department drove nowadays that sucked the county coffers
dry.

When Wolf had called him twenty minutes earlier, Ash had
been hunkering in his upstairs office for the fourth hour,
sitting in the dark with an aching back and a desperate need
for water. He had been about to go crazy. Not stir-crazy, but
actually crazy. The suspense had been tormenting him like
fingernails clawing inside his skull.

And now it was over. The phone conversation with Wolf
had told him as much.

"I need to come tell you some bad news. It's about your
son," Wolf had said.

"Why don't you just tell me now? What the hell is going
on?" Ash had said.

Wolf didn't tell him specifics, but Ash knew exactly what
had happened. So far, Ash was acting the part of a concerned

father well enough, but he was going to have his work cut out for him. He watched Wolf's SUV slow at the head of his driveway a quarter-mile away, then walked downstairs and began getting his mind right.

When Ash had been a kid, he'd been able to turn on the waterworks on command. It was a gift few had he realized later in life. Even world-renowned actors spoke of the difficulty of acting sad—with actual twitching lips and gushing tear ducts—but he had been able to do it. But this was going to be tough, because if he heard the news that his son was dead, then it was going to be a relief. Not exactly good news, but news couldn't get better for him at this point. Every single stroke of misfortune in the past few days, in the past few years, was now going to be wiped out.

Ash reached the bottom of the stairs, went back to the great room, which was now brightly lit like the rest of the house, and turned on some smooth jazz. He felt like he was getting ready for a date or something. When he felt the steel of the snub-nosed revolver that he'd stuffed in his pants dig into the small of his back, he paused and flipped the stereo off. What the hell was he thinking? He had just lost a son. He needed to act the part.

...

Wolf drove into the curving drive of Charlie Ash's ranch house. Long and sprawling, the layout of the house was two rectangular wings topped with A-framed roofs attached to a cylindrical center. On top of the cylinder was a pointed cone with a band of windows underneath, like a turret on a modern-day castle.

The windows in the center of the house sparkled with light,

and exterior halogens painted yellow smears on the snow outside.

He stopped in front of the house and looked down the straight shoveled walkway that ended in tall wooden doors on the front porch. Shutting off the vehicle, he peered into the woods as far as he could, then checked the road behind him, which meandered into the forest and out of sight. He wondered just where Stephanie Lang and the mayor had rendezvoused that night of the party. Then he figured it really didn't matter.

Stepping out of the SUV, a cold wind whistled past his ears, and he pulled his winter cap down. The moon was a yellow blob behind some high, thin clouds. The peaks to the west were invisible, which meant that low cloud, indicative of another front rolling in, enveloped the higher elevations. Forecasters were warning of accumulations of another twelve to eighteen inches.

Hopefully, it would hold off for the next couple of hours.

Wolf's boots crackled on rock salt as he walked the dry path to the porch. He stepped under the light in front of the door and pressed the doorbell. A song chimed quietly, barely audible through the heavy doors and rock façade.

The door clunked and then opened, and Charlie Ash stood in the doorway. He was fully dressed, wearing jeans and an unbuttoned flannel shirt on top of a T-shirt. His gray comb-over hair was firmly in place, looking wet from a recent shower.

He looked curious and concerned, but behind his gold-rimmed glasses his eyes darted around—like he was expecting someone to come out of the dark behind Wolf at any second.

Ash nodded. "Sheriff." His voice was hoarse and he cleared his throat. "Please, come in."

Wolf nodded back and stepped inside onto a thick brown rug. A crystal chandelier hung from a vaulted ceiling above, illuminating the entryway as light as day. It smelled like tobacco and leather inside, and there was no sound other than a soft whoosh of a nearby heating vent on the wall.

An expansive room behind Ash was full of leather couches and dim lamps with stained-glass shades perched on dark-wood. Off the room to the right was a brightly lit hallway that veered out of sight into the kitchen and dining areas. To the left, another hallway that was more dimly lit led to the wing with the bedrooms and the stairway to the office on the second floor.

Ash watched Wolf take in the interior. "Please, come inside. Can I take your coat?"

"No," Wolf said, standing still near the door.

Ash raised his eyebrows. "Okay."

"I didn't come to get comfortable and socialize. This is definitely not a time to get comfortable."

Ash blinked rapidly. "What's going on?"

Wolf turned his cheek and pointed at it. "Do you see this?"

Ash stepped forward and peered at Wolf's face. He squinted and shook his head, then pulled back with wide eyes.

"Is that blood?" Ash asked.

"That's your son's blood," Wolf said.

Ash's face dropped. "What?"

"Your son shot himself an hour ago. I was right next to him. I couldn't stop him."

Ash looked at the ground and gripped his head.

Wolf narrowed his eyes, studying his reaction. "He told me some things before he blew the top of his head off."

Ash looked up. "You fucking bastard. How can you talk about my son that way when he just—"

"Because you made him do it. And you can spare me the act of pretending like you care. I know about everything. I know about the sex tape you and Matt Cooper made of the mayor on Thursday night. I know about you blackmailing the mayor with it, and how Jen Wakefield watched it and then killed herself with her husband's gun."

Ash stood still and raised his lower eyelids.

"And when you learned about her accidental discovery of the sex tape—your little play to sell out Rocky Points gone wrong—you called Wakefield the next day, not even waiting twenty-four hours after her death before you made your demands to him. Did you know Kevin heard your conversation?" Wolf pointed up and glanced at the ceiling. "He was standing outside your office. Heard every word of it."

"Listen here—"

"Just shut up." Wolf stepped forward, snarling.

Ash backed up a step, then looked at the floor and smiled with a shake of his head.

"I can only imagine what Kevin must have felt when he heard you. Because you've done this before, caused someone to feel so terrible, so helpless and afraid about life that they killed themselves. You'd done it to his mother already." Wolf shook his head in disgust. "And you did it again to Jen Wakefield."

Ash rolled his eyes and snorted, but said nothing.

"I talked to Kevin tonight. Before he pulled the trigger. He wanted to get back at you, and that's why he's been killing all these people—Stephanie Lang for her role, Matt Cooper for putting that video camera in Wakefield's car, and tonight he got Wakefield for obvious reasons ... he was going to take you out next." Wolf narrowed his eyes. "Were you a little scared tonight? Because you knew exactly what was going on, didn't you? The way those Xs kept showing up at crime scenes, and in lipstick? Just like what you did to your wife that night she died."

"Ex-wife," Ash said. He stared Wolf in the eye. "She was my ex-wife. That was something I kept telling her but she wouldn't listen."

Wolf blinked.

"I'm confused, Sheriff." Ash tilted his head. "Am I supposed to thank you at this point? For what? For saving me from my psychotic son? Is that why you're here? For a thank-you?"

Wolf said nothing.

"Well, if you say he was out to kill me, then yes, thank you. But you know what I would love to know? What I would really love to understand? How you could even begin to substantiate any of the things you've been spouting off about for the last thirty seconds. My son goes off on a crazy killing spree and you want to blame me for it? Is that what's going on here, Sheriff?"

Wolf said nothing.

"A sex tape? Here's a question for you: what sex tape?" Ash smiled. "Do you have a camera with my fingerprints on it? Or a ... I don't know, some sort of USB drive with my prints on it? Or maybe a note or something that would have my fingerprints on it that would link me to something like this?"

"I never said anything about a USB drive or a note," Wolf said.

Ash flipped a hand. "I heard all about this alleged sex tape from Mayor Wakefield. He's been going bat-shit crazy the last few days. He makes a sex tape of himself and some girl from the restaurant and leaves it out for his wife to find, and, well, shit happens, I guess."

Wolf took a breath through his nose.

The heater clicked off and the house went dead quiet.

"Matt Cooper?" Ash asked quietly, though it was more a statement. "You say Matt Cooper was killed, too? And you say he set up the camera? Why? Why would he do that?"

Wolf didn't take the bait.

Ash clicked his tongue. "I guess we'll never know, seeing as my son killed him. And what are you suggesting? That I somehow hired Stephanie Lang to have sex with the mayor, and then paid Matt Cooper to set up the camera? Is there a stack of money or something? At either person's house ... stacks you could check for fingerprints?"

Wolf let his lips curl just a bit. The man was brazen, and he was also dead right in his calculations that Wolf had absolutely nothing on him for anything.

"I'll be getting to the bottom of what you've been doing, Mr. Ash," Wolf said icily.

"About what?" Ash asked.

"About the bribes, the corruption, the blackmailing, the—"

"I have no idea what you're talking about, Sheriff. And if you even think about throwing allegations around, I'll sue you for defamation of character so fast your badge will spin on the empty desk in what you used to call an office. Now that my son is dead, my position in the government of this small town is all I have. If you don't think I'll do everything in my considerable power to throw you out in the cold, out on a gas pump at the edge of town, then you're sadly mistaken."

Wolf stretched his neck.

"Well, I guess that was a little lie," Ash said. "I guess I've actually got quite a lot going on besides the government thing. You know, I've always been into real estate. Yeah, so I get to know everyone in town or in neighboring counties that have their finger on the pulse. That way I keep ahead of the curve, ahead of the next deal that will make me my next million, or two.

"Anyway, I got to know Mark Wilson." He paused and smiled briefly. "You know the man well. I actually have something, a little tidbit I heard while talking to him. And since you saved me from being killed by my psychotic son tonight, the least I can do is return the favor, as a friend, and let you know this juicy tidbit." He raised his eyebrows.

Wolf blinked, hearing a tiny shriek coming from his teeth mashing together.

"I was out at breakfast with Mark the day before he left town, and he was crying on my shoulder, so to speak. I've kind of established a relationship with him as a friend the last couple of years. I like to do that with certain contacts, keep them close. Anyway, he said Sarah broke up with him because she was still in love with you." He tilted his head and nodded. "She's still in love with you, and there was no way anyone could compete with that, he said. She's all tied up around your little finger, he said. And there was one other thing—what did he say? I don't know if she told you this or not, but she was screwing some other guy when you were in the army. That's what Mark said, and Sarah—"

Wolf slapped him on the face as hard as he could, the blow whiplashing Ash's head to the side with a force just less than enough to knock him out. The sound echoed between the walls in the confined space of the entryway, like a ricocheting bullet.

Charlie Ash bent over and howled in pain, cradling his face in both hands.

Wolf loomed over him, clenching and unclenching his

hand, feeling the sharp sting dissipate to tingling heat in his palm.

Ash stood up and straightened his glasses, eyes boring holes into Wolf's. His comb-over hair was flapping to the wrong side and his tongue pushed the inside of his cheek.

Wolf turned around, opened the door, and left.

As Wolf reached the SUV, he saw the interior of the house light up with two brilliant flashes accompanied by two muffled pops.

CHAPTER 30

ASH FELT dizzy as he watched the door close. The slap had jarred him, and he would find a way to return the favor in due time, in a way that would be the end of Wolf's career, but now he just needed food and water.

His face was numb to the touch. He needed some ice, too.

He walked to the front door and twisted the lock. His left eye dripped as he gazed out the entrance window, a new quirk from the thumping impact of Wolf's hand he hoped wouldn't last.

Wolf was sauntering away down the path outside. His walk was unhurried, like a smug bastard who'd just won a small, meaningless victory.

Ash reached up and flicked some light switches, sending the front porch and pathway into pitch black. *You're going down*, he thought with the strongest resolve he'd ever felt in his life.

He ripped off his flannel shirt and hung it on a hook, then walked into the great room and toward the kitchen for a proper meal and drink. *And three Advil.*

As he rounded the corner he almost ran straight into some-one. He stumbled to a stop and looked up.

Kevin.

Ash's heart thumped so hard he gripped his chest. Before Ash could react, a pistol had been pressed against his fore-head, pushing so hard that he felt a trickle of warm blood race down in between his eyes and down his nose.

"Kevin! What the ..." His throat was constricted and his heart was hammering in his ears.

His son, back from the dead, was standing right in front of him. The reality hit him hard.

Ash tripped and fell down on his butt and then rolled back-wards, crying out in pain as his tucked snub-nosed revolver dug into the small of his back.

"Stand up," Kevin said, warning him. "Stand up."

Ash got back up and shuffled in reverse, keeping his hands high. "Son—"

"Shut up," Kevin said. "Stand still. You're going to do what I say, or else I'm going to stick my gun in your ear and pull the trigger. Got that?"

Ash looked at the muzzle of the pistol and shook his head, thinking about how Wolf had just lied to him, and wondering just what the hell was going on.

"Got that!" Kevin screamed, and then he walked forward and fired two shots, one next to Ash's right ear, the other next to his left.

Ash cowered and twisted his face, pressing his palms to his ears. A metallic note screamed in his head, and his skull felt like it might just crack down the middle.

Kevin was moving his lips, but Ash heard none of it.

More talking. And then his son tilted his head back and laughed.

Slowly, Ash began hearing again, murmurs and muffled sounds like he was underwater. Then it was like he was breaking through the surface in ultra-slow motion—the trebles widening, sounding like rushing water in a stream.

"Sit down," Kevin yelled. He thrust the pistol at Ash.

Ash shuffled over to the couch and sat down with his hands in the air. He shook his head, unable to gain back his full-hearing.

Despite the damage to his ears, the initial shock of his son's assault was beginning to wear off. He was still his snot-nosed son, Ash reminded himself.

"What are you doing here?" Ash frowned, looking up at him. "Wolf just told me …"

"What?" Kevin asked, looking genuinely curious. "What did he tell you?"

Ash didn't say. He didn't say that Wolf had just told him that his son was dead. Had killed himself right in front of him. *What the hell?* Wolf was lying the whole time? What about that blood on his face?

Kevin was eyeing his father with amusement now. Other than digging the pistol into his forehead and shooting two shots near his ears, Kevin was keeping his distance, as if he didn't want to get sucked into any physical confrontation. As if Ash was going to jump out and grab him.

Ash kept quiet and looked out the window to the left of Kevin. He saw the bright snow of the back yard and the dark forest beyond.

"See this?" Kevin asked, holding up his pistol proudly. "A Sluice County Sheriff's Department-issue"—he read the side of the barrel—"Glock 17 … from Austria. Nice gun. Never fired one of these. I've been using one of your revolvers. Did you notice it was gone?"

Ash stared at him, feeling the burning in his shoulders from holding his hands up. "Where did you get that?" he asked.

"Ah, good question. I killed two cops." Kevin pointed it back at him and stared indifferently.

Ash caught movement in the window and looked again, this time seeing the taillights of a vehicle in the distance. They looked to be a Sheriff's Department SUV, and they were going full speed as they flickered into the forest and went out of sight.

Kevin followed his eyes and smiled. "Nobody saving you. Just you and me. And my Glock." His face became serious. "And in a few seconds, the fires of hell for both of us."

"You don't have to do this, son."

"Yes, I do have to do this. There's no choice now. You don't just kill two cops and live through the next twenty-four hours. In fact, I figure I have about five minutes before Sheriff-boy finds out about everything and comes screaming back here looking for me."

Ash narrowed his eyes. "How did you get here?"

"Took the SUV from Deputy ... Rachette, I believe his name was?" He raised his eyebrows. "Parked it in the woods. Sheriff just drove by it."

Ash felt a wisp of cold air and looked over toward the hallway to the kitchen.

"You snuck in the back," Ash said. "Used your key. I knew you would if you showed up." He looked down and saw Kevin's wet shoes, and the snow marks all the way up to his knees.

"You did it again, Dad," Kevin said, sounding like he was about to cry. "You ruined my life, and then you made Chris's mom kill herself and ruined his life."

Ash snorted. "Your mother killed herself, Son. Mrs. Wakefield killed herself. I didn't kill anyone."

Kevin snarled and shook the gun. "You killed them! You broke both of their hearts, and they had no other way out."

"Oh, shut up with your sniveling!" Ash stood up.

"Sit down!" Kevin yelled.

"Shoot me!" Ash reached up his arms and stretched lazily. "Oh, man. You had me holed up here all night. And I'm so hungry that I don't care anymore. You're going to kill me? Great. Let's get on with this. I'm ready."

Kevin looked unsure, glancing around the room.

Ash narrowed his eyes. "What's going on? After killing three people, now you're worried about killing your dada? Is that it?" He puckered his lips and sidestepped the footrest in front of him. "Don't want to kill dada?"

"Four people," Kevin said. "I killed four people."

Ash stopped. He watched Kevin's face twist into intense confusion for just an instant, and then melt into a cool look of confidence.

The look on Kevin's face made Ash blow snot out his nostrils, and as it flipped across his lip it made him burst out laughing; then when he wiped it with the sleeve of his shirt, mopping up blood that had trickled down his nose, that sent him into uncontrolled hysterics. He knew his son was going to kill him; Kevin had proven himself capable of that in the past few days, but the irony of the situation was just too much to handle. His stomach hurt as it convulsed, and if it weren't for the pain jabbing at his side he figured he would have laughed until Kevin shot him.

But he stopped instead and glared at his son with dripping eyes, chest heaving as he caught his breath. "Here's a little secret that is just going to kill you."

Kevin's cool expression wavered.

Ash stared at him, thinking about the significance of what he was about to say, knowing it might be the last thing he said on this earth. Finally, he spoke.

"I killed Mary Richardson," he said.

Kevin creased his forehead and his aim wavered, and Ash realized the truth might actually set him free.

Ash nodded. "I killed her. I drugged you, and killed her, and then put you next to her." He visualized pulling the revolver out of his beltline and firing. It was riding low and he'd have to rake it up his back with his thumb, and duck too, in case Kevin got a shot off.

"It feels good to finally tell you," he continued. "I was surprised when you started ..." Ash stopped talking.

Kevin's cool expression had returned and he was lowering his gun.

Ash fixed his gaze on Kevin. Then panic exploded inside of him as Kevin smiled.

"What the hell is going on?" Ash flicked his eyes around the room. Confusion pressed in, and as Kevin continued to smile, Ash knew he'd just walked into a trap, and he'd been an even more gullible fool than his son.

"You pieces of shit!" he yelled, and reached behind him, pulling the snub-nosed revolver out from the back of his pants. Before he could aim it, a blast of fire came from the hallway and he was punched in his shoulder with the power of a horse kick. Pain tore across his chest, down his stomach and across his genitals, up his neck and into his head. The hardwood floor swung up and hit him in the face, and then he lay still, blinking to calm the angry dots swirling in his vision.

CHAPTER 31

WHEN WOLF WALKED out of Charlie Ash's front door, he did so with a normal gait, trying to look neither in a hurry nor too relaxed. As soon as the lights went dark on the front of the house, Wolf swiveled and looked back.

Ash was framed in the entrance window, peering outside, looking like he was muttering something under his breath. Then he twisted and disappeared.

Wolf wasted no time; he sprinted to the SUV and opened up the back door. The cab light was off, so all he saw was movement.

"Okay, get up," he said.

The whites of Deputy Wilson's eyes appeared as he reared his head up from the backseat floor. He leaned and peered past Wolf toward the house.

"It's clear," Wolf said impatiently. "Get going."

Wilson opened the rear door, got in the driver's seat and fired up the engine. At almost the same instant there were two flashes inside the house and two pops of a gun, barely audible to Wolf over the roar of the Explorer's starting engine, but unmistakable nonetheless.

He froze and put his wrist to his mouth. "What happened?"

"He's ... I don't know," Rachette's voice was faint and raspy, more like a burst of static than a sentence.

Wolf put his hands over his ears and tried to understand as Wilson drove away.

"... him," Rachette said.

"What? Repeat."

"He's ... I think he was just trying to intimidate him."

Wolf took off in a high-knee run through the snow of the front yard toward the kitchen wing. His feet thumped with bad timing at first, but he got his rhythm and his quads and glutes burned as he kicked through the deep powder.

"I don't know," Rachette hissed. "He's already stuck the gun against his forehead, then he shot twice right next to his ears. What should I do?"

"Speak up, that's what you should do," Wolf said in between breaths. "That means Ash can't hear anything."

"Oh, yeah. Where are you?"

Wolf rounded the edge of the house and stopped just in time to avoid colliding with Patterson.

She looked up at Wolf with wide eyes and wiped a fresh dusting of snow off her face. Wearing large headphones, she was kneeling on the ground in a small dug-out clearing and had two glowing laptop computers in front of her, propped on piles of snow at eye level. She'd built herself a small audio-visual command center, like a kid would have built a snow fort.

"Sorry," Wolf said.

She nodded without speaking and then pressed some buttons.

New sounds erupted in Wolf's ear, and he nodded and gave the thumbs-up.

Patterson looked back to the video feed in front of her.

Rachette stood a few feet away with a hand on the door-knob of a side door. He swiveled out of the way, keeping his hand firmly on the knob.

Wolf walked up to the edge of the house next to the door and untied his boots as fast as he could.

Rachette pulled open the door and Wolf slipped out of his boots and stepped inside the dark room.

A second later the door sucked closed behind Wolf and he was left standing in enveloping warmth.

He froze, peering into the darkness to get his bearings. A bench was to his right, running the length of a long wall, and a row of coats hung along the opposite wall.

"You snuck in the back," Charlie Ash said in his earpiece.

Wolf cocked his head. The voice was faint and hissed with static, echoing like it was in a cathedral.

Wolf walked on moist socks across the tiled floor of the mudroom and entered the kitchen. It was brightly lit and very large, like half-of-Wolf's-house large. Wolf kept his eyes on the hallway ahead and shuffled forward, not worrying about the details of the immaculate space.

"Sit down!" Kevin's voice yelled, now just as clear in the hallway ahead of Wolf as in his earpiece.

"Shoot me!" Ash said.

Wolf pulled his pistol and peered around the corner. The hall extended far longer before exiting into the great room than Wolf had envisioned from the diagram Kevin had drawn. Wolf felt like he was losing time and needed to move fast.

Kevin had said, *Sit down*. Did that mean his father was coming at him?

Wolf ducked back into the kitchen and held up his wrist. "What's going on?" he murmured into the mic.

"You've gotta get in there," Patterson said quickly. "It looks like Charlie's stepping forward toward Kevin. Looks like he might make a move."

Wolf ran out into the hall and trotted along the right wall, then slowed as he reached the end. He inched forward until he saw Ash's right arm. Ash was right where they'd told Kevin to put him, but he was standing rather than sitting.

If this turns into an all-out brawl and either of them get hurt … Wolf didn't need to finish the thought. He'd already run over it in his mind a thousand times. He was treading on both sides of a fine line that divided ethical police work and vigilante justice. It was too late now to consider the consequences of failure.

Wolf stopped and listened closely, sensing the mounting tension in the room around the corner.

"Here's a little secret that is just going to kill you," Ash said, clear as a squad siren in Wolf's ears this time.

Wolf held his breath, knowing they'd roped Ash in. But doubt niggled at him. Ash had to suspect something was going on when he'd learned that Wolf was lying to him. And now he was up and standing in front of Kevin. Did he suspect the bullets were blanks and was about to charge his son?

"I killed Mary Richardson," Ash said.

Wolf closed his eyes and let out his breath.

"Got it," Patterson said into Wolf's ear.

"I killed her. I drugged you, and killed her, and then put you next to her," Ash said.

"Got that," Patterson said.

"It feels good to finally tell you. I was surprised when you started …"

The room fell silent and Wolf decided it was over.

"What the hell is going on?" Ash asked.

Wolf was going to enjoy telling him. He opened his eyes and stepped forward.

Ash was standing across from Kevin with his head cocked to one side. His forehead was creased, eyes darting around the room, and when he saw Wolf his face fell, like he'd just found a bomb with a ticking timer with three seconds left until detonation.

"You pieces of shit!" Ash yelled. Then he reached his right arm around to the back of his pants and pulled a pistol.

Wolf raised his gun, aimed and shot.

Ash's shoulder jerked back and he twisted and landed on the ground.

"What's going on?" Rachette screamed into the mic, and then Wolf heard frantic squeaking footsteps in the kitchen down the hall.

"It's okay," Wolf said into his mic.

Kevin stared wide-eyed at Wolf for a few seconds, then looked over at his father.

Ash was writhing in a growing pool of blood on the hardwood floor, spitting strings of spittle and obscenities out of his mouth.

Wolf walked to Ash and picked up the revolver, tucked it in the back of his pants, and then walked to Kevin with his hand out.

Kevin stood still, studying his father with a blank expression, and then raised the pistol to give it to Wolf. The index finger on his left hand was still taut on the trigger.

"Kevin," Wolf said.

Kevin blinked and looked at Wolf, and then gave him the gun. "Thank you," he said.

CHAPTER 32

THE LITTLE BOY sitting in the gondola car in front of Patterson wore silver-mirrored goggles and hadn't moved his head an inch in the past few minutes. She smiled again at him, receiving no response. Or at least none that she could see. The kid had a neck warmer pulled over his mouth, too.

Both parents were tapping thumbs on their phones, oblivious to the Colorado bluebird day with six inches of fresh powder outside.

Two kids? She couldn't even get this kid to acknowledge her. How could she expect to swoop into the lives of two children, as some sort of mommy-stand-in figure no less, and expect anything but a complete disaster?

She looked out the window of the gondola car and directed her thoughts to Edna Yerton.

Rachette had promised Patterson last night that he would check on the old woman this morning. He had volunteered because he was trying to schmooze Patterson rather than taking an easier and more appropriate approach ... like apologizing to her face about lying about Scott Reed's marital status.

But that's not how Deputy Tom Rachette worked. In fact, he was probably clueless that he had done anything wrong.

It doesn't matter now, she thought. Whatever was going on between her and Rachette, at least Edna Yerton would be the better for it.

Fatigue pulled at her eyelids as she watched a skier bounce effortlessly over the blanketed terrain below. Probably a local, she thought. Locals often skied mid-week to avoid weekend madness. And since she knew only a handful of townspeople at best, she had no clue who the man sailing down in a cloud of powder was.

And she was getting tired of that.

She was sick of nightly television shows for a social life and sick of being a stranger in her own town. But barhopping wasn't the answer. She was going to change things, and she would do it her way.

Her palms sweated under her gloves and her bowels squirmed. It was going to be nice when this was over, whatever came of it.

Then again, maybe she would just ride the gondola back down and save herself the embarrassment. *Oh, God. Kristen would give me hell for that.* She took a quaky breath and looked back at the boy.

Still unmoved. The kid was a rock.

The gondola bounced over a tower's cable wheels, and the little boy started to lean to his side. Then he slid forward, bonked his helmet on the window and hit his face. He jerked upright, reaching out his hands and wobbling his head.

Patterson blew air out of her nose and smiled wide as she realized the kid had been asleep.

The parents glanced at her and burrowed themselves back into their display screens.

When she looked back at the boy, he had pulled his neck warmer down and was smiling back, showcasing a mouth with more than a few missing teeth.

She shook her head, grateful that the gondola car was only another tower from the upper terminal. Staring at that gapped smile any longer and she would have probably started laughing uncontrollably.

The interaction with the child steeled her to finish what she'd come to do, and as the gondola slowed and the door clicked and opened, she took a deep breath and waved the family first. She gave a little wink to the boy as he left, and then followed the family out the door, leaving them fumbling with their equipment as she walked on.

The morning was bright, crisp, and clear, and not many skiers were milling around on top of the mountain. If she weren't on scheduled duty within the hour, she'd have been skiing.

She walked down the grated steps and onto the soft packed powder. Her heart fluttered and her breath caught when she saw the snow cat in the distance. She felt unnerved when she saw Scott Reed sitting on the wheel track.

He wore dark sunglasses, and he sat tall and stared in her direction, but he wasn't smiling. His eyebrows were knitted together like he was confused as to why she would visit him.

Her courage drained through her legs, and just when she thought she'd really screwed up his face lit up into a smile that made it seem the sun had risen higher into the sky.

"Hey!" he said, getting up from his seat and walking briskly toward her.

His ski pants swished as he stepped with strong legs, covering a lot of distance with each stride. He was wearing a gray hat, a gray heavy-knit sweater, and a blue-and-red scarf wrapped around his neck. It was pseudo-European looking, and Patterson realized that the man was a little bit of a fashionista. The thought made her smile even wider than she already was.

They were coming toward one another at speed, like in the movies when the girl flies into the guy's arms and they embrace for half the morning. She decided she had to control herself and slowed down holding out her hand in greeting.

He seemed to have had a similar thought, because he stopped quickly too, putting his sunglasses to his forehead with an awkward smile. His Caribbean-lagoon-green eyes darted around and he seemed a little embarrassed after looking so happy to see her a few moments before.

Or she could have been seeing things. Again. And it was time to put a stop to this torture.

"Hey—"

"Hey—"

They laughed.

"I saw you and didn't know if that was you or Rachette," he said.

She raised her eyebrows. "Oh, that's disturbing."

He laughed easily and shook his head. "No, sorry. I mean, I have terrible eyesight at a distance when I'm not wearing my contacts, which I'm not."

She laughed. "Ah, okay."

Their laughter wound down and they were left with a few moments of silence, but there was no tension, because he had an air of easiness that made her feel comfortable. He just smiled and looked at her, as if she could get on with whatever she was going to say when she was good and ready, and he had all the time in the world.

She looked down and pulled a straggly piece of hair behind

her ear. "Um, so I just came up here to ask you a few questions."

"Okay, great," he said.

She stared back for a few seconds, and then rolled her eyes. "Okay, listen. Are you married?"

"No. Why?"

"Because I heard you were."

"And you believe everything you hear?"

She stared up at those eyes again.

He stopped smiling and pulled off his left glove and displayed his hand. "See?"

"That's the oldest trick in the book for some men."

"Not for me." He held her gaze for a few seconds, and then concentrated on putting his gloves back on. "So ... it matters to you whether I'm married or not?"

She hesitated, and then she didn't. "Yes."

"Good." His smiled vanished. "Hey, is it true about Kevin Ash? He didn't come into work today and there's some serious rumors going around."

"Like what?"

"Like he was the one who killed Stephanie, Matt, and the mayor."

She looked back at the snow cat, wondering just how much information she could disclose. "You believe everything you hear?"

"Well, is it true?"

"If I said yes could I convince you to keep your mouth shut about it for a while?"

"You know," he said, "Kevin Ash was with me that night."

"What? Which night?"

"The gala night, Saturday. When I was driving Stephanie and that guy she was with. He was sitting right next to me in the snow cat. Said he was with a few other patrollers checking out the bowl underneath the lodge."

"Are you serious?"

"Yeah." He nodded. "He was sitting there chatting me up the whole time. When people were talking about what he did this morning, I got the serious creeps when I remembered that."

"And were you going to tell your local Sheriff's Department about this?"

He scratched his head and then shrugged. "I get off at noon today. I was sitting on the news, and was going to swing into the station and tell the prettiest deputy I knew about it."

Despite silently screaming at herself to not do it again, she rolled her eyes.

"And if Deputy Rachette wasn't there, I was going to tell you." His face was deadpan.

She laughed. "I've obviously made a mistake coming up here."

They laughed together and his face turned red, which made Patterson like him even more.

"But seriously," she said, "that is a good idea for you to come down. We'll need an official statement."

He nodded. "And when you get off work tonight, would you like to go get dinner with me? Or if that seems too forward, we could go get a coffee, or—"

"I thought you'd never ask," she said. Then the curious voice in her head took over. It wouldn't shut up.

"What?" Scott narrowed his eyes.

"I … never mind."

"What? What?" His eyes were alight with childish curiosity, and it made her smile.

"I guess I just wanted to know how old your children are. I

know it's a weird question, but I just want to know. It's just something I've—"

"What children?"

She closed her mouth.

"I don't have any kids."

Her face went red and her chest constricted. "You don't?"

"No."

"I thought you had two kids with your ex-wife."

"I've never been married. I thought we just discussed that."

She stood frozen in time for God knew how long, then shook her head. "No, you're right. Never mind. I was just misunderstanding something, something that ... I must have taken it the wrong way. Listen, I'll see you later at the station when you come in. Have a good morning."

"Wait, what if you're not there? Can I get your phone number?"

She gave him a contact card and backed away with what she hoped looked like a smile.

"Thank you. Tell Rachette hi for me."

She turned and left. "I'll be telling him hi all right," she said under her breath. "Upside his head."

CHAPTER 33

Two Months Later ...

Waves of snow descended the western slopes of the valley, pouring into the outskirts of Rocky Points. The first large snowflake hit the glass of Wolf's windshield and melted, and then another dozen left their marks.

The late April snow would be thick and wet, breaking branches and collapsing old roofs if it got deep, which the forecasters were saying was likely.

He turned on the wipers and scrolled through his phone contacts, stopping at the inch of screen that displayed Kristen Luke's and Sarah Muller's phone numbers.

For two months he'd been ignoring Sarah's hints that she might want to go for a drink or dinner. Or if he'd ever found himself alone with her, he'd pretend like he had to leave for fear she might start talking—telling him things he didn't want to hear.

Because the truth was, what Charlie Ash had said that night in the entryway of his house had made perfect sense to

Wolf. It had given perfect reason for Sarah's actions since she'd gotten sober.

But since that night he hadn't wanted to deal with the revelation. Not then, and not up until now. Not while he had more important things to worry about, like how he might have ruined the careers of three of his deputies.

Today was the day, he thought. Because everything else was coming to a head, and it might as well be the day. Because he was about to go talk to Burton—to face the consequences of his actions two months earlier—and he was ready to rip the band-aid off the Wolf–Sarah wound once and for all to see what was underneath.

Wolf pushed Sarah's name on the screen. He listened to the phone ring in his ear and watched the wipers leave long swaths of water as they squeaked back and forth.

"Hello?" Sarah answered.

"Hey."

"Hey."

"Can we talk?" Wolf asked.

There was a long pause. "Sure. I'm at the office, can you come over?"

"Be right there."

Wolf pulled back onto the highway and drove into town. A minute later he pulled into the parking lot of the Hitching Post Realty storefront office. With his front tire dropping into a hole filled with muddy water, he shut off the engine and got out.

By the time he'd opened the jangling glass door, his hair was coated with snow. Stepping into the warm office space, he brushed his head and wiped his feet on the welcome mat.

Sarah, Margaret, and a man Wolf failed to recognize looked up from their desks, which were all angled to face the large plate-glass window front of the office like they were plants soaking up as much light as possible.

"Howdy, Sheriff," Margaret said in a terrible Texas accent.

"Hello," Wolf said. He nodded at Sarah, who scooted back her chair and stood up. The man sitting at the other desk nodded and got back to pecking on his keyboard.

"How are things going?" Margaret asked, this time in a normal tone. She narrowed her eyes. "You talk to Burton yet?"

Wolf shook his head.

She raised her eyebrows and nodded, and then looked down at her computer screen.

Wolf blinked. "How about you? Business good?"

"Excellent as usual, but not as good as it could be. Hey, Barry,"—she looked over at the man at the desk next to Sarah's —"this is Sheriff Wolf. Sheriff Wolf, this is Barry Hashberger. Barry's a new one I recruited out of Vail."

Barry stood up and walked over with his hand extended. It was warm and dry and he shook with a firm grip. "Nice to meet you, sir. I've heard"—he stopped himself short —"about you."

"Nice to meet you, too."

Margaret cleared her throat. "I've told him the story about the Village Base Condos Deal and the corruption that came along with it, and the sheriff who uncovered the whole mess."

Wolf narrowed his eyes and nodded. "So you're glad the condo deal fell through and Klammer and Irwin had to skip town with their tails between their legs after all?"

"Hell, no I'm not glad. Like I said, business is not as good as it could be." She stared with a straight face and then tried to look happy. "I'm just kidding. We're starting another open-bid process as soon as we can get our godforsaken government back intact. And when we do, and someone else builds those condos, Hitching Post Realty will have those listings. Just a hell of a lot later, thanks to you." She bent down and squinted at the screen. "Ah! The Cherokee Trail counter just came in ... they agree to waive inspection."

Barry made a fist and held it in the air.

Wolf looked at Sarah.

She shrugged, zipped up her jacket and walked to Wolf with a smile. "Exciting in here, isn't it?"

Wolf nodded. "My hair is standing on end. See you guys later. Nice to meet you, Barry." Wolf waved and followed Sarah out the door.

Barry smiled and waved. Margaret kept her eyes on her screen and pointed in Wolf's general direction.

They walked through the snow to Wolf's SUV and got in.

"Where to?" she asked.

Wolf fired up the SUV and cranked the heat to halfway. He shut off the radio and looked out the windshield. The snow was falling so thick it was like looking straight at a waterfall, and the office window behind it was completely invisible.

"That night I busted Charlie Ash," he said, "he said something to me."

She stopped putting on her seatbelt and looked over at him.

"He said that you broke up with Mark because you were still in love with me, and he was sick of competing with me for your heart, and that's why he returned to Vail."

Sarah frowned. "You were talking about me and Mark with Charlie Ash?"

Wolf nodded. "He said he befriended Mark while he was in town."

Sarah swallowed and glanced out the windshield. "Okay."

"Ash was trying to egg me on, trying to get to me. And he

did a pretty good job of it, because he also said that Mark had told him that you'd cheated on me sometime in the past. When I was still in."

Sarah looked at him with an open mouth and wide eyes. The heater blew with a low howl and the wipers swished across the windshield.

Wolf reached up and turned off the wipers without breaking eye contact.

A tear fell down Sarah's cheek.

"That's the truth, isn't it?" he asked.

She kept her watery gaze on his and nodded. "Yes," she whispered.

Wolf took a deep breath and looked past her into the falling snow.

"I'm sorry." Her words were barely audible over the air vents.

Wolf sighed and closed his eyes, stretched his neck muscles, and then looked at her. "About what?" he asked. "About cheating on me? Or not telling me about it? Or not telling me about how we had a miscarriage? Or about something else? Something you don't have the guts to tell me about yet?"

She held his gaze. "I was going to tell you. I've been trying to tell you for months. Ever since Mark and I broke up."

Running his fingers over the two-day growth of stubble on his chin, Wolf sighed and gazed out the windshield.

The heater blew.

"I know you won't care to hear this, but for what it's worth, it was with some random guy. I don't even remember most of it." She talked to her hands. "I was so drunk, on pills ... it meant nothing to me, and I've been beating myself up for it ever since."

Wolf kept his eyes on the snow piling up on the windshield.

"I've been so ashamed. I ... was going to tell you so long ago, after I told you about the miscarriage. But then I just let things slip further and further away. And I felt so ... I knew I didn't deserve you for what I'd done to you when you were off fighting, so I chickened out."

He tapped the steering wheel with his thumb. "I don't know what ..." Wolf shook his head. "Who was it?"

"Nobody you know," she answered quickly.

Wolf looked over at her.

"Don't you want to know why?" she asked. "Why I did it?"

"What?" He shook his head and looked in the rearview mirror. He suddenly needed her out of the car. "Look—"

"You went back," she said. Her voice shook. "You just went back. You knew I was doing bad, and you left again."

Wolf stared at her. "I was serving my coun—"

"But you had a choice! You didn't have to do that last tour."

Wolf shook his head and leaned his head back. "I couldn't leave." Wolf closed his eyes. "I couldn't leave."

"Rangers lead the way," she said.

Wolf looked at her again.

She glared back at him defiantly, her wet eyelids narrowed, a stream of mascara running down one cheek.

Wolf looked at the steering wheel. "I've gotta go."

She climbed out and closed the door with a soft thunk, and then walked past the hood and disappeared into the falling cotton.

Wolf flipped on the wipers, backed into the lot and drove down Main.

He took a deep breath and shook his head, inhaling the flowery scent of Sarah, still strong in the cab.

Who? That's all he could think.

Why? Because he'd gone back. So she gave up.

He slapped the steering wheel, and then he slowed and took a left at a hand-painted sign that said *Beer Goggles Bar and Grill* with an arrow pointing left down a dirt road.

The narrow bridge over the Chautauqua River creaked and clacked as Wolf drove across it.

The road on the other side was muddy, cratered with potholes, and Wolf's SUV rocked side to side as he pulled into the lot and parked. He stepped outside and shut the door, squinting as the huge, wet flakes slapped his face.

The snow was still melting on contact with the ground, and the saturated rocky dirt shifted under his boots as he walked over and around puddles to the entrance.

Inside, bluegrass music pumped out of a speaker right next to his head. It smelled like beer and bar food and his mouth watered.

There were ten or so patrons in the restaurant, and a few quiet types sitting at the bar sipping beers. Former sheriff of Rocky Points, Hal Burton, was wedged into a corner booth against the windows on the left side. He looked up and saw Wolf, nodded, and got back to studying the menu.

Wolf looked at the melting snowflakes beading on the glass next to Burton and thought of Sarah's wet eyes.

"Sheriff," Jerry Blackman, the owner of the bar, leaned over the counter and held out his hand.

Wolf snapped out of his thoughts and shook it. "Hey, Jerry."

"Get you a drink?" he asked.

"I'll take a Coke," he said, noticing the tall, half-drunk beer sitting in front of Burton.

"You got it." Blackman grabbed a glass and twisted away. "I'll bring it over."

Wolf walked over and slid into the booth across from Burton. "What are you looking at the menu for?"

"I'm hoping some inspiration will jump out at me," he said, not raising his gaze. A few seconds later he slapped the menu closed. "Nope. Bacon cheeseburger again."

Wolf smiled.

Burton looked out the window and grabbed his beer. He tilted it up and poured it through his thick gray mustache, and when he came up for air he had a line of foam on it.

"I see you're sticking to your diet," Wolf said.

"Shut up." Burton belched and set down the glass, holding up a finger in the direction of the bar.

The truth was, Burton did look like he was sticking to his diet. His once over-ample frame was now just ample, and his face looked to be thinner, the skin drooping more underneath his chin rather than ballooning out.

"You look pretty good, actually," Wolf said, studying him.

"Lost twenty-two pounds so far. I've been starving myself for the last day for this meal, so shut up and quit lookin' at me like that."

Wolf smiled and looked out the window. The Chautauqua was running fast and high with the arrival of mid-spring warmer temperatures. The banks on either side were still piled with snow, and sheets of dripping ice reached out over the water, the icy liquid passing underneath in rippling waves.

"Snow's comin' in again, eh?" Burton asked.

Wolf adjusted his focus and looked at the flakes flying by the window. "Yep. Gonna be big, they say."

Jerry came over with another beer and a Coke. Burton and Wolf ordered the bacon cheeseburger and fries.

Then they sat in tense silence for a few minutes. The speakers played "Touch of Gray" by the Grateful Dead, and the clank of silverware hitting plates filled the other gaps in sound.

"Jesus, you aren't even going to ask me about it?" Burton leaned his elbows on the table.

Wolf shrugged and took a sip of his Coke.

Burton narrowed his eyes and leaned forward.

Wolf met his glare. "Okay, how did it go?"

Burton leaned back and shook his head, mumbling something R-rated under his breath. He reached down and pulled a manila folder off the seat next to him and pushed it across the table.

Wolf took it and opened it up.

Inside was a black-and-white copy of the formal reprimand issued by the Sluice County Commissioner's Office upon the recommendation of the Incident Review Board tasked with his "misconduct in the line of duty"—a form filled out and given to Wolf by the Commissioner of Sluice County himself. It was something that Wolf had seen more than a few times in the past month, and had been thinking about almost continuously since it had been delivered to him.

It was a constant reminder that Wolf's future as sheriff of Sluice County looked tenuous at best.

Wolf flipped to the back page and realized that it had been stapled in the corner to the page in front of it. This page was a typed letter, signed in ink by Commissioner Heller and a couple of other names he recognized.

Wolf read the letter, word by word, then set it back inside the manila folder and closed it. Then he looked up at Burton.

"Complete dismissal," Burton said, bouncing his thick eyebrows. "Huh? Who's got your back?"

Wolf exhaled and looked back out the window. "I don't like people fighting my fights for me."

Burton scoffed. "Jesus ... I didn't fight your fight, you dumbass. I had your back," he said, poking his finger onto the table. "You've been fighting for a month, and I jumped in and took a shot where I saw an opening."

Wolf pulled his eyebrows together and looked at Burton.

Burton nodded. "Big difference."

"What about Rachette, Patterson, and Wilson?"

"Nothin's ... whoa, here we go," Burton leaned back and Jerry Blackman clanked steaming plates of food on the table and shoved them into place.

"Anything else?" Jerry asked.

"No thanks," Wolf said.

"Yeah, I'll take another," Burton said, pointing at his three-quarter-full beer. "I'll be ready by the time you get back."

Jerry disappeared and Wolf stared at Burton.

"Don't worry—Cheryl's pickin' me up in an hour. Gave me the day pass to have some drinks."

"Rachette, Patterson, Wils—"

"Oh, yeah. I talked to Heller." Burton shook his head. "He's got no beef with what you did. And he's sure as hell not going to throw those deputies under the bus. Everyone knows it was just Ash's last-ditch effort to get even with you, and they ain't gonna give that guy the satisfaction. Not that conniving, murdering son of a bitch. Rachette, Wilson, and Patterson have received the same letters confirming full dismissal of any wrongdoing."

They ate their food in silence, listening to bluegrass on the stereo and watching the sky thicken even more with dropping flakes until the river was barely visible through the curtain of snow.

Relief enveloped him, and he actually felt his pulse slow with each minute.

He had been agonizing up until now, living in a personal hell ever since that night they'd tricked Charlie Ash into confessing. Agonizing because, for following Wolf's plan, three deputies had been put at risk of being fired. And because it had immediately become clear that the fates of Wolf's and his deputies' careers were going to be connected by the powers that be.

What bothered Wolf the most was that he had foreseen the problems that would certainly arise that night. He'd had a clear glimpse of the future, but he'd ignored it. He'd been too caught up with justice and not enough with what the law dictated he could or couldn't do. When Kevin had confessed to killing Mary Richardson, all while holding his gun left-handed and not right-handed like the Lake Tahoe killer Chief Gunnison had described, Wolf had simultaneously seen the truth and the window of opportunity to bring justice to Charlie Ash open wide.

Charlie Ash, though in county custody and confined to a hospital, had delivered a crushing blow when everything had been over and done with. The official complaint alleged that Wolf and his subordinates had deprived Ash of his constitutional rights when they'd used unlawful means and deadly force to elicit a statement from him. And Ash, under extreme duress and fearing for his life, had *"intentionally offered a false statement in an attempt to save himself from bodily harm and imminent death at the hands of an individual known to Wolf and his deputies to be violent and mentally impaired."*

Ash, calling on any and every political connection he had,

had demanded his own release, and that Wolf and his deputies be dismissed at once.

And now this letter in the manila folder, and the same letters for Rachette, Patterson, and Wilson was the paddle to get them off Shit Creek once and for all.

When Wolf and Burton had finished their food, there wasn't a granule of salt left on either plate, and only then did Burton open his mouth to speak again.

"I was talkin' to Heller. You know, you oughta be proud of what you did." He picked his teeth with a toothpick. "That ... Ash-hole woulda still been chairman of our county council. Runnin' around, takin' bribes." He shook his head and took another long pull of beer. "And all the while a cold-blooded murderer? Nobody would have ever been the wiser if it weren't for you."

Wolf wadded up his napkin and set it on his plate. "Lot of dead people in Rocky Points. A lot of risk I put on my deputies."

Burton stared at Wolf. "You can't take responsibility for what Kevin did, killing all those people. You can blame Ash for that. What you did was ... noble. You figured out Kevin Ash was the one killing and was going to kill his father next, and you saved Charlie's life rather than standing by and letting him die.

"Sometimes, things just work out where you're always puttin' someone at risk. Especially when you're in the leader's chair. If you wouldn't have clipped a wire on Kevin, set up those video feeds and done that?" He shook his head. "A murderer would be free. Right here. Right in our government. Right in our town."

Burton drained his beer and got started on the next one.

Then he stared at Wolf and put a palm on the table. "You can't always keep your partners from risk."

Wolf looked up at him. Burton was staring at him with wide, unblinking eyes, and Wolf understood. Burton was referring to Wolf's father. Burton and Wolf's father had been partners back in the day, and if Burton had been with Wolf's father that day so many years ago, his dad might still be alive.

Wolf had beaten himself up for years for not being able to solve the case of his father's death, but Burton had beaten himself up about it even more—all for taking a sick day on that fateful day Daniel Wolf had been killed.

"What matters is you." Burton poked his index finger at him. His lip started quivering, along with his voice. "You're the type of guy that makes sure you're there for your partner—your *partners*—in the end. That's what I've always seen in you, and by God that's why you're sheriff of this county, and not some other …"

Burton paused and then drowned the rest of his sentence with a pull of beer.

Wolf turned and looked out the window. He watched the streaks of water running down the glass, and he thought again about Sarah's streaming eyes. His breath caught when he remembered her defiant glare, and the way she'd told him there was a *reason* for her cheating on him when he'd been off risking his life halfway around the world. Like it had been a premeditated thing.

Burton slapped his palm softly on the table, bringing Wolf back to the moment, trying to hammer his point home in Wolf's head.

"I know." Wolf nodded. He scooted out of the booth before he had to look at a second set of crying eyes in one day. "I've gotta go. Tell Cheryl hi for me." He picked up and waved the manila folder. "And thank you."

Burton smiled and sat up tall, raising his beer. "I was happy to be able to jump into that fight and throw a couple uppercuts, just like when I was in the older days."

Wolf stared at him. "You're hammered."

Burton nodded and smiled. "I am."

Wolf walked away, dropping fifteen dollars on the bar in front of Jerry Blackman on the way by. Wolf had given up arguing with Burton about splitting checks and had learned to resort to other means to cover his share.

Outside was dead quiet, which seemed counterintuitive with the snow falling so intensely, dropping so hard he couldn't see the SUV in the lot. He walked over the wet grit, stepping through puddles, making his way in the general direction of his parking spot, and finally found the Explorer after a minute of wandering aimlessly in the whiteout.

Luckily, Cheryl was coming to pick up Burton because the man wouldn't have stood a chance navigating this weather without her help. Not after four beers, or had it been five? Who was he kidding? It would probably be seven by the time the old man's wife came to pick him up.

That was a woman who stood by her man, Wolf thought. Her imperfect, jackass of a man … a jackass with unbreakable loyalty and a good heart.

Wolf sat in the SUV and shut the door. He ruffled the snow off his hair, and then wiped the beads of moisture from his face and stared in the rearview mirror. He sniffed and caught the faint aroma of Sarah's perfume again. He wondered how long it would linger. He suspected for quite some time.

As he stared at his reflection, he got that feeling again. Like he'd been missing something. Something that had been staring him in the face, but he was too preoccupied to see it for what it was.

Was it that he needed to stop beating himself up for his failed marriage? That he needed to forgive himself for putting his partners in danger?

You're the type of guy that makes sure you're there for your partner—your partners—in the end.

Wolf narrowed his eyes, glaring at his own reflection.

Or was it that he knew Sarah had been acting out of desperation, because in the end, he hadn't been there for her? For his partner?

Of course it was. It was all those things.

Wolf looked out into the veil of snow, shrouding everything he would have rather liked to see—the road, the potholes, the bridge, other cars ... where the hell he was going. The uncertainty could have been enough to drive him back into Beer Goggles for five or six beers.

But instead, he fired up the engine and backed out through the ruts and potholes.

Because he had to get back to work.

THE END

ACKNOWLEDGMENTS

Thank you so much for reading Deadly Conditions. I hope you enjoyed the story, and if you did, thank you for taking a few moments to leave a review. As an independently published author, exposure is everything, and positive reviews help so much to get that exposure. If you'd be so kind to take a moment to leave an honest review, I'd be so grateful.

I love interacting with readers so please feel free to email me at jeff@jeffcarson.co so I can thank you personally. Otherwise, thank you very much for your support by other means, such as sharing the books with your friends/family/book clubs/the weird guy who wears tight women's yoga pants who works at the deli, or anyone else you think might be interested in reading the David Wolf series. Thanks again and I hope to see you again inside another Wolf story.

Would you like to know about future David Wolf books the

moment they are published? You can visit my blog and sign up for the New Release Newsletter at this link – http://www.jeffcarson.co/p/newsletter.html.

As a gift for signing up you'll receive a complimentary copy of Gut Decision—A David Wolf Short Story, which is a harrowing tale that takes place years ago during David Wolf's first days in the Sluice County Sheriff's Department.

SHERIFF DAVID WOLF looked up and saw the line of trucks and SUVs thundering down the dirt road at five-alarm-fire speed. Letting up his bodyweight on the wriggling animal underneath him, he hissed in pain as a hoof glanced off his knee. The dust from the slowing vehicles washed over the volunteers inside the cattle pen, and then moved on to envelop the rest of the crowd gathered on the surrounding lawn.

"Who the hell is that?" Deputy Tom Rachette squinted and waved his hand.

"MacLean," Wolf said.

The calf bleated, protesting the ropes expertly lassoed around its head and hind legs. The two men controlled their horses, pulling the ropes with practiced precision.

Rick Welch, third-generation owner of Triple T Ranch, quickly shaved the calf's right rear haunch and a volunteer weekend cowhand approached with two smoking branding irons.

"God damn it," Rick mumbled through clenched lips, waiting for the cloud to pass.

Luckily, a light morning breeze dispersed the dust, and the air became breathable again.

The unplanned break over, Wolf sagged his weight onto the animal and held tight. At six foot three and two hundred pounds, he'd always carried a muscular physique with little effort, or, in the case of his years as an army Ranger, with tremendous effort, but now that he was almost forty-one years old, his muscularity hid the fatigue within that came after rigorous activity. The morning's work had his shoulders and abdominal muscles screaming for mercy. As sheriff of Sluice County for the past three years, he was lucky if he managed to break away three times a week for weight lifting, and the cardio ... well, he figured his cardio was living in the mountains of Colorado.

He'd lost count of how many calves they'd done so far, but he knew there were plenty more to go. Even with the second and third team of horsemen and volunteers working just as hard inside the pen, it was going to be an all-day job that might go into tomorrow.

Deputy Tom Rachette, a fit young man in his mid-twenties, seemed to sense Wolf's slowdown and squatted next to him, gripping the calf's hind legs and stilling the animal for good. Rachette was shorter than average, but in Wolf's estimation, the deputy was built like a bull, and he had tenacity and strength rivaling that of most larger men.

"Thanks," Wolf said through gritted teeth, a fresh twinge of pain shooting through his lower back.

Triple T Ranch had the largest herd of cattle in Sluice County, and it was a community operation to get the cattle branded every year. Wolf hadn't missed the event for seven years running, and Margaret Hitchens, town real-estate agent and self-appointed chairperson of the Wolf-for-Sheriff election campaign, had turned the branding into a rally for votes, complete with food and games for the entire family outside the cattle pen.

Margaret had seen to it that the *Sluice Sentinel* had run announcements in the three weeks leading up to the event, and nearly every display window and cork board in Rocky Points featured one of Margaret's come one, come all invitations. Over fifty men, women, and children had shown up.

And now there were a few more uninvited ones.

"Okay!" Rick shouted.

The ropes slackened. Wolf slipped the loop over the rear hooves and he and Rachette jumped up, clearing out of danger.

"Sheriff Wolf!" a deep, jovial voice called from the other side of the fence.

Wolf turned with little enthusiasm toward a rising commotion.

A videographer scrambled with a tripod and camera, and an army of still photographers darted this way and that, kneeling and climbing into photo-opportunity positions.

Wolf instinctively glanced at Margaret, who was already out of her lawn chair and charging towards MacLean, a suspicious crease on her brow beneath her cowboy hat.

"What's this?" she demanded.

MacLean looked over at her like she was an attacking rabid dog, then smiled pleasantly.

"Margaret, I heard about the cattle-branding and thought I'd volunteer." He raised his voice for everyone to hear over the mooing. "That is, if you'll have me."

Photographers snapped photos. The videographer panned from MacLean to Wolf.

Margaret scoffed and walked away.

Wolf walked to the fence with an outstretched hand caked with dried mud.

MacLean knotted his hand with Wolf's and shook vigorously. His smile was confident, his steely eyes either ignoring or oblivious to the cool reception of every person surrounding him.

The cameras whirred and clicked.

Releasing Wolf's grip, MacLean hopped over the fence with considerable grace for a fifty-five-year-old. His brand-new work boots stomped down on the dusty earth and he bent down, grabbed a handful of dirt, and rubbed it across his chest, leaving a skid mark on his expensive white button-up shirt.

"Mr. Welch!" MacLean boomed, marching toward the owner of the Triple T Ranch with his now dusty hand.

Rick fumbled with the branding irons, leaving MacLean holding out his hand without a partner to shake it. Finally, they shook and MacLean beamed a smile framed by his perfectly trimmed silver goatee.

The photographers pounced.

Wolf heard a ping on the fence and a collective gasp. He turned in time to see a photographer's head whipping back as he landed on the ground. The camera-wielding man's smooth-soled shoes were no match for manure.

The guy bounced up without hesitation and snapped some shots.

Wolf turned on his heel and plucked Sarah from the crowd.

Standing in front of her chair to get a better look, she met Wolf's gaze and smiled.

They gravitated toward one another at the fence line. He watched her and took a cleansing breath, feeling a jolt of energy. The combination of the crisp air and watching her move was better than ibuprofen or any other pain reliever. As far back as high school, when he'd met his sweetheart turned wife, turned ex-wife turned—whatever it was they were now —she'd always liked to dress the part of a cowgirl, and with her worn jeans, frayed hat, button-up embroidered denim shirt, she wore the look just as well as she had back then.

They met at the fence and she handed him a water bottle.

"Real nice of him to show up," she said. "What an asshole. No wonder this guy's winning. Good God, there's like ten photographers. Is he shooting another commercial?"

Wolf drank the cold water and let the sun warm his skin. It was clear blue skies with visibility as far as it got to the north and south, with pine-tree-covered mountains socking them in to the east and west. The dung-scented air was warm with a steady cool breeze, making it biting cold in the shade, typical of early June in the middle of the Rockies.

Sarah's jeans stretched against her thinly muscled leg as she propped a boot on the fence and she smiled up at him.

"You look like a dust bunny. Here,"—she reached through the fence and ruffled his hair, sending a cascade of dirt onto Wolf's shoulders—"let's unveil that gorgeous dark hair of yours for the cameras, and let's wipe your face. It looks like one of those cattle pooped on it."

Wolf closed his eyes and let her delicate hands do their brusque work. "I think one of them did."

"—Wolf?"

He turned around at the sound of his name.

MacLean stood with Trevor Lancaster, the undersheriff of Byron County. Lancaster was Wolf's age—younger, taller, and more muscled than his boss. Wolf couldn't help notice the way the man raked his eyes up and down behind Wolf, taking in Sarah's figure with unreserved curiosity.

Besides Lancaster, all eyes were on Wolf.

"What's that?" he asked.

"I said," MacLean yelled over the cows, "why don't you and I mount up and rope one of these calves? Show 'em how it's done?"

MacLean was oblivious to the glares he received.

"I don't think you or I could show any of these men anything they haven't done themselves over fifty times already today."

MacLean's smile wavered for an instant, but he shrugged and walked toward a horse and grabbed the reins from the dismounted cowboy. The sheriff of Byron County climbed on with expert speed and grabbed the lasso off the saddle horn.

Wolf turned back to Sarah and handed her the water bottle.

She smiled and winked. "Go get 'em, Sheriff."

Wolf looked at Sarah's beautiful Colorado-sky-blue eyes, her tanned face flecked with tiny circles of sunlight passing through the holes in her cowboy hat, and at that moment thought he could wrestle down a bull with his hands. Then when he tried to think of the last time he'd thrown a lasso and came up with no memories, his confidence came down a few notches. With a sigh he turned around.

"All right, Sheriff Wolf!" Margaret Hitchens thrust a fist into the air and tried to rally some cheers from the crowd.

Travis Chapman hopped off his Mustang and gave Wolf the reins. "You got this?"

"Nope," Wolf said, climbing up without hesitation. The beast beneath him twisted and bucked, and Wolf managed to keep his seat, though barely.

Chapman finally calmed the Mustang down and handed up his coiled lasso.

Wolf took it, let out some slack, and twirled it in a slow circle, getting his bearings with riding a horse and twirling a lasso—two actions alone he hadn't done in years.

"You be the heeler?" Sheriff MacLean winked at Wolf.

Wolf smiled. Roping the heels meant he'd have to lay the lasso loop as a trap in front of the moving calf's rear legs and then snag the legs as it moved through the loop. Though looping either the head or heels was no easy task for the unpracticed, the former was the more difficult task. Successfully heeling a calf was something he'd seen the men today fail to do on numerous occasions. They were professionals. Wolf, most definitely, was not.

"Sure," he said, getting the feeling that this politically masterful opponent of his had just roped him.

MacLean turned and pursued a calf without hesitation, tossed the lasso and snagged its head in a swift fluid motion. He yanked the line and stopped his horse. The calf twisted, turning its hind legs toward Wolf.

Wolf rode into place, feeling wobbly in the saddle as the huge Mustang accelerated.

He twirled the rope above his head, at an angle towards his left shoulder, like his father had taught him all those years ago. Then he rode up alongside the left hind leg, just like he remembered, letting the loop grow with each twirl. He watched the calf hop, the hind legs leaving the ground in a steady, predictable rhythm. And then he threw.

And he whiffed.

"Come on Wolf!" someone yelled from the crowd.

"You can do it sheriff! Waaahooo!" Margaret Hitchens's voice was easily picked out of the silence.

Wolf tried again, missing the mark one more time, and then again. This time the toss was good, but he was late pulling the slack.

"You gotta flatten your toss!" MacLean said.

Wolf chuckled to himself as he reeled in the rope. *I've gotta flatten your face.*

Amid a deafening uncomfortable silence, Wolf missed again.

"All right," MacLean declared. "I'll take the heels. You got the head."

Ah. Okay. Easy enough, Wolf thought. He felt like he was thirteen all over again, tossing a rope at a wooden dummy with his father barking at him.

"Okay, you got this!" Deputy Rachette started a renewed wave of banter. "Come on, Sheriff!"

"Yay, Sheriff Wolf!"

Wolf took a deep breath, twirled the rope above his head, this time keeping a nice bend in his elbow with each revolution. He picked an easy target: a calf that was standing still, unobstructed in the confusion of moving cattle.

The rope hit the rear half of the animal and dropped to the ground.

MacLean laughed. "Okay, let's give back the pros their horses. We could be here all day!"

Wolf ignored him. He whipped back the rope and stretched the loop out, twirled it over his head twice and tossed it. Sailing through the air, the loop went over the head of a brown-and-white spotted calf and landed around its neck. He pulled back, tightening the slack, and then wrapped the rope around the saddle horn. He steered his horse the opposite way, whipping the calf around and presenting the hind legs to MacLean.

"Hey! Now we're talkin'!" MacLean yelled.

A split second later, Wolf's rope yanked back incredibly hard—too hard—almost sending him off the saddle as the Mustang twisted back. At that second, he saw the calf in the air, both hind legs securely roped and pulled back, the animal poised to land on its side.

"Whoa!" Wolf pulled up on the reins, but too late—the calf was stretched inhumanely thin, and just when Wolf thought he had ripped the animal in half, the Mustang stopped and backed up a few steps.

MacLean wasted no time turning and dragged the calf backwards towards the men with the branding iron.

Wolf followed, keeping total slack in his rope, more than a little relieved that the calf was struggling against the tow.

As the men branded the calf, MacLean sat tall with a self-satisfied grin plastered on his face.

Once again, Wolf felt bested by this man, in an arena he was unfamiliar with.

Being appointed sheriff of Sluice County, just like Hal Burton before him, and Wolf's father before Burton, Wolf had never had to pander to the masses, never had to act a part; he'd simply shown up for work and done the best job he could.

Now that the smaller Sluice County was merging with its neighbor to the south, Byron, things were changing. Big time. Down in Rocky Points, just a block and a half from the station, a three-story monstrosity of a municipal building and new sheriff's office, complete with state-of-the-art jail cells in the basement, was going up in record time. And with the new structure came something even bigger. An election. And a campaign. *Multiple* campaigns, because the people of the newly formed Sluice–Byron County were voting not only for a sheriff but for other seats in the new county government too.

It was now spring and the election would be held in mid-summer by special order of the governor of Colorado. With the political atmosphere like a mosh pit at a thrash-metal concert, Sheriff Will MacLean seemed to be at home amid the chaos.

Wolf wondered just how MacLean planned on cutting and pasting all this video footage, what exactly he was going to do with all these photos.

No doubt something awe-inspiring, just like the rest of the man's campaign for sheriff had been thus far.

Wolf felt no awkwardness when it came to mountain living. But the pixels captured through those lenses said otherwise. That's all that mattered. The airtime on television that MacLean's campaign could buy would undoubtedly show the people otherwise.

"And that," Margaret Hitchens yelled, "is Sheriff Wolf's attitude towards his job in action. Never give up! Never give up!"

A lone whistle pierced a smattering of applause.

Wolf felt his face go red as he jumped down and handed over the reins.

"Sheriff Wolf!"

Rachette had his cowboy hat off, waving it in the air with one hand and holding a radio in the other.

Deputy Patterson stood next to him with excitement painted on her face, and not because of the recent action. She held her radio, too.

"What's up?" he asked as he reached the fence line.

Patterson climbed two slats of the fence and leaned toward him.

"We have a dead body," she said. "Correction: almost a dead body."

Go to Amazon.com to get the next David Wolf Mystery and continue the adventure!

CPSIA information can be obtained
at www.ICGtesting.com
Printed in the USA
LVHW090538250320
651144LV00001B/136